The Calling

The Andovia Chronicles Book 1

Tiffany Shand

DEDICATION

For my mum, Karen.

ACKNOWLEDGMENTS

Editing by Dark Raven Edits and Lauren Blanchard

Cover Designs by Kristina Romanovic

CHAPTER 1

"She must be put to death for her crime," said the village elder. "Traitorous little wretch — killing the man who took her in and raised her as his own all these years."

Nyx Ashwood froze as she stood surrounded by her tribesmen. Her mouth fell open at the man's words. *What? No, this can't be happening. I haven't done anything wrong.*

"I was only protecting my sister," Nyx protested. "Harland tried to—"

"Silence," the village leader, Jarrod, snapped. "You killed one of your own people with forbidden sorcery. You will pay for your crime." He towered over her with his massive frame, his dark eyes flashing. Long black braids trailed down his neck, his breath stank of ale and a bushy beard covered half of his weathered face.

Sorcery! Ridiculous. She didn't have magic. Her abilities came from a curse, not from any magical talent. Now that very curse might cost Nyx her life. Everyone in the tribe possessed a spark of magic that allowed them to use basic spells. They viewed anything beyond that as evil. Nyx knew she shouldn't have been surprised. The villagers had been looking for an excuse to get rid of her for as long as she could remember.

She sat huddled in the corner of an old barn the villagers often used for meetings. Her wrists were raw from where they had been bound with tight rope, and they had tied her to a post so she couldn't even fly away. Her jaw and limbs ached from where one of the men had beaten her. Worse still, she couldn't remember everything that happened the night before. She had woken up in the tavern early that morning with Harland's wife, Mama Habrid, screaming at her. Mama Habrid had accused her of murder, and Nyx had seen Harland's body slumped over on the other side of her foster sister's room.

Why couldn't she remember anything? She had known people were looking for her last night and her trading contact, Traveller, had been killed. After she had discovered Traveller's body, she had fled from the cave the trader had been staying in. After that... After that, everything had turned blank.

Cracks of light crept in through the broken walls, and Nyx flinched as a rat scurried past her. Poor creature. They had been treating her worse than vermin. At least the rat had a chance to run away. She didn't have that option, not with all the men here.

She is guilty.

We should have gotten rid of her years ago.

I always knew that changeling was nothing but trouble.

Their thoughts buzzed through her mind so loud she wanted to scream. Nyx hated being around so many people. It made it hard for her to concentrate and consider her next move. With her hands bound, she couldn't touch anyone and use her influence on them either. Mama Habrid must have warned them about that too. She had always been so careful about keeping her curse a secret from people because she knew they would condemn her to death if they thought she had magic.

What she wouldn't give for some wine, or better yet, the drug Nilanda to dull it all out, but there was no chance of that.

Her mind raced with questions about the night before. She had heard her sister screaming and knew she had to stop their foster father, Harland, from hurting Kyri again. Everything after that remained a blur. What happened? What had she done?

She did remember Harland choking Kyri then... nothing. She knew she must have intervened somehow. Nyx guessed she might have used her influence, as she often did, to rein his temper in.

Everyone kept saying she had killed him, but how? Her curse worked by tormenting her with other people's thoughts and sometimes allowing her to bend people to her will, but she didn't have the ability to kill anyone. While she might be able to get someone to hand over coins and other possessions, she couldn't force them to commit murder for her.

Nothing she said or did would make the villagers change their minds. If only she could get her hands free, perhaps she could force them to release her. Doing so always drained her of energy, but it wouldn't harm them. The effects had always only been temporary. Usually, she got someone to do whatever she wanted them to do and then let them go. No harm done.

Nyx had to get out of there. At seventeen, she was too young to die. She had barely even begun to live. The life she had endured so far had been one of hardship. With Harland gone, she had hoped she and her foster sisters could finally have a better future and get away from this awful place, but there would be no chance of that unless she found a way to escape. Eight men stood between her and the door that led out of the barn. A quick glance around showed her nothing but a few cracks and loose boards. There was nowhere big enough for her to crawl through, not without being seen.

Nyx curled her long wings around herself, hoping they would provide her with a little warmth. She shivered as a cool breeze blew under the door and through the cracks in the walls. She had no idea what time of day it was. She had lost her sword last night too. Being without the weapon she had considered a part of herself for the past two years left her feeling naked and empty.

"She must be put to the flame," another man spoke up.

Flame? Nyx's heart pounded in her ears, and her blood went cold. They were going to burn her alive? Good gods, she hated fire. It had always terrified her. Worse still, her sister, Domnu, had said she had seen Nyx being put to a pyre in a vision she had had last night when some strangers had come looking for her. They couldn't put her on a pyre. If she had killed Harland, it had been self-defence. Nyx thought she would remember something as important as that. She sometimes blacked out when she used her influence – especially if it had taken more energy than usual. Maybe she had been too exhausted to stay conscious. Or perhaps her mind had blocked out the event.

Had she stabbed him? No, she hadn't seen any stab wounds on him earlier that morning. Hit him over the head with something? No, they kept insisting she had used magic to do it. If she ever killed anyone, it was more likely to be with the end of a blade, not with her curse.

Nyx pulled her knees up to her chest and buried her face in her hands. This had to be a nightmare and one she prayed she would wake from soon.

Someone chuckled. "Oh, you can't deny what you did to me, girl. Even if your mind blocks it out, you know you have blood on your hands."

Nyx looked up to see Harland's glowing form standing a few feet from her. He looked just as she had remembered with his mop of long grey hair, straggly beard and ice-blue eyes. He wore the same clothing that he had on the night before: a rumpled, dark red tunic and muddy black trousers.

Impossible. She had seen his body when they dragged her out of the tavern. His eyes had been glassy and lifeless, and the dead didn't come back to life. No, he wasn't alive, but his presence sent a chill over her.

"You're dead," she whispered. "How can you be here?"

"Yes, I am. No thanks to you." Harland leaned back against the wall, yet his glowing presence cast no shadow, nor did the arguing village men notice him. How could they not see him? He was right there. Was she imagining this?

"You are a spirit," she kept her voice low so no one would overhear her. "Why have you come back for me? I didn't do anything to you. If I did, it wasn't intentional. I'm not a murderer."

"I've come to let you know I will be waiting for you. Fire is an awful way to die, but it is no more than what you deserve. I didn't deserve to die, yet you used your unholy curse on me." Harland gave her a bright smile. "Don't keep me waiting too long. I have big plans for you on the other side." Then he disappeared in a wisp of smoke.

Was this to be her fate? To die on a pyre and be subjected to Harland even more in the next life than she had been in this one? No, Nyx would not endure that. She had been a slave for as long as she could remember, sold to Harland and turned into what he wanted her to be. Now that time was over.

"You can't kill me," she told the villagers again. "I didn't—"

Why wouldn't anyone listen to her? Usually, the village elders gave anyone accused of a crime the chance of a trial first where they could speak in their defence. She should have known they would never give her such an opportunity. Nyx was considered little more than a gutter rat.

"Quiet, girl," Jarrod growled and turned back to the other men. "Get everything ready. She will burn at noon."

The other men trailed off as Jarrod dragged her outside the barn and past a row of tiny makeshift houses. The tribe liked to move around depending on the season, so they were all made of wood. Faces and accusing eyes stared out at her from the windows, and their thoughts echoed through her mind.

They all thought she was guilty and were happy to condemn her. Her skull pounded from the onslaught of their voices, buzzing like a swarm of bees through her mind.

Noon? That meant she only had a short time to escape. They had spent the past few hours debating what to do with her. She had woken up to the sounds of Mama Habrid screaming. Her foster sister, Kyri, had been huddled in the corner, too terrified to say or do anything. Kyri hadn't even done anything when the men came and dragged Nyx away.

Jarrod tied her to a post made of thick wood. It would take a lot of strength to pull it out of the ground. As Jarrod stalked off, Nyx tugged at the ropes around her hands. They were too tight to pry loose. Her long plait fell past her shoulders, despite the fact her hair often changed colour. It had settled on dark pink. In times of distress it always returned to its natural shade of blonde.

Nyx unfurled her wings and flapped them. She rose off the ground a little, but the rope held her to the post. Her wings weren't strong enough to get her free. She had always felt like there had been something tying her to this place, and now there was.

Curse it all. There had to be some way out.

"Nyx?" someone hissed.

Nyx turned to see her foster sister, Domnu, lurking beside one of the houses. Domnu's dark blonde hair billowed around her face, and her dark green eyes were filled with fear. She didn't have wings like Nyx did, and her long woollen dress hung loose around her thin frame.

Nyx stood out with her large wings. Long veins ran down the back of them and shimmered with iridescent colours. Her fae features had always made her look unusual among the humans here. "Dom, help me," Nyx whispered. "Please."

Domnu gripped the side of the wall. *I can't. There are too many people around,* she thought at Nyx. Since Nyx could read their thoughts, her sisters had learnt to use it to communicate with her when they didn't want anyone to overhear them.

Nyx's foster sisters were the only people who knew about her curse. Aside from Harland and Mama Habrid, who had taken her in as a foundling.

"Please, they're building a pyre." She gave her sister a beseeching look. "If you don't help me, I will burn. We always promised we would be there for each other. Doesn't that mean anything to you?"

Domnu paled. *I'm sorry, Nyxie, I don't know how to help. They will kill me if I try to help you escape.*

"You get away from there," someone yelled. "You shouldn't be around her." One of the village men had spotted Domnu and advanced towards her.

Domnu hurried away before the man had a chance to reach her.

Nyx wished Domnu would have a vision telling her this would turn out alright. But Domnu couldn't control her power any more than Nyx could control her curse. Domnu wasn't fae, but she did have the ability to see the future. The familiar feel of Domnu's presence retreated further away. She wouldn't even stay close to be there when they put Nyx to death.

The men began stacking up piles of wood in the village square.

Bile rose in her throat, and tears stung her eyes. No, she wouldn't cry. Harland had always said crying was a weakness, and she wouldn't give the villagers the satisfaction of it.

Nyx half expected Harland to walk around the corner and demand to know where she had been all this time. She had chores to do in the tavern at the insistence of Mama Habrid. Harland always put her "talents" as he called them to good use by travelling around from village to village picking people's coin purses. She had a quick hand and knew how to distract people.

Gods, please help me through this, she prayed. *Don't let them put me to the flame.*

Last night had been normal at first. She had been sweeping the floors in the tavern and avoiding Mama Habrid and Harland as much as she could. Harland made her go around to the tavern's patrons every evening, picking their coin purses. She only slipped out a few coins here and there so people wouldn't notice. There was big money to be found in the larger villages. If she ever got caught, she had a way of making people forget, thanks to her curse.

It had been a normal evening until those people had come looking for her. Three youths: two male and a female. They had known her

6

name and had been there when she found the body of her trading contact. Had they been responsible for killing Harland? She had no way of finding out now and wondered if those strangers would appear at her execution just as Domnu had foreseen.

Mama Habrid would love any excuse to get rid of her. Nyx had always been Harland's favourite since she brought in the most money. Unlike Domnu and Kyri, who could only use their gifts in a limited capacity to make good coin, Nyx's ability could never be turned off.

Think, she told herself. *There must be another way out of this.* Her curse would do her no good here except perhaps to warn her when people were coming. So many thoughts buzzed through her mind like a swarm of bees flocking to a hive. It made it almost impossible to concentrate.

She tugged at the ropes again, yet the knots refused to budge. Her heart stopped when she caught sight of the pyre they had already erected. More men brought in piles of wood. Gods, were they really going to do this? Would they really burn her alive? Nyx averted her gaze, unable to look at it. She could imagine the flames licking at her flesh, burning through skin and bone.

She had been an outcast all her life. Someone had abandoned her in the woods when she was a child. That was why they had given her the name Nyx, which meant strife, and the last name of Ashwood after the tree she had been found under. They called her a changeling because of her wings, but no other baby had been taken in her place.

The thoughts of two men grew louder. Two burly men rounded the corner and yanked her off the post.

They dragged her through the village and up to the platform. One by one, the rest of the villagers flocked out of their houses to come to watch the spectacle. Would no one here help her? Nyx had always known they disliked her and feared her for her strangeness, but she had no quarrel with them. She had never done anything to hurt them aside from stealing a few coins on Harland's orders.

Gods, this could not be happening.

Horrible way to die, the first man thought.

The witch deserves it, the second man thought. *She's been a plague on our village since the day she arrived here. We should have gotten rid of her years ago.*

Their whirling thoughts pounded through her head like a heavy drum.

Nyx struggled, but the men kept a firm grip on her. They tied her straight to a post and placed kindling around her feet. She had to concentrate. Her curse did nothing to help her, so she would just have to find another way to escape.

Nyxie, I'm coming!

Wait, that sounded like Domnu.

Domnu rounded the corner and swung a broom straight at the first man, knocking him to the ground. Nyx spun and kicked the second in the stomach as Domnu cut at the rope binding her to the post. "Run, Nyx!" Domnu cried.

Nyx hesitated. She couldn't leave her sisters behind. Who would be there to protect them now? If she ran, they would have no one to take care of them anymore. Mama Habrid would sell them on the slave market now that Harland wasn't around to keep her in line.

"Go, now," Domnu hissed. *Hurry. There's a pack with your things in it on the woodland trail. Go and get it. Don't worry about us. You must leave.*

Nyx turned and ran. Shouts rang out behind her.

She sprinted away from the village. She knew where Domnu meant. Nyx spent more time in the forest than she did at the tavern. It was the only place she could find peace away from the constant bombardment of thoughts.

The villagers would be right behind her; she had to hurry. Where would she even go from here? Nyx had only a little money from what she had stolen and kept for herself, but it wouldn't get her far. The fae were considered slaves here on these islands, as were anyone who looked different or possessed some type of magical ability. Even if she did escape, it might not be long before someone tried to grab her and sell her back into slavery.

Nyx headed straight for the tree line and ducked behind a large oak. She glanced up and scanned the trees for any sign of the local dryads who inhabited the nearby forest. Aside from her sisters, they had been her only friends and treated her with kindness.

"Willow? Serophene?" she hissed. "I need your help."

None of the dryads appeared, and her heart sank. Had they given up on her too? She called out for them in her mind instead. The dryads didn't need to communicate in words, so perhaps they were just hiding for fear of the villagers seeing them.

Nyx waited a moment, but no one appeared, nor did she feel their presence nearby. They must be hiding deep within their trees or they didn't want to come out to aid her.

Voices echoed behind her, but she had grown fast at running over the years. Her wings added to her momentum. She didn't dare risk flying or they would see her. She would have to get somewhere safe before she attempted that.

Nyx stopped, breathing hard. She had to get her hands free.

"From light to bright," she muttered a spell to conjure a small flame. Fire terrified her, but it was the only way to get her hands free. Light burned straight through her ropes, and she rubbed her aching wrists. Grabbing her pack, she swung it over her shoulder. It only had a few spare clothes and some coin inside. She had never been one for luxuries. She slipped her blade into her belt but prayed she wouldn't have to use it.

Nyx had to keep moving or they would catch up with her. Their thoughts became so loud she clutched her head and tripped over a tree root.

Someone, please help me. I don't want to die. Gods, why can't I stop their thoughts? I don't want to hear them!

Footsteps echoed behind her.

We are gaining on her.

She won't get far.

Her wrists ached, as did her limbs. She knew she would be covered in bruises.

Nyx made her way through the woods rather than keeping to the trail. Leaves crunched under her boots as she rushed by several trees. Their gnarled limbs seemed to reach for her as she ran, the branches snagging on her tunic. She knew these woods better than anyone, so it was easy to find her way. A quick glance upstream revealed no sign of the dryads. They had made it clear they wouldn't help her.

The villagers would expect her to follow the trail that led to the road onto the next villages several miles away. She couldn't go that way. No one would offer shelter to a changeling. They would turn her over in the hopes of getting some good coin.

She would make for Dead Man's Cliff — a treacherous area known for landslides. If she could jump from that, maybe it would give her enough momentum to fly.

Where is that damned girl? She will pay for what she did.

Nyx pushed their thoughts away. Finally, the cliff was in sight.

Nyx sighed with relief. She had made it. If she survived the fall, she would have a chance of freedom. Where she went from here didn't matter as long as she kept away from that pyre.

Someone threw themselves at her, knocking her to the ground. Nyx let out a cry of alarm as the man wrestled with her. "Thought you could escape from us, didn't you, witch?" he snarled and punched her. Nyx's head reeled back, and stars flashed before her eyes. He drew a knife and slashed her. "I should kill you now for what you did to Harland. I always knew you were a threat."

Nyx raised her arm to shield herself, a trickle of blood dripped down as the knife slashed through her skin. She gripped his arm and thought, *Let me go.* She willed her curse to force the man to comply. Energy reverberated through her body, making her gasp and he drew back in alarm. She brought her knee up and kicked him in the groin. Good thing she had only wanted something minor from him or it would have drained a lot more energy – energy she needed to escape.

The man cried out in agony and slashed at her again. The blade tore through her wing.

Nyx yelped and clutched her damaged wing. Her fingers came away sticky with blood, but she didn't have time to worry about it as she hurried to the edge of the cliff and clutched her bleeding arm.

We've got her now, someone thought.

Nyx flexed her wings. *Gods, please protect me.* She jumped, wings flapping wildly. The harder she flapped made no effect as she didn't gain any momentum.

My wing must be more damaged than I thought. Gods help me! I'm going to die. This is it. She closed her eyes.

Air rushed around her. She braced herself, expecting the ground to reach her again. At least this way she had chosen her death, and it would hopefully be quick, not prolonged in agonising pain like it would have been if she had burned.

Instead, her descent slowed. *What's happening?*

Something had a hold of her, not her wings which still flapped uselessly.

Why aren't I falling? She sensed someone nearby, and strange words carried on the air. Blood pounded in her ears. *Why am I not hitting the ground?* Although she felt someone's presence, she couldn't hear their thoughts.

The ground reached up for her, and she closed her eyes, bracing herself for the inevitable impact.

When it came, she landed soft and gentle. Nyx opened her eyes as a boy — no, young man — peered down at her then clamped a hand over her mouth. "Shush," he hissed.

"You!" It was the same person she had seen the night before. He had long blond hair, piercing blue eyes, and wore an expensive cloak, velvet jerkin and brown trousers. He looked too well-dressed to be from the lower realm.

Nyx yanked her knife from her belt and held it to his throat. He waved his hand and knocked the knife away with a blast of invisible energy as if the blade were nothing but a minor inconvenience. "I am here to help you," he said.

"No, you're not. You killed Traveller and probably Harland, too. You're going to make my tribe burn me alive!" She gripped his arm. *Get away from me!* She screamed the words in her mind and willed her curse to hit him and force him to get away from her.

Energy surged through her body, making her gasp as a concussive wave burst from her, like thunder without sound.

The man flinched and gritted his teeth. "Your powers don't work on me, Nyx."

Her eyes widened and a memory of the night before flashed through her mind. She had lost control of her curse when she had seen Traveller's dead body. The man hadn't been affected by her influence then either, even when he had tried to hit her with a lightning bolt.

He clamped a hand over her mouth. "If I move my hand, will you promise to be quiet?"

Nyx frowned. He was touching her, but she couldn't hear anything from him. How was that possible? Why wouldn't her influence work? That had never happened before.

She nodded.

He drew his hand away from her mouth and offered it out for her to take. "What are you doing?" Nyx growled.

"Helping you."

Her eyes narrowed. "I don't want your help." She scrambled up. "Who are you? Why did you come looking for me?"

"You're bleeding." He pressed a hand to her arm and said strange words. Warmth washed over her skin as the cut stopped bleeding.

Nyx stared at her arm in disbelief. "How did you…?"

Shouts echoed close by.

We've got her now.

Nyx grabbed her fallen pack and looked around, but there was no sign of her knife. She turned to run.

"Wait," the man said and gripped her wrist.

Nyx yanked her arm free and ran. She would not let herself be anyone's prisoner. The gods only knew what he wanted. She'd only taken a few steps before she came face-to-face with an enormous white wolf.

Nyx clapped a hand over her mouth to stifle a scream. Good gods, she had never seen a wolf this big before. It looked almost the size of a man with glowing amber eyes, all rippling muscle and thick fur. *What is that?*

The wolf stood there, staring at her. Nyx half expected it to pounce on her and rip her apart with its massive jaws.

"You don't understand —" Nyx protested.

Jarrod himself and the rest of the villagers swarmed around them in a circle, some carrying knives and makeshift weapons like pitchforks.

Nyx spotted her sword in Jarrod's belt, and her chest tightened. *He has my weapon.* She had to get out of here. It didn't matter who the strange man was, even if he had saved her life.

"Trust me," he told her and said more strange words. Light flashed over her skin.

Nyx stared down in horror. Her skin had darkened and she now wore a long velvet gown and a thick woollen cloak, yet the clothes felt the same. She couldn't feel the strange new garments. Gods, what had he done to her? Her long hair had changed to a deep shade of bright red: the same colour as the girl she had seen in the cave last night along with the blue-eyed stranger.

"What have you done to me?" she cried.

"Quiet," the man hissed. "Don't say anything. I'm keeping you alive."

Alive? For what purpose? Nyx froze as several of the village men approached them. Their thoughts buzzed around her mind. *Where did the changeling go? Who are these newcomers? Why are they here?*

Nyx wanted to run but knew the blue-eyed stranger would stop her again. Power rolled off him in waves. What was he? She had met a few magic users over the years, but none of them had been as

12

powerful as him.

"Can I help you?" the man asked with a charming smile. He took hold of her hand, and her mind went silent. All of the thoughts she had been picking up on vanished.

What was he doing? Why couldn't she hear anything? She realised he must somehow be suppressing her curse or perhaps neutralising it.

"Where is the changeling?" Jarrod demanded and drew her sword. "I know she fell down here. Did you let her get away? She is a killer, and anyone caught helping her will be put to death as well."

Nyx made a move to flee, but the man tightened his grip.

Let me go, she thought and willed her curse to force him to comply once again. Nyx had to be touching someone to make it work. Doing so would drain her energy, but she didn't care. At least she would be able to get away. She wasn't about to be captured by the villagers or this strange newcomer. Energy reverberated through her fingers. The man flinched but didn't relinquish his grip.

Argh, why wouldn't it work? She wanted to scream in frustration and demand to know who the stranger was and why he was there.

"Who?" The man frowned, unfazed by what she had just done. "Oh, you mean the girl who fell out of the sky? I believe she ran that way." He motioned in the opposite direction.

Jarrod gave Nyx a hard look. "Who are you people? I haven't seen you before, and I know every face from the surrounding villages."

Nyx noticed the wolf had retreated. Where had it gone? It had been right there. Perhaps the stranger had somehow hidden it behind his magic as well. Also, where was the girl that she now looked like? Nyx hadn't seen her since last night.

"We are travellers passing through. This is my wife."

Wife? Nyx flinched. Had he changed her appearance to protect her or would he want something in return?

"As you can see, there's no changeling here."

Jarrod hesitated and gave Nyx a scrutinising look. Her heart pounded in her ears like a heavy drum. He couldn't recognise her, could he? She looked like someone else now. "The changeling will be put to the pyre for what she did."

Oh, gods. Nyx kept her gaze averted as blood pounded in her ears.

"What did she do?"

"She used sorcery to kill a man. She is dangerous and deserves to die for her crime," Jarrod snapped. "You folks had better be on your way. Strangers aren't welcome here."

"Sir, we have her here," one of the village men called and dragged someone along with him.

Nyx gasped when she caught sight of a girl that looked just like her — the real her. Right down to the dark pink hair streaked almost black with dirt and the large iridescent wings. Good gods, how was this possible?

The other Nyx struggled against his grasp but didn't say anything. She shot the man holding the real Nyx a look. Something seemed to pass between them.

Jarrod's smile gleamed. "Good job, Percival. I knew that little rat wouldn't get far. Let's hurry up and take her back. The sooner she burns, the sooner the stench of her evil will be gone from this world."

"Wait a moment." The man held up a hand and took a step forward, dragging Nyx with him. "What do you mean to do with her?"

"She is a murderer. She killed a good friend of mine — a man who took her in as a foundling and was a father to her. She destroyed him with her unholy magic." Jarrod grimaced, and his eyes flashed with anger. "We will take her back to the pyre where she will finally pay for her crime."

Nyx opened her mouth to speak, yet no words came out. Something sealed her lips in place, preventing her from speaking. What had this newcomer done to her? She needed to tell them the truth. As much as she wanted to escape, she didn't want this strange doppelgänger to die in her place.

"How did she kill him?" the man persisted. "You say she used magic, what kind?"

"The victim's wife claims the girl is cursed. She can somehow overhear people's thoughts and used her wickedness to destroy a good man. We found him dead during the night, blood streaming from his ears and eyes. There was also the body of a trader found near the woods who was known to have dealings with the girl," Jarrod answered. "She's been a curse on our tribe since the day she was found. You had better not interfere with this, boy."

Nyx flinched at Jarrod's words. No, she couldn't have done that. Her curse had never worked that way. It had never hurt anyone except herself. Her revulsion gave way to anger.

Interfere? You fool. Can't you see he's doing just that? Nyx wanted to scream.

She hadn't killed Traveller or Harland either. Traveller had already been dead when she had followed the blue-eyed stranger and his companions to the cave and stumbled upon the body there.

"In that case, why not let me kill her for you?" the man said. "I am a druid, and I despise people who use magic to harm others." Fire formed in his free hand and Nyx instinctively drew back.

What game was this strange druid playing? Surely he wouldn't kill her or the impostor disguised to look like her?

Jarrod sneered. "Why would you do such a thing? You don't even know this criminal. And I want the satisfaction of doing it myself."

"I don't have to know her; I can sense when someone has fresh blood on their hands, and she deserves to die for her crime. So, let me take care of the problem for you." The druid held out his hand, making Nyx wonder if the flames hurt his skin.

Jarrod hesitated and rubbed his bearded chin. "Will she suffer?"

The man gave an evil smile. "Even more so than if you put her on a pyre. This way, she will be suffering for an eternity in the underworld."

"Very well. Kill her then." Jarrod walked over, grabbed hold of the Nyx doppelgänger and shoved her towards the druid.

The other Nyx shook her head and opened her mouth to speak, but that was when the druid struck. He hurled the fireball towards the other Nyx. She screamed as the flames hit her in the chest then exploded her body in a fiery blast.

Nyx looked away and stifled a cry of alarm. Tears pricked her eyes. Would the druid do the same thing to her? At least it would be a quick end. Maybe she wouldn't even feel anything.

Jarrod frowned. "That's it? You said she would suffer first!"

"And she is suffering in the flames of eternal fire. We'll be on our way now." He gripped Nyx's arm and led her away.

Jarrod and the other villagers trailed off. Not one of them stopped the druid to ask him any questions. The fools. They had always been so distrustful of newcomers. Why hadn't they asked more questions?

"It's alright," the druid said.

Nyx yanked her hand free from his grip. "Who are you? What are you?" Only the distant murmur of the villagers' thoughts echoed in her mind now. "What have you done to me?"

"I'm not your enemy, Nyx Ashwood. In fact, I just saved your life," the druid replied. "If I hadn't changed your appearance, you would no doubt be burning on a pyre now."

Her mouth fell open. "How do you know my name? Who are you?"

"My name is Darius. I know a lot more about you than you can imagine, Nyx. I was sent here to find you and take you into custody."

Custody? Nyx's head spun. None of this made any sense. "What do you mean? Are you going to kill me?" she demanded. "Tell me who you really are."

Darius shook his head. "No, you're much too valuable to be killed. I am Darius Valeran." He slapped a metal cuff around her wrist. "You are a prisoner under the laws of the Archdruid and shall be brought before him to face judgement."

CHAPTER 2

Darius Valeran wondered what he had done to deserve being sent after this fae girl. His brother Gideon had forced him to come all the way to the lower realm to find the suspected mind whisperer they had heard rumours about.

All colour drained from Nyx's face when he mentioned who he was. "You're the Archdruid's son?"

"His second-born son, yes." A pit of guilt formed in his stomach at the sight of the metallic cuff he had slapped on her wrist. It flashed with spelled runes that would not only block her powers, but also prevent her from running off. If she tried, she wouldn't get far.

His friend and travelling companion, Ranelle, swooped down from the treeline. She still looked like Nyx's true appearance. She grinned at him. "Good job, Valeran. That was a nice bit of magic. But did you have to pretend to kill me?"

"You're immune, Rae. I think we pulled the trick off well." Darius flashed her a smile.

Nyx gasped and clapped a hand over her mouth. "Why does she look like me? What in the gods' names is she?"

Ranelle waved her hand, transforming back into her true self. The glamour faded, revealing a tall young woman with pale skin, long fiery red hair and pointed ears. Her green eyes sparkled, and she wore a long green tunic dress and brown hose with boots. Long black leathery wings rose from her back.

Nyx took a step back in horror. "What is that?"

Ranelle put her hands on her hips. "You are terrible at

introductions, Valeran."

Darius sighed. "I didn't expect to have to pull off a fake execution." He had spent over a day travelling here from the islands of Andovia. The plan had been simple: find Nyx, catch her committing a crime and then arrest her and take her back with them.

That had been his brother's idea. It had worked, just not the way Darius had intended. He only had moments to cast the glamour on Nyx and for Ranelle to pull her own glamour before those villagers caught up with them.

"Would someone please tell me what's going on?" Nyx demanded. "You can't arrest me. I'm not a criminal."

Darius pulled out a scroll from his coat and held it out to her, although he doubted she could even read. "This states you are now a prisoner of the Archdruid. He has authority in any realm, and we already know you are a thief and a murderer."

"I'm not a murderer," Nyx snapped. "I didn't kill Harland or Traveller!"

Darius gave her a hard look. "We know you didn't kill the trader, but I went to the tavern last night and saw them bring out your father's body. Only a mind whisperer could have done that."

"A what?" Nyx demanded. "Harland wasn't my father, and I didn't kill him. Now change me back, so I can look like myself again!"

Power hit his senses so hard Darius almost flinched. It hadn't taken him long to find his quarry. The hardest part had been trying to capture her last night. The girl was like a beacon with power washing over her like waves hitting a rock. Darius had been intrigued when they had learnt of a potential mind whisperer. He hadn't expected for her powers to be so uncontrollable, though. How she hadn't killed her entire tribe he didn't know.

"It's just a glamour." Darius didn't understand her alarm. She should be grateful he had saved her life.

Nyx glared at him. "Which is?"

"An illusion that masks your true appearance. I didn't have to save you, but I —"

"Change me back."

"It would be safer if you waited until we were away from these parts. Someone might recognise you and alert those villagers to the fact that you're not dead."

"Change me back right now. I'm not going anywhere with you."

Darius sighed and waved his hand. The glamour faded, Nyx returning to her usual self.

Nyx looked herself up and down, spinning around to see if any of the glamour remained.

"You are coming with us. I didn't travel all this way for nothing," he snapped.

"Let's all try to calm down, shall we?" Ranelle suggested. "Hello Nyx, it's nice to meet you. I'm Ranelle Alrin — a friend of Darius'. Don't mind him; he's not very good with introductions."

Darius didn't see the point of being polite or making introductions when it came to a criminal. He had thought this would be a quick and easy trip. Instead, he had spent the night traipsing around looking for her and for an evil spirit. He hadn't even wanted to come here. Why couldn't Gideon have come himself? He was the one who wanted the mind whisperer after all.

Why are you being nice to a criminal? Darius demanded of Rae.

Because she's scared and confused. Can't you see that? Ranelle glared at him. *Plus, you don't know the circumstances of what happened.*

Darius didn't need or want to know. He had seen the evidence for himself. The girl was out of control, and everyone around her was at risk of being killed by her overwhelming abilities.

"I don't understand any of this." Nyx shook her head. "Why would the Archdruid want me? I'm no one important."

"It's not the Archdruid who wants you. It's my brother Crown Prince Gideon Valeran. Maybe he can tell you why he wants a mind whisperer."

"What's a mind whisperer?" Nyx demanded. "Because I'm not one."

"It's someone who can listen to and influence people's minds," Ranelle explained. "Like you can."

"Why did you pretend to kill me?" Nyx glared at Darius. "None of this makes any sense."

"If I hadn't, the villagers would have tried to burn you, then you would have used your power on them the same way you did your father." Darius glared back at her.

"I didn't —" Nyx protested.

Darius waved his hand in dismissal. "I saw what you're capable of and what you did to that man last night. There's no point in denying it. Now you're coming to Andovia with us." He pulled a clear crystal out of his cloak.

A beam of light shot up from it as he set it on the ground. The beam expanded into the image of a young man with long dark blonde hair, a chiselled face and green eyes. He wore a long velvet black tunic and black hose.

"Here is the mind whisperer just as you asked for." Darius motioned to Nyx.

Gideon grinned, his gaze assessing Nyx. "Excellent work, brother." He then turned his nose up. "Scrawny thing, isn't she?"

Darius rolled his eyes. He didn't give a damn what the girl looked like. It was hard to tell underneath all that dirt anyway. He just wanted to get home to Eldara and back to his usual job acting as a Captain in the Forest Guard. Darius had more important things to do than picking up criminals in the lower realms.

Nyx stood there, either too stunned or overwhelmed to speak. Darius didn't know which.

"You are Nyx Ashwood?" Gideon arched an eyebrow. "You're not what I expected."

Darius bit back a laugh. What had Gideon expected?

"Have you had a chance to test her powers yet?" Gideon asked Darius.

"No, we ran into some problems." Darius didn't need to test Nyx's powers to feel them. She had hit him with her magic when she used her compulsion against him earlier.

"What problems?" Gideon glowered between Darius and Ranelle. "I told you not to take that shifter and that wyvern half-breed with you." His lips curled.

"I am not a half-breed," Ranelle muttered under her breath.

"You told me to—" A scream from Nyx cut Darius off, and he spun around to see the wolf blocking Nyx's path. "We'll be back in Andovia soon." Darius picked up the crystal, and the image winked out. "This is Luc." Darius motioned to the giant wolf. "I'd suggest not running off. You won't get very far." He stuffed the crystal back inside his coat. "Come, we need to get moving, or we'll be late for the ship."

"Ship?" Nyx frowned. "Where are you taking me?"

"To the islands of Andovia. Would you prefer I take you back to the pyre?"

Nyx flinched. "No. What happens after that?"

"That is up to my brother. I'm only the messenger. Let's go."

"Half-breed," Ranelle grumbled. "One of these days, I'll —"

"Do what?" Darius arched an eyebrow at her. Ranelle knew full well she couldn't argue with Gideon, not if she wanted to become a scholar as she planned.

Nyx glanced around, no doubt looking for a way to escape.

Keep an eye on her, Darius thought to Luc.

Darius trudged off along the cliff path with the wolf trailing at his heels. Nyx and Ranelle followed along behind them.

"Shouldn't we tend to her injuries?" Ranelle touched Darius' arm.

Darius narrowed his eyes at Nyx. He'd already used magic to seal the wound on her arm. "Do you have any other injuries?"

She crossed her arms and raised her chin. "No." She glowered at him. Despite being covered with dirt he could see she had long dark pink hair that trailed past her shoulders and dazzling blue eyes. Her large iridescent wings flashed with different colours as she moved. He guessed she was some type of fae but couldn't tell what kind since there were thousands of varieties.

"You could be more grateful. I did save your life back there," Darius grumbled.

"I could have saved myself. I would have been fine if you hadn't come along." Her eyes flashed, and red shimmered through her hair. "How did you even know I was falling?"

"I heard you calling for help," he admitted. "And like I said before, we've been watching you."

"That part I still don't understand," Nyx snapped. "Why would your brother want me? Like you said, I'm a common thief."

"Your powers make you important. That's why my brother sent me all this way to find you." His jaw tightened.

Good thing he, Luc, and Ranelle had been nearby waiting until they could get to Nyx. Gideon would never forgive him if he had let Nyx slip out of their grasp.

She froze. "What? How? Are you cursed too?"

Darius bit back a laugh. "No, we were waiting for the right moment to come and get you, and your call was loud enough for us to hear. Even Luc heard it."

It's Lucien, not Luc, the wolf groaned. *How many times do I have to tell you that?*

Darius chuckled in his mind. *You like it, admit it.*

Lucien huffed. *Why are we helping her? Haven't you helped enough damsels in distress on our travels? This is becoming a bad habit for you.*

She's the only damsel — I mean girl I've helped. And I didn't have a choice, did I?

Right. But —

Darius cut the connection so he wouldn't have to hear any more complaints.

"In case you're wondering, we were sent to find you. I'm glad we managed to save you before those villagers..." Ranelle shuddered. "Look, Nyx, I know it may not seem like it, but look at this as an opportunity."

Nyx scoffed. "To do what? Be sold to someone else?"

"You're not a slave," Ranelle protested.

Nyx narrowed her eyes at Darius. "And I suppose he's not a slave master?"

Darius flinched. He opposed slavery more than anyone. "Actually, I'm not. I'm a Captain in the Forest Guard."

"Yet you're still treating me like a slave."

"How else do you expect to be treated after you committed murder?" Darius retorted. "My brother doesn't usually send me to fetch prisoners, but he considers you important, so here we are."

"And I want to know why the son of the Archdruid is interested in me. I steal things to survive. What is so special about that?"

"Interesting. You don't know what kind of fae you are then? What are your other powers?"

Nyx gaped at him. "My what? I have no powers."

"You called for help with your mind. Not many Magickind can do that over distances. Nyx? Is that short for something?" Ranelle asked.

"No, it's just Nyx." Nyx eyed the wolf. "Is he your pet?"

Darius and Ranelle both laughed, and Lucien growled. "Spirits, no. He's my friend," Darius said.

Nyx didn't look like a criminal, but then again criminals rarely ever did.

"You can hear people's thoughts, right?" Ranelle arched a brow. "How long have you been able to do that?"

Druids were trained to read people's thoughts – one of the Archdruid's new rules – but only the most powerful had much luck with it.

Nyx hesitated. "Hear and see. I'm cursed."

Darius frowned. "That seems an odd thing to be cursed with. Who cursed you?"

She shrugged. "I don't know. The fae, I guess. I've always heard things."

Nyx was probably born with power then. Darius wondered if she could be a mind whisperer like Gideon suspected — but that was impossible, especially after the last realm war.

Nyx stumbled and winced.

"We are far enough away from the village now. Let me look at your wounds," Ranelle said. "I've seen you clutching your arm."

Nyx froze. "What? I don't need tending to. I'm fine."

"Your wing is damaged. I can see it. If we don't heal it now, you might never fly again." Ranelle put her hands on her hips.

"I'm fine," she ground out.

Darius sighed at her stubbornness. "I have some basic healing skills. I won't hurt you."

Nyx shook her head. "No."

Why wouldn't she let him treat her wounds? Was it because of modesty? He had noticed her wincing. Darius thought back to their earlier encounter with the villagers. She had heard their thoughts. Perhaps touch made it easier for her to hear more? "Give me your hand."

Nyx frowned. "Why? And also, no."

I've decided I like this girl, Lucien remarked. *She isn't a simpering fool like the girls who flaunt themselves at you.*

Darius suppressed another sigh. The sooner he caught up with his mentor, Ambrose, the better. Then he would get home to Andovia, and this girl would be Gideon's problem.

"I want to try something. You can't hear my thoughts, can you?"

Nyx hesitated and nodded. "No, why is that?"

Darius suspected he was somehow immune to her powers. He didn't know how or why, though. Perhaps Ambrose would know.

Despite the cuff, waves of power still pulsed from her, not as strong as before but strong enough. How was that possible? The cuff was supposed to repress all magic.

"Some druids are taught how to protect their minds with a mental shield. It also prevents anyone from reading us." He held out his hand. "Take my hand and see if you hear anything – if you're worried about how your power will react to me."

Nyx reluctantly took hold of his hand. Warmth flared between their fingers. Nyx stood there as if waiting for something to happen. "I don't hear anything – not even distant echoes. When you touched me earlier the villager's thoughts faded."

They stood there for a few moments.

"Aren't you supposed to be tending to her wounds?" Ranelle asked.

Darius pulled back. "Right, so can I look at you now? I mean, examine you?" Holy spirits, why did he keep stumbling over his words?

If looks could kill, Darius was sure he would be dead from Nyx's glare. "No, I told you I am fine," she hissed.

Darius pulled off his pack and rummaged around in it until he found some jars. "Here. Use these for your bruises and cuts." He held out the jar for her. "I need to look at your wing to assess the damage."

"I'll tend to you. Don't worry, he won't do anything to you," Ranelle added.

Nyx sighed and lifted up her tunic. She turned around. "Look then."

Darius glanced over at Lucien. Nyx's back was covered in bruises. Someone had beaten her — no wonder she didn't want to be touched.

Anger surged through him. *I should have killed those villagers,* he thought and wondered where the sudden anger had come from. He didn't want to feel sorry for this criminal, not after what she had done, but he hated seeing anyone mistreated.

Her wings unfurled and rose higher. They shimmered an iridescent purple. Looking at them didn't show what kind of fae she was.

The man who had attacked Nyx had cut through the middle of her wing, so the skin now flapped around like a broken leaf.

Can you tell what she is? Darius asked Lucien. Lucien came over and sniffed Nyx, he drew back.

"What is your wolf doing?" she asked.

"He is curious about you." Darius glanced over at Luc. *Well?*

Lucien pressed his nose into Nyx's hand, and she patted his head. *She smells of the wind, grass and something else,* Lucien said.

What?

I don't know. I've met dozens of fae, but she doesn't smell like any of them.

How is that possible? We've been all over the islands, and you grew up near Fae.

Nyx ran a hand over Lucien's head. "You're so soft."

Lucien grunted. *Would you please tell her I'm not a pet and that I don't like being touched?*

But you are pretty in that form. Women will start falling at your feet.

Lucien turned away from Nyx and growled at Darius. *I, unlike you, am not a philanderer.*

You keep telling yourself that, my friend.

Ranelle stifled a chuckle and turned her attention to Nyx's wing. *Wolfsbane, can you heal this?*

I don't possess the skill of healing yet. Plus, I doubt even my power would work on her.

"This wing needs more than a salve can heal." Ranelle frowned. "I don't suppose you can heal yourself?"

Nyx shook her head. "No, that's not part of my curse."

"I doubt you're cursed. Everyone has natural gifts." Darius rummaged around in his pack for another jar.

"I don't have a gift," she growled.

He finally found a jar of a potent healing balm that had been made by the fae. It might be enough to start repairing Nyx's wing, at least until they reached Andovia.

Ranelle undid the jar and rubbed it over Nyx's wing.

Nyx yelped as light sparkled over the broken skin. "What did you do?"

"Look, it's working." Darius motioned to her wing. The tear had knitted into a thin line.

"Am I healed?"

"No, but it's better than before." He shoved the jar back into his pack.

Time to get moving. He only hoped they didn't run into any more trouble along the way.

CHAPTER 3

Nyx couldn't believe she had become a prisoner, to a Valeran no less. Gods, how had she ended up as their property? She couldn't decide what to make of the druid, Ranelle, or that strange wolf of theirs. The beast looked at Darius as if they were having a silent conversation. For all she knew the wolf could talk.

The dusty road that stretched out before them offered no scenery but a scattering of trees on either side. The noonday sun rose high in the sky. It looked like any other day, but her life had changed so much within such a short time.

She had to admit she had felt better after Ranelle had used that healing stuff on her. Darius hadn't done anything to hurt her, but that didn't mean she would trust him. Nyx never trusted anyone. Look at her sisters. Kyri hadn't even come forward to defend her or to speak about what had happened, yet she had been the only other witness in that room. If only she had had a chance to talk to Kyri, or even Domnu again before she had been forced to leave. Her sisters might not have been related to her by blood, but they were the closest thing she'd ever had to family. They meant everything to her, and now she might never see them again.

Nyx could never go back to the tribe – they weren't forgiving people. Darius was right about one thing: she had nowhere to go, but that didn't mean she wanted to go anywhere with him either.

"So how did you find me?" she demanded. "How did you even know about me?" Even if he was a Valeran, she didn't care. She wouldn't treat a slave master with respect — he deserved none.

"You'll have to ask my brother about that." Darius shrugged.

"And what happens to me when we get to these islands?" Nyx had heard of Andovia but didn't know much about the place other than the fact it was the continent in the upper realm. She lived in the lower realm, and the upper realm had never been much of a concern for her. That was where the Archdruid and other wealthy people dwelled.

Darius shrugged. "Again, it's up to my brother to decide your fate. I am only the messenger who was sent to bring you back."

"What gives him the right to do that? I don't live in Andovia. I'm not subject to your laws." Her hands clenched into fists. "Nor did I do anything wrong last night. You were the ones chasing me, remember?"

"Everyone in the lower realm is subject to the Archdruid's laws, and you are also a fae."

Nyx scowled. "And you're treating me like a slave."

"You are a criminal. If you wanted to keep whatever rights you thought you had, maybe you shouldn't have committed murder."

Nyx opened her mouth to protest then closed it. What good would arguing do? Nothing she said would convince this druid of her innocence. One way or another, she would get away from him. She had been sold into slavery before and she would get her freedom no matter what.

"You know I didn't kill Traveller, so who did? Was it you or one of your friends?" she demanded. Her mind drifted back to the strange shadow creature she had seen. "Or was it that shadow that kept appearing?"

"None of us killed that trader. Did you see the dark spirit?"

Nyx hesitated. "I felt it, but I don't think I saw it. Did you bring it there to find me?"

Darius gave a harsh laugh. "No. Things are a lot more complicated than that. I am not surprised you sensed it with your powers. Too bad we lost it after it fled from the cave."

She stared at him, incredulous. "I don't have powers. I'm cursed." She had tried asking Harland about the curse a few times, but he had always said it was because she was an unholy thing.

"Curses are meant to punish and inflict suffering. You don't have any of that."

Good gods, she couldn't stand this man. The more he spoke, the more she wanted to slap him. "You have no idea what it's like to be at the mercy of people's thoughts all the time," she growled.

Ranelle laughed. "I like this girl. Nyx, you should stay with us."

Darius scowled at her.

Ranelle seemed nice enough, but Nyx didn't know these people, nor would she trust them either.

Nyx couldn't fathom what the Archdruid's son might want with her of all people. Maybe the man was soft in the head. What could he know about her anyway? She always kept to herself. It wasn't like she went around telling people about her curse. People would think her insane or worse, despise her more than they already did.

Her tribe had despised her and people from the neighbouring villages had given her a wide berth. Most of the tribes in this area were simple people who possessed only a spark of magic that allowed them to do basic spells.

They didn't welcome people who looked different from them, especially someone who had wings. Nyx had pointed ears once too but someone — probably Harland or Mama Habrid — had cut them off when she was a child. Now her ears looked rounded, and she had scars covered by her hair.

Her heart clenched when they got to a small crossroads. There were no signs, but she knew this place well. Turning left led to the main road away from all the nearby villages and into the city.

Harland had only taken her to the city a few times, but she had been too overwhelmed to pay much attention to anything. Too many minds, so much noise she had collapsed from the intensity of it. If he weren't dead now, Harland would have taken her there today as he had planned. Her pickings from the surrounding villages hadn't proven very fruitful recently, and he had insisted on going there to find richer coin purses. That was why she had gone out last night to see Traveller and get some of the Nilanda. The drug was a powerful sedative.

Nyx had to get away and find an escape route. This might be her only chance. That damn wolf had stopped her earlier, but now it trailed along with Darius. She didn't have any idea what the fae prince wanted with her nor did she want to find out.

Ranelle chatted away, but Nyx was too busy looking around to pay attention to what she said.

How would she get away?

The druid had power, it rolled off him in waves of energy. The wolf terrified her and Ranelle… She stared at the young woman. What were those leathery wings of hers? Was she a demon? Or something else?

Ranelle caught her staring. "Is everything alright?"

"What…are you?" Nyx murmured.

Ranelle laughed and tossed her long hair over her shoulder. "I'm a hybrid. Half-fae, half-wyvern."

"Wyvern?" Nyx gasped. She thought of the images of great scaled beasts she had seen on items sold by travelling merchants. Wyverns were just a legend; great fire breathers that ruled the skies and fought during the realm wars.

"But wyverns aren't real… are they?" Nyx looked Ranelle up and down, half expecting her to change into a scaly beast.

Ranelle laughed. "Oh, we're real. I'm just… unique. I can't change into full wyvern form. I only have wings." Her wings folded back, then disappeared.

Nyx gasped. "How…?" She had never imagined someone's wings could disappear. At times she had always wanted to be able to hide her wings so she wouldn't stand out so much among humans.

"I can pull them back into my body." Ranelle shrugged.

Darius and the wolf trudged ahead then turned right into a vast forest. Nyx didn't know whether to be relieved by that or not. The druid had said it would block her powers, but she didn't feel any different. Her curse still felt active, though she couldn't hear anything from Ranelle or the druid himself. Would her influence work? She had tried it on the druid earlier, and he had somehow resisted her. She had never met anyone immune to her influence before. How was that possible?

Even Harland hadn't been able to resist. Not that it had done much good. Nyx hadn't been able to use her influence to stop him from abusing her sisters. The man had a short temper, and the smallest things set him off.

Nyx winced. Now Harland would never do anything again. Her gut clenched. She pushed those thoughts away. Nyx had to focus, she had to escape.

Darius had magic. The wolf could no doubt rip her apart if it chose to. Ranelle – aside from her wings, what could she do?

"Do you have power too?" Nyx asked and bit her lip. She needed to know what she was up against if she had any chance of escaping.

"I can conjure fire." A fireball formed in her hand. "Earth and fire are my talents. Watch." She motioned with her hand, the tree branches they passed twisted and bent around each other.

Nyx flinched. So Ranelle had powers, too. "Do you know what they are going to do with me? Am I going to be a slave to the Valeran brothers now?"

Ranelle shook her head. "I don't know, but Darius would never treat you like a slave. He despises slavery."

"What about his brother?"

Ranelle bit her lip. "Gideon…can be difficult."

"Why does he want me?"

"Because you're a mind whisperer. Those were thought to be extinct."

"They must want me for something else or the druid wouldn't have come all this way to find me. So, tell me what you know." Nyx resisted the urge to reach out and use her influence on Ranelle. For all she knew it might not work and she didn't want to provoke the druid's ire.

Normally she never had to try and listen to anyone's thoughts. They came to her whether she wanted to hear them or not. Reading the druid wouldn't work. She had known that when she touched him earlier.

"Ranelle, please, you have to tell me the truth." Nyx gripped the other girl's arm, and her power flared free. "I'm afraid." *What do the Valeran brothers want with me? What will they do?* Power pulsed from her into Ranelle. "Tell me."

Curse it, she hadn't even meant to use her influence.

Ranelle became dazed. "They think… you're part of the prophecy."

"What prophecy?" This was news to her. How could she be part of any prophecy?

"This prophecy speaks of two chosen to defeat the darkness." Ranelle fell under her gaze.

"What will they do with me?"

"Test your powers to see if you are the one the prophecy —"

"No!" Darius yelled and bounded back towards them.

Luc shot forward, knocking Nyx to the ground. She let out a cry of alarm as the wolf's massive body slammed into her.

"Rae?" Darius knelt at her side. "Are you alright?"

The wolf growled, his hot breath on Nyx's face as his amber eyes bore into her.

Get off me! She screamed inside her mind. Energy reverberated through her skull, hitting the wolf. Luc howled, and his paws tightened on her chest. *Get off! Get away from me!* The band on Nyx's wrist snapped off.

A flash of Harland's empty eyes went through her mind.

Oh, gods, no!

Harland.

Had she really killed him?

She did not want to be dragged off to some strange new world and be subjected to the gods only knew what. Nyx screamed out loud, letting her rage and her inner turmoil out. A blast of blinding energy hurtled the wolf away from her. Blood roared through her ears as energy reverberated around her like thunder without sound.

Ranelle cried out and clutched at her head.

Luc lay on the ground, writhing in agony.

Darius winced and called out something to her, but she couldn't hear him over the roaring in her ears.

Harland appeared beside her. "Killer," he taunted. "You killed me after everything I did for you."

"No!" More power flooded out of her like a dam overflowing and bursting.

"Nyx!" Darius winced, his long hair flapping around his face. "Nyx, stop!"

"Killer, you destroy everything around you." Harland smiled. "You may have killed me, but I will never leave you. Never."

She couldn't stop. The roaring in her ears grew to a crescendo.

Luc rolled over, pawing at the ground.

Nyx wanted to run. This was her chance to escape, yet she couldn't move. Her limbs were heavy, and the roaring in her ears threatened to overwhelm her. Why had Harland come back? He was dead.

"Oh, I'm real, girl."

"Nyx?" Darius' hand clamped down on her arm. All at once, the roaring stopped, the world fell silent. Nyx gasped for breath and gulped in lungfuls of air. "Holy spirits," Darius breathed.

"What did you do?" Nyx asked him.

"I stopped you. Blessed spirits, you could have killed them both!" He glared at her. "What were you thinking?"

Nyx looked past Darius' shoulder. Ranelle sat up, blood dripping from her nose and tears running down her cheeks. The wolf lay the ground, unconscious. Guilt formed a pit in Nyx's stomach.

"Please let me go. My sisters are all alone. I have to protect them." Tears stung her eyes.

Darius glanced down at the broken band. "That's impossible. How did you…?" He sighed. "Nyx, I can't let you go. You're too dangerous for that. You've seen what your powers can do." He motioned to Ranelle and the wolf. "Once we get to Andovia, I promise I'll find someone to help you control this." He gripped her hand. "Your powers are dangerous. You could have killed us all if I weren't somehow immune to your magic."

"I just wanted to know the truth," she hissed. "I never meant to hurt anyone. My curse can't harm others… can it?"

"I'm not sure what it can do, but it does have the potential to kill, like it did last night. Can you stand?" Nyx wobbled as he pulled her up. "I suppose things just became much more complicated."

CHAPTER 4

After making sure Nyx had her powers under control, Darius turned his attention to his friends. "How do you feel?" he asked Ranelle.

"My head hurts." Ranelle wiped her bloody nose with the back of her sleeve. "I'm fine, though. I'm not enslaved."

"Enslaved?" Nyx peeked out from where she had sat back in the grass and buried her head in her hands. "What does that mean?"

Darius cast his senses out then scanned Ranelle for any signs of damage. He found nothing. Lucien now lay human and naked on the ground.

"It means you need to stop using your powers and learn more self-control. You can do a lot more than compel others." He thanked the spirits neither of his friends had fallen under her control. If she had used the full force of her power and enslaved them, he would have had to kill Nyx to release them from her hold. Darius doubted she would be able to remove her influence by herself since she had so little control.

Nyx gasped when she scrambled up. "Why isn't he a wolf anymore? What did I do?"

"He took the full force of your power," Darius said without any kind of malice. "It must have forced his body to change back."

Ranelle sniffed and rose too. "Lucien is a lykae – a shapeshifter," she explained to Nyx.

"I'm…sorry. I never meant to hurt anyone," Nyx moaned and shook her head. "This doesn't make any sense. My influence always wears off. Always. I make people forget when I've used my curse on them."

"Don't use your influence on anyone," Darius warned.

Nyx growled at him. "Are you going to start answering my questions then? Because using my so-called power seems to be the only way for me to get any answers."

Darius' jaw tightened. "I don't have all the answers you want. Some of them will have to wait until we see my brother."

"It's alright. We know you can't control it," Ranelle said.

"Luc?" Darius examined Lucien's naked form. He didn't sense or see any sign of injury. "Luc, can you hear me? Are you alright?"

"How many times do I have to tell you not to call me Luc?" Lucien grumbled and groaned. "What did we do to provoke such an attack?"

"Nothing. She can't control her powers." Ranelle crossed her arms and glowered at the naked man.

"How do you feel?" Darius asked his friend.

"Like I have fallen off a cliff." Luc scrambled up. "Holy spirits, it was like being hit by a whirlwind full of lightning bolts."

Nyx stared at the ground, avoiding Darius' gaze.

Darius waved his hand, and a pile of clothing appeared. "Get dressed. We've been delayed long enough."

Darius wondered what he should do about Nyx. He could conjure another cuff, but her power would seep through it. Instead, he went over and took hold of her arm. "You had better stay close to me whilst we move."

Her eyes narrowed. "Afraid I'll run off, druid?"

"You had your chance to run before."

"I couldn't, in case you hadn't noticed." She tugged at his arm. "I don't need to be held hostage either."

"You used your powers to read Ranelle. Look what happened."

She flinched. "I didn't mean to."

"I know that, which is why you need to learn to control your gift."

"Gift?" Nyx snorted. "How can you call that a gift? You have seen what a nightmare I am. Why would you want to let me near your brother?"

"Andovia is the only place you can learn about who and what you are. No one in this realm understands you, do they?" Nyx looked away, but that answered everything. "There's more at stake than just you here. Things are happening in Andovia and…" Darius trailed off.

"And what?"

"It's complicated." Darius wondered how much he should tell her. Did it even concern her? She knew nothing about their lands.

Once Lucien was dressed, the four of them trudged off. This part of the lower realm looked so barren in comparison to the lush greenery of Eldara. He would be glad to get home again and back to work.

Darius kept Nyx close, although she refused to hold onto him. He would have to keep an eye on her in case she did try to make a run for it again. Once they reached a clearing in the woods, Darius could create and activate a transportation ring. It had to be precise or the magic wouldn't work. Transport rings had limited capability and could only be used over shorter distances.

"Are you tired?" Darius decided to break the awkward silence between them.

Nyx narrowed her eyes. "Why?"

"Because you used a lot of power earlier, and I'm guessing last night too." Darius needed to know more about her power if he was going to help her. Hopefully his mentor, Ambrose, would know what to do to help her get her gift under control.

"I don't remember much about what happened last night," she growled.

Darius' eyes widened. Was that because she didn't want to remember? Or had something happened to make her forget? It seemed doubtful.

"What is the prophecy about?"

"How do you know about that?" Darius gaped at her then he shook his head. "That's why you read Ranelle. Spirits, Nyx, you have no idea how dangerous you are. You can't keep using your powers on anyone just to get what you want. Your magic is dangerous and puts innocent lives at risk."

She glowered at him. "I couldn't control what happened earlier. And it's not like you're forthcoming with answers."

Ranelle and Lucien trailed behind them, bickering as usual.

"You have to stop actively using your power," Darius said. "Not only can your power kill, but it can enslave people too."

"That's ridiculous," Nyx snapped. "I hear thoughts. That's all."

"You can compel people too – like you tried to do with me. Your compulsion runs much deeper than that. Your power can enslave someone to your will. It's a natural part of being a mind whisperer."

"How?" She furrowed her brow.

Darius sighed. "I don't know how it fully works. We only have legends to go by. You're the first mind whisperer in a generation."

"What happened to the other ones?"

Darius hesitated. He couldn't admit his family had wiped them out. Nyx distrusted him enough already.

"What's the prophecy about?" Nyx repeated. She then froze and spun around.

"What's wrong?" Darius frowned.

She shivered. "Something doesn't feel right."

Darius paused and sent his senses out. A chill ran across his mind. No. This couldn't happen now. They were out in broad daylight. *Rae, Lucien, we're not alone,* Darius warned.

Ranelle and Lucien stopped their bickering and went on alert.

Lucien sniffed. *I don't sense anything.*

What is it? Rae asked.

"What is going on?" Nyx demanded. "I can hear you talking to each other. You're all on edge, why?"

"We need to keep moving." Darius motioned for them to follow. "Pick up the pace." He took hold of Nyx's arm and tugged at her. "Come on."

"I'm not a hound you can order around, druid."

He repressed a sigh. Spirits, he would be glad to get rid of this girl. He let go of her. *Can you hear me?* Darius lowered his mental shield in the hope her power would pick up on his thoughts.

Nyx gasped. *Yes. How...?*

Good, then believe me when I tell you we need to move. Now!

The four of them sprinted through the woods.

Darius used his mind's eye to scan the area with his senses. The clearing lay up ahead. Once there, he could set up a circle and get them to the port, then they would be safe. Or at least he hoped so. Darius did not want to deal with any darklings.

I will tell you about the prophecy later, he told Nyx.

You had better, druid. Nyx gripped his arm. *I feel something.*

What? He frowned and tugged on her arm so they could get going again. *We need to keep moving.*

Cold, iciness. Nyx shuddered as she trotted beside him. *Do you know what it is?*

It's — Darius grabbed hold of Nyx, pulling her tight against him as the ground in front of them gave way. Green plumes of smoke rose from the gaping void where the ground had been.

Nyx stifled a cry of alarm. "What happened?"

"It's a rift. An opening where the veil between our world and the next meet."

A mass of darkness shot out from the abyss.

No. Darius' blood went cold. The mass grew denser.

Ranelle took to the air and fired an arrow that went straight through the growing mass.

The mass then broke apart and formed into several wispy beings with glowing eyes.

Darklings.

Darius muttered a curse. He shoved Nyx to the side then dove out of the way too. A piercing shriek rang out.

So much for daylight serving as protection. Darius had never expected a rift to open here in the lower realm. So far they have been limited to the islands of Andovia. Had something or someone followed them here?

Ranelle fired another flaming arrow. It, too, shot straight through the darkling.

What are these things? Nyx yelled at him.

Darius winced. *Darklings – evil spirits. They are what killed the trader last night.* He didn't have time to tell her what little he knew about the creatures.

Lucien moved with supernatural speed as he shot out of the way from another darkling coming at him.

Darius gasped as tendrils of smoke wrapped around his throat.

Nyx screamed as a darkling came at her. Light burst from her hand.

A ball of blazing blue fire swirled around them. It first hit the darkling choking him, then the others. The darkling screamed and shot back into the rift.

A man with long flaming red hair stood there, glowing staff in his hand. "Seems I've arrived just in time," Ambrose said.

CHAPTER 5

Nyx stared at the spot where the strange shadow creature had been. "What was that?" She let out a breath she hadn't known she'd been holding. She coughed as green plumes of smoke rose from the gaping hole that lay a few feet away from them.

"That was a darkling." A tall redheaded man with a braided beard stood before them. He clutched a wooden staff with a glowing orb atop it and wore a deep forest green robe. "That," he motioned towards the rift, "is a rift caused by a tear in the veil of existence."

Energy crackled around him so much it made Nyx's temples throb. Good gods, what was he? He had so much power she had to take a step back, but it did little good to ease her pain. Nyx rubbed her aching forehead. "Which is what?" She had no idea what the man was talking about.

"That is a long story. This rift leads into the underworld. The veil is a boundary between this world and the next. The boundary has been tampered with and dark things that are not meant to walk in this world have come through."

Nyx pushed her long hair off her face. None of this made any sense to her. She had thought the druid coming to find her had been strange enough. Now they had started talking about rifts and evil spirits.

"Ambrose. Thank the spirits you are here," Darius breathed.

Who were these spirits the druid kept mentioning? The gods? Nyx didn't bother asking. Why did it matter? She had to concentrate on getting away from these people, but she kept getting distracted. First by losing control of her powers and now by this newcomer's strange roiling energy.

The newcomer shook his head. "I can't leave you alone for one moment, can I, boy?"

"Gideon sent me to find the mind whisperer. This is Nyx Ashwood." Darius motioned to her. "Nyx, this is my mentor, Ambrose Brethian. He is a druid from Eldara — one of the Andovian Islands."

Ambrose motioned to Ranelle and Lucien. "Why are they here? I thought you were coming to find the mind whisperer on your own?"

"We wanted to come along," Rae said. "It's not often we get to visit one of the lower realms. I needed to get out of the library for a bit."

"We had to make sure he doesn't get into trouble," Luc added and grinned. "He would be lost without us."

Their thoughts buzzed through her mind, and Ambrose's energy grew more intense. Oh, for the love of the gods, how much more discomfort would she have to endure today? Losing control over her so-called power had been hard enough.

A wave of weariness hung over her like a heavy cloak. Ambrose's power struck her like an oncoming storm. Did all druids have this much power? If so, she didn't want to be around any more of them. She had to get away, but Darius was so close to her and with the other druid there she didn't know if she would get far.

"How did you know where we were?" Darius asked.

Nyx backed away further and glanced around for any possible escape route. Her wing ached from where it had been torn earlier, so she doubted she could fly. When one of her wings had been torn before, it had taken days to heal properly. It didn't matter where she ran though as long as she got away from these people.

"I've been tracking rifts for the past two days." Ambrose frowned. "Are you alright, child?" He made a move towards her and Nyx stepped back.

"Please stay away from me." Nyx raised her hands. She almost didn't care if she lost control of her power again. She needed this man to keep away from her. His energy hurt so much.

"Nyx's powers are much stronger than we expected." Darius took hold of Nyx's arm as she turned to leave. The world at once fell silent, and the pain in her head settled to a dull ache. She didn't know whether to be relieved or annoyed by that. She chose the latter. Why did this druid have to keep doing that? The silence might be a blessed relief, but she did not want him touching her. People never came near her, nor did she welcome the feeling.

"We can't leave the rift open." Ambrose gripped his now glowing staff. "This is worse than we feared. I had hoped this problem would be isolated to just the Andovian islands. I didn't realise it would spread to the lower realm so fast."

Darius frowned. "What do you suggest we do? We haven't been able to close any of the rifts before now."

Ambrose ran a hand down his long beard. "Perhaps a shield will help. We can't stay here in the lower realm to monitor things, but I don't want things to become as bad here as they are in Andovia." He raised his staff. "It may not stop the darklings, but it should slow them down." Energy pulse from his staff and a glowing layer of light shimmered over the rift.

Nyx's mouth fell open. Incredible, she had never seen anyone use magic like this before. She was tempted to ask Ambrose about how it worked but decided against it. Darius was too busy explaining Nyx's powers for Ambrose to answer her questions.

They moved past the rift and trudged onward.

Did anyone not know about her? she wondered. As much as she wanted to use her power again, she couldn't risk losing control like she had earlier. The gods only knew what they would do to her if that happened.

Nyx didn't know what to make of the newcomer either. He had power, that was for sure. Lucien was a little gruff. Ranelle seemed nice before Nyx had almost killed her. The druid was another story. He was just like his awful father. She didn't want to know any more about him.

Ambrose's energy hit her hard again as he came closer to them and Darius let go of her arm. Ambrose stopped and drew a large circle on the ground with the end of his staff, marking it with strange symbols.

"What's that for?" Nyx frowned.

"It will transport us near to the port where we will catch our ship," Ambrose replied, and Nyx winced. "Are you well, child?"

How could she explain to someone that their energy hurt her? This had never been a problem before. Only people's thoughts bothered her.

"No, I'm cursed and your... your energy hurts me."

"Ah, you can sense power. That doesn't surprise me. I find your energy quite...uncomfortable myself."

"My what?" She rubbed her aching temples.

"You are like a fire, burning with it," Ambrose told her. "Perhaps that is what my magic feels like to you. When we get on the ship, I'll see what I can do to ease your discomfort." Ambrose motioned for them to go inside. "All of you step into the circle."

Darius took hold of her arm and dragged her into the circle.

"Watch it, druid," she grumbled.

"We both know you'll try to escape again." Darius gave her a look as if challenging her to deny it.

Nyx glowered at him. She had been considering that possibility. She still needed to get away from these people, but Darius wouldn't let go of her. Damned druid. Nyx cursed. Why wouldn't her influence work on him? Especially now when she needed it most.

Ambrose said some strange words and the circle illuminated with light.

"Why are you holding my hand?" Rae demanded of Lucien.

"I'm not. You grabbed my hand," Lucien grumbled. "We both know you're scared of transporting anyway."

"I am not. That was you, Wolfsbane."

Nyx made a move to run for it, but Darius kept a firm grip on her arm.

Light blazed around them, and Nyx's body became weightless for a moment.

Nyx gasped as the light blinded her. Her head spun from the strange sensation, and her stomach recoiled. She thought she might be sick.

They reappeared in an alleyway. The smell of steaming food and the sound of voices hit her hard as Darius relinquished his grip on her. They had to be in the city.

Good gods, Nyx had never been able to cope in the city. Too many voices and the energy crippled her. "How do you expect me to get through this place?" she hissed at Darius. They had no idea how the curse affected her despite claiming to know about mind whisperers.

41

"You can hold on to me."

She rolled her eyes. "Oh, that makes me feel so much better, druid."

"You'll be fine." Darius gripped her arm and the circle faded.

They passed through a bustling cobblestone street. This didn't look anything like the city of Lyrelle where Harland had taken her a few times. This place seemed much cleaner with large stone buildings, houses with proper roofs and a bustling marketplace. Lyrelle had a market too, but most of that had been old junk. This place had food, clothing, jewellery and everything in between. Some of the jewels even looked real. Harland had always taught her how to know the difference between the good stuff and the bad stuff. There was no point in stealing things if they weren't worth good coin.

Nyx waited for the drone of voices to hit her like a swarm of angry bees.

It didn't.

Nyx had to find out why Darius affected her this way. Was it because he was a druid? No, that seemed unlikely since Ambrose didn't mute out her power. Was it because he was a Valeran then? Perhaps, but she didn't know enough about them to be sure.

Nyx's mouth fell open at the sights and sounds. Her stomach groaned at the smell of different spices. She hadn't eaten anything since last night and hadn't realised how hungry she felt until then.

People held out gems and other objects. Nyx wanted to stay and look at everything, taking it all in now that she could absorb things without being overwhelmed by her curse. But Darius tugged on her arm every time she tried to stop and stare at something. What she wouldn't give to use her influence on him, but at the same time he was probably the only thing dampening her curse.

"Come on, we can't miss the ship," he told her.

"It's all rubbish anyway," Lucien remarked when he caught Nyx's wistful gaze.

Rubbish? The stuff she had glimpsed in Lyrelle was rubbish, but this was exciting. She wanted to look and explore. More than anything, she wanted to get away from these people.

"Says someone who doesn't appreciate fine things." Ranelle scowled at him.

"Not all of us like horde junk, dragon lady."

Ranelle swatted him over the head. "I'm not a dragon,

42

Wolfsbane."

Lucien winced. "No, you're a —"

Nyx stopped listening and forced herself to focus. She had to escape. This seemed like a good place to do it. At least now she could concentrate enough to get a good look around. The question was how would she get the druid to let go of her? She could get lost in the crowd and find somewhere to hole up for a while.

This might be her last chance to escape before they got on that ship and took her to Andovia. She didn't know enough about the upper realm to understand what kind of challenges she would face there. At least here in the lower realm she knew what she was up against. She still had her pack with stolen money in it that she had been saving for a time when she could escape from Harland. Nyx had never imagined it would turn out this way. At least the druid and his companions hadn't bothered checking to see what was inside it.

Nyx imagined a wall around her — sometimes that helped when her curse overwhelmed her. She focused on a wall of solid stone. Nyx tugged her arm free from Darius' grasp. She stepped forward and gasped. Voices hit her so hard she couldn't breathe.

Should have made him…

How much does he want for that?

These apples are a bargain.

Oh, good gods. She needed to run, to hide in an alley somewhere away from the chaos of so many minds. Had the druid brought her here on purpose? He must have known she would be overwhelmed by such a place.

"Just breathe." Darius took hold of her arm.

The voices lessened but didn't fade until he took hold of her hand. It felt strange to be so intimate.

"I am not holding hands with you," Nyx hissed.

"Skin to skin contact will make it easier for me to neutralise your power," Darius said. "Is that better?"

"No." She wanted to run, not be stuck with him and led into a new life of untold dangers.

Bloody druid. Power or not, she would get away from him, one way or another.

CHAPTER 6

Darius kept a firm grip on Nyx's arm as they passed through the city. Merchants called out and showed off their wares. People pushed through the bustling crowd. This place was much smaller in comparison to the cities of his homeland.

Nyx looked both uncomfortable and fascinated. "This is…extraordinary." She gasped at the sight of several ships. The wooden vessels groaned and swayed as they bobbed up and down on currents of air. Their massive, coloured sails were flapping, and gold sparks whirled around them. "What are those?"

"Ships." Darius bit back a smile.

"No, ships float on water. I met a sailor once in a tavern, and his thoughts were fascinating," Nyx said. "These don't look like any kind of ships I've seen."

"They float on air instead of water."

Nyx bent to peer under one of them. "How do they stay upright?

"We use old magic," Ambrose answered. "The ships are similar to sea vessels; except they navigate through the air instead of water." They headed for a smaller ship with the name *Affinity* emblazoned on the side. Ambrose hurried along the walkway and ascended the ship.

"We should have flown in by dragon. It would have been so much easier and quicker," Lucien grumbled. "I hate these things."

Darius knew his friend always got airsick whenever they flew on these vessels, but he enjoyed them. They weren't as exhilarating as flying on a dragon, but they were ideal for long distances and more comfortable. Dragons would have drawn too much attention if they

44

had brought them and these vessels were better equipped for carrying large groups of people.

He kept a firm hold on Nyx, both so she wouldn't get overwhelmed by the people, but also so she wouldn't make a run for it. Darius had seen her eyeing potential escape routes already, and he knew she would try escaping again. At least on the ship, she would have nowhere to run.

As they walked up the gangway, Nyx paused halfway up. "Isn't there another way to get to your islands?" Her face turned white.

"Not unless we flew by dragon, but my father couldn't spare any." Darius didn't mention that he hadn't asked his father if they could use any dragons. He knew full well that he never would have agreed.

"How safe are these ships?" Nyx asked. "Will it fall out of the sky?"

"No, my dear. They're very safe and even fare well during storms." Ambrose gave her a warm smile, but it didn't put her at ease.

"Can't you druids transport yourselves from one place to another?" Nyx stared at the other druid in disbelief. "Like you did earlier? Why can't we travel that way?"

"Transportation circles only work over certain distances," Darius replied. "They can't transport us from one realm to another. That requires a lot more power."

They all stood and watched as the crew untethered the ship and set sail. The ship shuddered and groaned as the moorings were released and it took to the air. Darius almost laughed at Nyx's open-mouthed expression as the ship left the dock. After all, he had been travelling on them from a young age since his parents often used them to go to faraway lands.

"How long does it take to get to your islands? I don't want to spend days cooped up on a ship. I thought your brother wanted to see me right away?"

"They're not my islands and it'll be about an hour or two depending on the wind."

Her eyes widened at that. "How fast do these things travel? Isn't wherever we're going hundreds of leagues from here?"

On an ordinary ship, the journey to the upper realm and islands of Andovia would have taken several days.

Darius nodded. "It is a long way, but as I said, these ships travel fast."

"Ranelle, Lucien, I trust you can keep yourselves occupied for a while?" Ambrose asked them. Both teens stared at each other, then gave a curt nod.

"Good. Darius, Nyx, come with me." Ambrose motioned for them to follow.

"Doesn't holding onto me all the time bother you?" Nyx whispered.

Darius frowned, thoughtful. "I have to make sure you don't run away."

She scowled at him. "Doesn't it bother you that you're taking me away from my family?"

"It doesn't matter what I think. The law is the law, Nyx." He had to obey his brother's orders whether he wanted to or not. Besides, he couldn't leave her wandering around the lower realm putting people at risk. Darius hoped she would realise the potential danger of her powers sooner rather than later.

"Never mind the fact my sisters will be sold back into slavery?" She crossed her arms. "Guess I shouldn't expect someone like you to care."

His nostrils flared. "What does that mean?" Darius did not want to waste time or energy arguing with a criminal. When Gideon had sent him to retrieve her, he hadn't expected her to be so irritating. His brother would be in for a shock when he did meet Nyx in person. He almost pitied Gideon for that. He would be glad to get home and be rid of her once and for all. Why did he have to be the one to deal with her? He was part of the Forest Guard on Eldara, not a lowly foot soldier who carried messages and retrieved people for his lord.

"I meant given who your father is, I shouldn't expect you to be any different."

Anger heated his blood and his fists clenched. "You don't know anything about me, so don't presume I'm anything like my father."

Holy spirits, this girl is infuriating.

How dare she compare him to his tyrannical father. Darius had always vowed to be different from his parents. They both might have been dark magic users, and that same darkness ran in his blood, but that didn't mean he would be anything like them. He kept to the true path of what being a druid was meant for: protecting nature, taking care of others and using the powers that came from the natural elements, not from those darker places, as they did.

"Are you coming?" Ambrose called out.

Darius sighed and stalked off after his mentor. He waited, half expecting Nyx to jump over the side of the ship.

She glared at him, then stomped over.

Darius and Nyx headed into a large cabin filled with several seats stuffed with pillows. He would have been glad to retreat to one of the cabins for a while to get away from Nyx. Why did he of all people have immunity to her power? He didn't understand it. There was nothing special about him that would give him the ability to neutralise her. He might have a block on him to ensure he never came under the influence of a mind whisperer. Still, he had never heard of that neutralising a mind whisperer's power entirely. Darius would have to investigate the matter further when he got home.

He would be glad when he no longer had to deal with her. Darius had his own affairs to tend to, like solving the murders caused by the darklings and finding out what had caused the tear in the veil.

"Now what are you doing?" Nyx wanted to know. "Are you going to interrogate me?"

"No, we're going to test your powers," Ambrose answered.

"Why does he block my curse?" She motioned towards Darius. "Is it because he's a Valeran?"

Darius scowled at that. Was he to be blamed for every bad thing because of his infamous family name? He gritted his teeth and muttered a curse under his breath. Dangerous or not, he wanted Nyx gone. Who was she to judge him anyway? She had killed that tavern-keeper — although Darius suspected the world would be a safer place without that slave trader in it.

Ambrose chuckled. "I'm not sure what it is about him that disables your powers yet. But I doubt it is because he is a Valeran."

Darius bit back a smug smile and slumped into a seat. At least he didn't have to hold onto her for a while. Nyx didn't seem so overwhelmed now they were on the ship and there were only a few crew members on board. If she was, she didn't show it.

Darius wondered how much control she had over her abilities. Judging by how she lost control earlier today, he was amazed she hadn't enslaved or killed anyone before now.

"What makes you believe you are cursed?" Ambrose asked her.

"I can't imagine anyone being born with this gift. Plus, Har – the man who raised me said I was cursed. How could this be a gift? I am tormented by other people's thoughts."

"You don't seem to mind using your influence on people, though." Darius leaned back in his seat and crossed his arms.

Her scowl returned. "I do what I must to survive."

"Influencing others couldn't be part of a curse. You use it to your advantage too much. How could you not know the danger that comes with such power?" Darius let his arms fall to his sides. "Mind whisperers are taught from an early age to –"

"Up until last night, I had never even heard the term mind whisperer before. I've been a slave for as long as I can remember. There was no one there to train me."

Darius opened his mouth to ask her more questions, but Ambrose cut him off. "The man you killed." Ambrose didn't say it with any malice. "Did you lose control of your power last night?"

Nyx paled. "I – I don't remember. But I didn't kill him. I might be a thief and use my powers to cheat sometimes, but I don't kill people." Her hands clenched into fists. "And if I did do it, it was only to protect my sister."

Ambrose frowned. "You have a sister? Does she have the same abilities as you?"

Nyx shook her head. "No, we aren't related by blood."

Darius noticed she hadn't mentioned that her sisters did have abilities. He had seen that for himself last night when he had gone to the tavern looking for Nyx. "I need to test you to find a way for you to control your gift," Ambrose said. "How often do you lose control? Do you have lapses in time too?"

Darius hadn't considered the possibility of Nyx truly not remembering what she had done. He thought she might have lost control but had suspected she was lying when she said she had forgotten last night's events. Now he didn't know what to think. She hadn't had any lapse in time earlier when she lost control.

Nyx shrugged. "When I get upset or angry. I'm fine if I stay away from people." She shot Darius another glare.

"And you were with your foundling family for how long?"

"Since they found me under an ash tree when I was ten. That's why they named me after it."

"I'm going to remove the shield I placed around me and see what you can sense." Ambrose raised his staff. "Try not to resist me. I'm going to use my senses. I will not harm you."

Darius straightened in his seat. If she lost control, he would have to neutralise her power again. He would be ready for that – even if he didn't want to touch her again. Once they got to Eldara he would figure out why he could neutralise her power. He didn't know if it was a blessing or a curse. He suspected it meant he would have to spend more time with her even after he handed her over to his brother.

"How did you manage your gift when you were around people?" Ambrose asked.

"It has gotten worse over the past year or two. So, I sometimes take a sedative – that's the only thing that helps." Nyx took a seat as far away from him and Ambrose as she could get.

"What sedative?"

"Nilanda."

Darius' mouth fell open. Nilanda was one of the most potent sedatives and usually only used in healing houses. It was also a dangerous drug because it could sap magical abilities.

"How often do you take that stuff?" Darius asked her.

Nyx shrugged. "Only when my curse gets overwhelming. Or when I have to go to the city. Otherwise, I can't cope with all of the voices."

"Nilanda is dangerous —" Ambrose began.

Nyx held up a hand to silence him. "I know what effects it can have on people. It's never taken my curse away, which is a pity. And I haven't had any adverse side-effects from it either. So, there is nothing to worry about." She fiddled with a leather band on her left wrist. "Harland would… he would hit my sisters if I refused to go with him. It was the only way I could protect them."

Darius flinched. He knew full well what it was like to endure abuse. Pity for her swelled in his chest, though he pushed the feeling away and reminded himself she was still a killer.

"I will scan you with my senses now." Ambrose gripped his staff.

Nyx shrank back in her seat. "Will it hurt? If it does—"

Darius didn't want to risk her losing control again. *We need to be careful. Her losing control is not an experience I want to relive. Her power felt like it would tear me apart.*

Ambrose clutched his staff tighter. *I know. But we'll never know the true extent of her power unless I test it for myself. I doubt she is cursed, but I have to check just to be sure.*

Can I join senses with you? Darius asked. *I am curious about her power, even if I don't like the idea of her using it on anyone.*

Ambrose gave him a slight nod.

"No, this will not hurt, Nyx. All you may feel is a slight tingle." Ambrose raised his staff and the walls around them flashed with light. "This room is now shielded so you will not be affected by the minds of those on board."

Nyx arched an eyebrow. "I still hear them, but not as much as before."

Ambrose and Darius both cast their senses out. Their powers joined together as they connected through a familiar mental link.

"Try not to resist us," Ambrose repeated. "It's a small test. Think of it as if we're looking into a pool and seeing what's inside it."

Nyx tensed, as though bracing herself.

The true extent of her power hit Darius like a tidal wave. He winced as he walked over to Ambrose's side. *Whoa. I had a hard time reading her before but... how have people around her survived for so long? From what I sensed; they only possessed a spark of magic when I was in her village.*

Incredible, so much raw power. Ambrose sent his senses out further. *I haven't met a mind whisperer in decades, but her magic is very strong.*

Darius' eyes widened. He had no idea how Ambrose could have met another mind whisperer since they were supposed to have been extinct for at least a generation.

Stop that! Nyx's voice echoed through their minds.

Darius and Ambrose stumbled backwards as a blast of energy assaulted their senses.

"You do have some control," Ambrose observed. "Well done. I didn't expect you to be able to do that. Are you certain you have no training?"

"How do I have control?" Nyx furrowed her brow. "I didn't do anything. And no, I've never had any training. I've been a thief for as long as I can remember."

"You told us to stop." Darius rubbed his now aching forehead. His senses reeled from the sudden onslaught of energy.

"You blocked us both, we heard your mental command." Ambrose looked flabbergasted. *She has power, that's for sure. It's a good*

<50">
50

thing you came for her when you did.

"I did what?" Nyx asked.

You don't think she's cursed, do you? Darius asked and hoped Nyx wouldn't be able to overhear their conversation.

"Just try not to resist us. We need to probe a little deeper to see if there is any sign of a curse."

I don't feel any dark magic from her, and I would know it, Darius added. *I grew up around it.*

I doubt it's a curse, but I need to be sure. Ambrose sent his senses out again.

Nyx took a deep breath and reluctantly nodded.

Darius sent his still-reeling senses out again and raised his mental shield further in case Nyx lost control. It might not affect him, but he didn't enjoy the feel of it.

Energy pulsed from deep inside Nyx, reverberating through their combined minds. Darius and Ambrose drew back from the feel of it.

"You're very gifted, my dear." Ambrose pulled his senses back, so Darius did the same. "And you are not cursed. Your gift is natural."

Nyx groaned. "I was afraid you'd say that. Can you get rid of it?"

"Why would you want that?" Ambrose gaped at her. "You use your abilities, don't you? How do you think you would adjust to life without them?"

"Because I don't want to endanger people or be enslaved to his blasted family because of it." She inclined her head towards Darius. "I'm sure I would be just fine without my abilities."

Darius supposed that would make Gideon lose interest in her but doubted it would gain her any freedom. Not after she had committed murder.

"That won't grant you your freedom," Darius remarked. "Not after the crime that… took place." He decided not to antagonise her further about Harland's death. It would be better not to make her angry again or she might lose control.

"It would be like saying you wanted to cut off one of your limbs," Ambrose remarked. "Would you want that? It would be a useless thing to do. It's not like you would be cutting off something defective. Your power is as much a part of you as breathing."

Nyx shook her head. "But I'm tired of being at the mercy of everyone else's emotions. I want to be alone in my mind and not have all this noise around me."

"Removing your gift could have terrible consequences. Perhaps even death. No one is ever stripped of their powers unless they have committed a heinous crime or they are not of sound mind."

Nyx sighed. "You don't know if you can teach me to control it. You haven't encountered any mind whisperers for centuries. That's why you're so desperate to have me."

"You read my mind?" Ambrose arched an eyebrow.

"I don't have to. I am a thief. I'm good at reading people."

"We will test your abilities more when we get to Andovia," Ambrose said. "At least there we can be in a more controlled environment away from other people in case your power slips again."

Nyx slumped back in her seat. "Guess I'm stuck with you now, druid."

"I suppose you are." Darius got up and went over to Ambrose, who was staring out of the window.

"We can't let my brother learn how powerful she is," he said, and conjured a ward so Nyx wouldn't overhear them. "I dread to think what he might do if he knew. I suspect he wouldn't kill her but will try to use her powers for himself."

Ambrose nodded. "Nor your father. You know how he and your grandfather wiped out the mind whisperers. He will not be happy when he learns of her." He gripped his staff tighter. "We won't be able to keep that a secret from him – not now that Gideon knows of her existence."

"But how can we stop them? We can't hide her power." Darius gripped the railing. "Gideon might sense her before we even reach the islands."

"I have been thinking about that. A shield would be too obvious." Ambrose rubbed his chin.

"Perhaps we could put the shield on her clothing or…" Darius shook his head. "No, she would need to keep it on all the time. There is too much risk of her taking it off or losing it. A shield would be better because it would be wrapped around her skin."

"Gideon would sense a shield. Besides, Nyx's power would eventually seep through. We would need something to suppress her power, but not leave her vulnerable so she can't sense potential danger." Ambrose frowned. "Perhaps you are the key."

"I can't hold onto Nyx all the time. The moment I let go of her, her power would seep out. Why do I neutralise her power?" Darius frowned.

"At first, I thought it might be the mental shield your father gave you. I can't be sure. Your very touch neutralises her power. Perhaps your blood would have the same effect." Ambrose glanced over at Nyx. "We will test it more and find out how you do it when we return to Andovia."

"How am I supposed to use my blood? I can't use it on her or it might neutralise her power forever." Although he had to admit part of him would be relieved if she did lose her powers. At least then she wouldn't be a threat to anyone.

"Use it on something of hers. Something she has on her. You'll think of something."

Darius only hoped that was true and he could figure out something before he came face-to-face with his brother again.

CHAPTER 7

Nyx had no idea why Darius had taken off the bracelet she wore. It was a thin band made from leather that Kyri had made for her. It might not look like much, but he took it despite her protests only to bring it back moments later. He had done something to it, but she hadn't seen what.

Damned druid, just because he thought he owned her now didn't mean he was entitled to touch her things. He told her to put it on. Nyx had half a mind not to. Perhaps he had done something to glamour it to hide any changes he had made. After what she had seen earlier that morning, nothing would surprise her. She couldn't throw it away, though. It meant too much to her.

She had tried questioning Darius about what would happen to her once they reached Andovia, though he refused to supply any answers. Nyx gasped as the floating ring of islands came into view. They looked smaller than she had expected. "You never said the islands of Andovia were floating." She gripped the railing and leaned forward. Incredible, she had never seen anything like them before. Then again, she had never been on a ship that could fly either. The islands looked like they should fall out of the sky, yet some of them had cascading mountains on top and areas of lush green grass.

Darius joined her. "This isn't Andovia. This is the Ring of Sorrow — a ring of floating islands that serve as a boundary between the upper realm and the lower realm."

She raised an eyebrow. "Why are they called the Ring of Sorrow? They look incredible. I can't see anything sorrowful about them."

"Watch." Darius motioned to the islands. The ship banked a sharp left as one of the islands moved so close to them Nyx gasped.

"Is it going to hit us?" She took a step back, bracing herself for an inevitable impact. Perhaps she would meet her death today after all, only it would be on a crashing ship and not on a pyre.

Darius shook his head. "No, the crew are skilled at navigating their way around these islands. Many ships have perished here, though. It's even worse down below."

Below them, an ocean of blue stretched out with the roar of crashing waves and the faint cries of gulls. Strange, Nyx hadn't realised the sea was there. Seeing it was something she had always wanted to do. She had never thought it would be under this kind of circumstance. Nyx had known there would be no way of escaping while she was stuck on the ship. She might be able to fly, but she had never flown long distances before, and doubted she could with a damaged wing. Nor did Nyx fancy the idea of being forced to stay on one of the floating islands. She had considered the possibility, but now she knew she would get hurtled off one of them.

Nyx needed to be somewhere close to land to make her escape. She knew the druid and the others would be keeping a close eye on her though. The druid knew she would bolt at the first opportunity. That didn't mean she would stick around for long. Nyx had to get away before she came face-to-face with the other Valeran brother. Somehow, she suspected he would be a lot worse than Darius. Now that they knew about her so-called powers, she dreaded to think what they might force her to do with them. Other people using her powers had never been much of an issue until now. Harland had only used her to make good coin and manipulate people to get what he wanted. At least he had never forced her to harm anyone.

She shivered. Nyx still struggled with the thought of him being dead. As much as she despised the man and longed to get away from him, it still felt surreal. Even if she didn't remember what happened, she knew she hadn't killed him.

One way or another, she would get away from these people. She guessed she would have to wait until they reached land. But what then? She would be alone in a strange place with no idea where to go or how to get back to the lower realm. From everything she had heard, she knew the upper realm was a strange place and ripe with slavery. Nyx had no idea what to expect when she got there. Fae were often sold into slavery, and she didn't want to risk being captured by someone else. She had already endured that experience as a child with Harland and didn't want to relive it.

Nyx hoped she had enough coin stashed away to buy a ticket for safe passage on a ship. It didn't matter where she went as long as she got out of the upper realm and back to Joriam to find her sisters. It would be difficult being around so many people, but she would endure it. Maybe she could find a merchant or the captain of the ship and force them to take her where she wanted to go. The possibilities were endless. Now that she knew she had magic and what she was, she realised how limited her life had been before. Why had she been so focused on stealing coins when she could do so much more?

Her mind raced with thoughts as the ship steered its way around the ring of floating islands. The druid insisted once they were past the almost impenetrable barrier of rings they would soon arrive in Andovia. She needed to be ready. Getting off the ship would probably be the best time to make a run for it – either then or once they got into a crowd of people.

More islands hovered by, some even floating below them close to the waterline. As the *Affinity* rounded another mass of land, the ship slowly descended and drew closer to the water. Nyx leaned over the edge to get a better view. Below them, fish jumped out of the water along with the shimmering outline of what she thought was also a fish until it emerged on the surface and shook a spear at her. It looked to be a half-humanoid, half-fish creature. Nyx gasped. "What is that?"

"It's one of the merfolk. We are passing over the realm of the Undersea where they live. They are not very fond of ships," Darius replied. "That's another reason why we use flying ships and not sea vessels. Too many of them get attacked and often sunk because of our feud with the Undersea realm."

Nyx had heard of the merfolk in some of the village's old tales, but she had always thought they were a myth. She never imagined an entire realm could exist below the waves. Up ahead large islands loomed into view. Dark shapes moved through the air, and large buildings dwarfed the landscape. On the central island, something glittered like a diamond.

"What's that?" Nyx motioned to the shining object. It couldn't be a building, could it?

"That's the Crystal Palace on the main island of Avenia. The glowing towers are in its capital city Alaris."

"This is incredible," Nyx breathed then shook her head. No matter how magical this place looked, she had to remember she wasn't here to stay.

"It's nice to look at, but don't let its beauty fool you," Darius muttered under his breath.

She frowned at him. "What does that mean?" Dread gnawed at her stomach like icy fingers. What was he talking about? Could this new place be even worse than she had imagined?

He shook his head. "Not everything is as wonderful as it looks here."

"What kind of world are you dragging me into, druid?" Nyx put her hands on her hips. She knew beauty often hid deception, but if there was further trouble in this new realm, she wanted to know about it. It was all the more reason for her to get away from the druid before it was too late.

"I'm not dragging you into anything. If you had laid low and kept your powers to yourself, you wouldn't be coming here now. You have no idea what kind of danger you are in just being what you are."

Nyx glowered at him. "Then why don't you let me go? Your brother is probably going to kill me anyway."

Darius returned her glare. "Because you are still a criminal and a danger to everyone in this world. I can't let you go and put thousands of lives at risk."

Nyx gritted her teeth. If he let her go it wouldn't mean she had to be around people. She could easily live alone in a forest away from everyone. That way she wouldn't be a danger to anyone, and she wouldn't have to suffer through the constant onslaught of people's thoughts. Once Nyx got back to her sisters they could all leave and live off the land somewhere far away from the laws of any realm.

"What happens to me now, then? Am I going to be taken to prison?" Nyx asked. She wanted to know what she might be up against when they got there.

"You're not going to be locked up." Darius shook his head. "Put your bracelet back on."

She narrowed her eyes. "Why? What did you do to it?"

He raised his hands. "Nothing. Just… you don't want to lose it, do you? You might drop it."

"You are a terrible liar, druid. And if I'm not locked up, I guess I'm going to be put to work then. Or forced to do something awful."

"No one will force you to do anything."

Nyx scoffed at that. "You forced me to come here. You already said your brother wants me for my so-called power. We both know he won't want me to do anything good with it, so don't bother lying."

Darius sighed and looked away.

Nyx reluctantly put the bracelet back on. She wondered how she would cope with all the minds on the island. They couldn't guarantee a way to control her curse. She refused to call her ability a gift. It was a burden and an unbearable one at that.

"Welcome to the islands of Andovia." Ambrose came out on deck too. "This is said to be the birthplace of magic."

Nyx believed that well enough. Energy seemed to pulse all around the islands. She expected it to overwhelm her, yet it didn't. Odd. Intense energy always overwhelmed her. Even Ambrose's energy didn't affect her the way it had earlier. Perhaps he had raised his shield.

"So all the Andovian are fae?" She arched a brow.

Ambrose shook his head. "Not quite. Most of the original Andovians were forced into slavery during the last great realm war when the Andovian queen was killed. Since then the Archdruid has ruled these lands."

"Thank the holy spirits we're back." Lucien gripped the railing. He had looked green throughout the journey. "I'm never going on one of these things again."

"I offered to make you an anti-sickness charm," Darius pointed out. "You refused. So, you only have yourself to blame, my friend."

"Magic doesn't work on me." Lucien slumped onto the deck and placed his head between his knees.

The ship slowly began its descent. The closer the islands got, the more it filled her with dread.

"Once we are docked, I must go to the Crystal Palace." Ambrose gripped his staff tighter.

"Palace?" Nyx frowned. Although she had glimpsed the palace earlier, she hadn't expected to go there, though it made sense as Darius' brother likely lived there.

She would have to be ready when they reached the ground to make her escape. Nyx swung her bag over her shoulder and fiddled with her bracelet. She considered taking it off again, but if she did the druid would probably nag her more.

"It's where the Archdruid and the fae queen hold court," Darius explained. "My brother will want to see you, but I want to return home first to check on things."

"Your parents." She had heard of the Archdruid being married to a fae queen, yet the druid didn't look like any of the fae she had seen before.

He shook his head. "No, the fae queen is not my mother."

"So, she's his mistress? And your mother is his wife?"

Darius rubbed the back of his neck. "In the eyes of the fae, the queen is his wife. My father is also married to my mother, who is a sorceress."

"How does that work?" Nyx imagined it must be hard enough having one spouse. Two would be impossible.

"It's complicated. My mother considers herself his true wife, as does my father."

Nyx didn't ask anything further. What a strange world she had been dragged into. She still expected to get overwhelmed by thoughts as the ship came closer to the island.

A few stray thoughts buzzed around her mind, but nothing more than usual. Nyx didn't know whether to be relieved or alarmed. The druid had done something to her bracelet, she knew it. Why did he want to make her powerless now? Was it so he could have her instead of his brother? No, he seemed to want to get rid of her. The whole reason they had come to find her was because of her abilities and whatever that mysterious prophecy was about.

She had even heard Darius and Ambrose talking about darklings too. They had mentioned murders and how the creatures were killing people. They didn't seem to know who or what might be causing it.

"What did you do to my bracelet?" she hissed at Darius.

"Nothing." He forced his face to become passive, but she could see right through his innocent expression.

"I'm not a fool, druid. It's different, I can feel it. I will use my influence again if I have to."

Darius gave a harsh laugh. "That won't work on me — you should know that by now."

"What did you do?" She gritted her teeth. Her power roared just below the surface and ached to get out. Once they were off the ship,

59

it would be time to go, and she would be ready. Still, she wanted to know what damage the druid had done.

"It's just a spell to make sure you don't run off. Even if you take it off, the spell will still prevent you from escaping."

Her heartbeat quickened at that. The *Affinity* landed with a loud thunk, waves crashing against the sides as it entered a small dock filled with water. Metal creaked and groaned as clamps locked the ship into place.

The crew lowered the ramp after the ship settled.

"Come along," Ambrose called and motioned for them to follow.

The moment they stepped off the ship, Darius put a hand on her arm. "Don't think of trying to run away," he said. "You are spelled now, and I'm not in the mood for chasing after you."

Lucien and Ranelle came up behind them. Lucien looked more like his usual self now. As a shifter, she knew he could probably track her too, regardless of any spell.

Would running or flying be the best option? She flapped her wings, relieved to find they still felt intact. Maybe her injury from earlier that morning had healed enough for her to fly now. She'd always been a fast healer.

Nyx trailed after the druids as they disembarked onto the island of Avenia.

Thoughts still buzzed at the edge of her mind, yet the voices sounded far away. The bracelet must suppress her curse. But why? They wanted her to control it, didn't they? Her curse had always been good for one thing: showing people's true intentions. Now it was failing her when she needed it most.

Was that why Darius had enchanted it?

No, Darius was immune from her power, and Ambrose had a strong shield around his mind. With enough force or perhaps if she touched him, she would get through it.

Nyx fiddled with the bracelet. It wouldn't come off. She knew the druid must have enchanted it so she couldn't remove it either. She gave him another glare. First, he had dragged her all the way here. Now he had cursed one of her most treasured possessions. Nyx would find a way to escape and get revenge on him.

They passed through the cobblestone streets. Colour adorned the people, the houses and everything in between.

Everything looked so bright here.

Nyx was in awe and wanted to take everything in. Everything back in her realm had been dark and earthy. No one had been able to afford anything bright. The tribe had thought such things frivolous. She reminded herself not to get distracted. This would be the perfect place to get lost in the crowd.

"Lucien, Ranelle, you should return to your duties now," Ambrose said. "I have things to take care of with the high council. Darius, why not head home? You and Nyx can freshen up whilst you're there."

Nyx's stomach dropped. They were leaving her alone with the druid?

Ranelle and Lucien said their goodbyes and wandered off. Ambrose trailed off too.

"Come." Darius motioned for her to follow him.

"Don't think I will just obey your orders if you bark them at me."

Darius sighed. "Are you always this irritating?"

She flashed a smile that showed too much teeth. "I do my best. Where are we going?"

"Over to the island of Eldara — it's where I live with Ambrose and the other druids."

Her mouth fell open. "You don't live there?" She motioned to the glistening towers of the Crystal Palace.

He snorted. "I did once. It is not as wonderful as it looks, believe me." He sounded sincere this time.

"Aren't you taking me to your brother to show off your new prize?"

Darius narrowed his eyes. "You are not my prize. I was only following orders. I thought you might want to clean up and have some food. Then I'll take you to my brother."

"Oh, so you'll make sure I look good first?" She sneered. "Why have you suppressed my power? What kind of game are you playing, druid?"

Darius sighed. "No game, can we please get moving?"

Nyx crossed her arms. This was her chance, she realised, to get away for good. Everyone looked fae with pointed ears, horns and other strange abnormalities. She would not look out of place among them with her wings. Anywhere else in the lower realm people would have spotted her easily, but not here. Her mind raced with trepidation, and she forced the feeling away.

Nyx finally spotted an opening. Darius was focused on where he was going instead of her. Finally, the chance for freedom.

She tugged at her bracelet. It refused to budge.

Oh well, it would have to wait until later. Once she was somewhere out of the way, she would get it off. Nyx made sure her sack was secured. She couldn't risk losing it during her escape.

It was now or never.

"Lord Darius?" someone called out.

Nyx faltered as she turned to make a run for it.

A gangly male fae with pointed ears came over. He gasped for breath. "Prince Gideon requests you come to the palace at once."

Nyx bolted and made it a few paces before something barred her way. A wall of invisible energy prevented her from moving forward. She turned and slammed into it again. No matter what direction she went, something blocked her.

The messenger scurried off.

"We've got to go to the palace." Darius' jaw tightened. "There's no time to go anywhere else."

Nyx's shoulders slumped. He knew she would run, and he'd stopped her.

Like it or not, she was stuck with him. Now it was time to face the other Valeran brother.

CHAPTER 8

How he hated this place. On the outside it looked beautiful, but it held a wealth of dark magic inside. Hidden behind pretty glamours, jewels and finery. Darius despised everything about the fae court. He had always been glad when his father travelled. His mother insisted he remain with her until he had grown old enough to leave.

His home was on Eldara, among the trees, nature and the openness. Being surrounded by his fellow druids and not among people who desired nothing but power and status was where he belonged.

As they approached the giant double doors leading to the palace two guards dressed in shining silver armour approached them. Both were fae men with golden hair and a silver glow to their skin. The guards scanned him, then waved them through. They used their senses but wouldn't detect any threat from him.

"Why are the guards glowing? Do you see it?" Nyx hissed at him.

Darius nodded. He guessed she had never seen people like these before or been into the upper realm. "The ruling fae here are called Silvans. They are one of the oldest and most powerful races of fae."

"Why don't they have any wings?" Nyx frowned.

"Not all fae have wings. Most of the ruling class do not. In fact, they consider having wings a sign of inferiority." He wouldn't go into depth about what the people here thought about the different kinds of fae. Nyx would find out all of that herself soon enough.

Her eyes widened. "Why? I thought any race would be glad to rule the skies."

Darius gave a humourless laugh. "Oh, the Archdruid rules the skies here, but not with the fae. With them." He pointed upwards where dark shadows moved over the city and roars echoed in the distance like thunder. "My father controls both the land and sky. One day soon he will no doubt rule the seas as well. I hope to the spirits that day doesn't come any time soon."

"What are they?" Nyx asked, then gasped. "Are those dragons?"

He nodded. "Most of them are the Dragon Guard – my father's army. He has thousands of warriors stationed here in the upper realm and in the lands beyond."

"But you're not in the Dragon Guard? I thought someone like you would relish the chance to do that. I know full well what the Dragon Guard does. News travels fast even in the lower realm." Nyx's hands clenched into fists. "They raze entire towns and villages to the ground."

Darius' stomach clenched. He didn't want to think about the many atrocities committed by the Dragon Guard. It was one of the reasons he had decided against joining them. "Don't pretend to know anything about me."

They passed through a long hall. Tapestries and golden statues lined the walls. More guards were stationed throughout. Darius knew Gideon would be in the council meeting along with the queen and the other council leaders. It felt odd being back here. Gideon must have had his spies on the lookout for him since Darius kept his presence shielded. Blast it all, he should have transported himself and Nyx over to Eldara when they landed. At least that would have bought him some time and allowed him to coach Nyx on how to deal with Gideon.

Would she have listened, though? Doubtful. But he had hoped to explain a few things to her, and to clean her up a bit. Nyx did look worse for wear with her torn, bedraggled clothing and dirt-smeared skin. Darius didn't care about such things, but Gideon would.

Thank the spirits he had used his blood on her bracelet before they got off the ship. At least her powers would be under control. He hoped it would last and it would keep her power hidden from his brother and everyone else in the council meeting chamber. It wouldn't surprise him if her magic somehow managed to seep through whatever immunity he had. Her power was so strong he doubted anything could contain it.

Nyx didn't say anything as they carried on down the hall. Two double doors led into the council meeting chamber. The meeting was already in session.

Darius wouldn't go in that way. His stepmother would be furious if he walked in unannounced. He opened the door to the antechamber, and Nyx followed him inside, glowering at him. The small room held little more than a couple of chairs and a table where people or guests that were brought before the council were made to wait. A tapestry depicting the islands of Andovia covered one wall.

It was typical of Gideon to force him to wait. Darius knew he couldn't do anything to object. Like it or not, Gideon always came first, and Darius was used to being second in line.

"Stop that," Darius snapped when he caught Nyx tugging at her bracelet.

Her eyes narrowed. "I know you bewitched it. I don't understand why."

Darius sighed. "Would you believe it's to keep you safe?" He didn't see the point in lying to her now. But he knew he had to be on his guard, even the walls had ears in this palace.

Nyx snorted. "You wouldn't do anything to protect me." She crossed her arms. "So, what did you do to it?"

"Does it matter? You'd only see me as your enemy anyway."

"You're hardly an ally, are you?"

"I'm not your enemy." He might not like the fact she was a criminal, but that didn't make them enemies either. Her power could be useful in the right hands, and he couldn't help but think of all the good she could do with it if she chose to. Instead of all of the bad things she had been doing.

"You brought me here." She glowered at him.

"No, your actions did that." He glared back at her.

"Oh, so it's my fault I can't control my damned powers." Nyx fiddled with her bracelet again, but it refused to come off. "Did you enchant this so it stays on my wrist?"

"It's for your own good." He decided against telling her how the bracelet would suppress her power. Time would soon tell whether his plan had worked or not. If Gideon discovered the true extent of her power, he wouldn't be able to do anything to save her.

"How so?" Nyx put her hands on her hips. "I didn't get over —"

Darius clamped a hand over her mouth and stifled her cry of

alarm. *Be quiet. There are people here that will listen to everything we say. If you want to stay alive, you will keep your power hidden and your mouth shut.*

Nyx's eyes widened, and she slapped his hand away. *What are you talking about? Why would anyone overhear us?* she demanded. *Besides, why would you want to keep me alive? You want to get rid of me.*

Darius sighed. *You are right. Perhaps I should just let my brother have you and do whatever he wants. Forgive me for trying to keep you alive.*

Give me one good reason why I should believe anything you say. You are a Valeran. Nyx crossed her arms.

Believe it or not, the last thing I want is my brother to have your power on his side.

Nyx scoffed at that. *So, you want my power for yourself then? From what I've seen and heard, you have to live in your brother's shadow. You want to use me against him, don't you?*

That sounded so ridiculous Darius laughed. *You couldn't be any further from the truth. I don't want to use you for anything. Spirits, I'd be glad if you hadn't set foot here. You need to learn to control your powers and Ambrose might be the only one who can help you do that. I've suppressed your power because that might be the only thing that keeps you alive.*

You really expect me to believe that?

Believe whatever you like. Darius gritted his teeth and stormed into the passageway. He hurried up the steps to the balcony that looked down on the council meeting hall. At least up there he could get away from her. Everything about her infuriated him, especially the fact that she thought he was a true Valeran. It made him wonder why he had bothered to help her.

The high council sat down below. A vast blue diamond shape covered the tiled floor, and high arched windows let in cool streams of light. A table stood in the centre of the space and flags fluttered overhead depicting symbols for each race.

A petite woman sat at the head of the room. Her rose gold hair shined like polished marble, and her pointed ears stood stark against her pale skin. A white crown glittered around her forehead.

Nyx stomped up behind him and stopped short. "Who are they?"

He motioned to the woman. "That's the queen."

On the queen's left sat a young man with a handsome chiselled face. His dark blond hair was tied back, and his dark green eyes were creased with a frown. He wore a dark green tunic and a glittering symbol of the Awen hung around his neck. Nyx would no doubt recognise Gideon from the projection she had seen earlier that morning. On the queen's right sat an ethereal looking woman with silver hair and azure eyes. Her long white gown cascaded down her body like a waterfall.

"That's Irena of the Silvan fae. She is a leader too and a distant cousin of the queen."

Next to them sat a man with a long, black bushy beard. He wore a rumpled grey tunic and brown trousers. He looked out of place among the two stunning women.

"That's Alaric, leader of the shifters and chief overseer. He is Lucien's mentor."

"Is he a Lycan?"

"Lykae," Darius corrected. "No, he is a fae shifter. The lykae are kindred of them. Different Magickind can become overseers – they are guardians. They guide and protect important people throughout their lives."

"Who does Alaric protect?"

Darius shook his head. "No one – I suspect he did once. Now he leads the shifters on Migara and trains new overseers." He didn't see the harm in telling her who each of the council leaders were. It stopped them from arguing for once.

The fourth person had pale, almost opaque skin.

"Is that a man or a woman?" Nyx frowned.

"That's Navi, an ice elf, and I don't know if they are male or female. They like to be referred to as they." Sometimes Navi looked male, sometimes female.

"Is Ambrose a leader too?"

Darius shook his head. "No. He will step in as a leader on rare occasions, though."

"Is that all of them?" Nyx leaned a little closer then drew back when Gideon turned his head in their direction.

"Yes, there used to be five, but now that only happens when my father is present." Darius looked down again, surprised to find Ambrose absent. Had his mentor come and gone already?

The double doors burst open and, as if on cue, Ambrose rushed in.

Odd, where had the other druid been? What had taken him so long? Ambrose had left them at the dock a while before the messenger had come to find Darius.

"Forgive me for being late." Ambrose gasped for breath and sweat beaded on his brow. He bowed his head in respect to the leaders and scrambled around the table to reach an empty seat reserved for guests.

"Was your ship delayed?" Gideon glared at the other druid. "I ordered you to come here once you arrived." Gideon had never liked Ambrose since he got more respect from the other druids than Gideon ever would. They had wanted Ambrose to serve in Fergus' place when the Archdruid was away. Gideon had been furious at that. Ambrose had refused, even though he despised the way Fergus did things.

"No, I had another matter to attend to and was delayed. Again, my apologies." Ambrose gripped his staff, still breathing hard. "I didn't mean to be gone for so long. Has something happened in my absence?" He edged towards the seat but didn't sit down since Gideon was also standing. "Has another rift opened?"

"Where have you been?" Gideon asked. "You've been gone for days and didn't once report in about where you were going or what you were doing."

Darius gripped the balcony rail harder. Since when did anyone need Gideon's permission to leave the upper realm? He shouldn't have been surprised though. Gideon did everything in his power to make the old man suffer.

"I've been tracking the rifts that have been opening up here and in the lower realms." Ambrose took a seat in an empty chair that was usually reserved for Gideon, who now sat in the Archdruid's seat.

Typical Gideon. He had to be in the place of power.

"There have been more deaths. My apprentice was also attacked by a darkling."

Gideon's icy gaze shot up to Darius. Blast it all, Darius hadn't wanted his brother to see him or Nyx.

Darius shot the prince a glare. *Go about your meeting. When it's over, I can finally leave.*

"I have seen the darklings on Migara," Alaric spoke up. "We gave chase, but our magic had little effect against them.

"No one was hurt?" Queen Isabella asked with a slight lilt to her voice.

"Yes, one of the shifters was killed. When are you going to take the threat of those evil spirits seriously?" Alaric leaned forward in his seat.

Gideon scoffed. "They are nothing but wandering spirits. They are of no threat to anyone. The veil is thin on this point of Erthea. Spirits are always coming through — that is nothing unusual."

"What about the rifts?" Navi asked and played with a strand of their long hair. "Have more emerged? Those are not natural. We have never had rifts open up before."

Irena leaned forward. "Yes, I would like to know about this too."

"The rifts are nothing to be alarmed about," Gideon insisted. "Rifts open up in the land sometimes."

"The veil between the worlds —" Ambrose protested.

"Enough!" Queen Isabella raised her hand. "Until you bring proof of this, it is not a concern of this council. You are always trying to bring such trivial matters before us. If you're so concerned, you and the other druids can handle it."

"But what of the prophecy?" Alaric asked. "What if this is the dark time it speaks of? This could be the start of something terrible coming, and we need to be prepared for it. Our world barely survived the last dark age."

"There's no proof of that." Gideon sat down and leaned back in his high-backed chair.

Then why did you send me to find Nyx? Darius wondered. *You believe the next dark time is coming, brother. You just don't want the council to know it.* Gideon would want to sweep in and save the day so he would look like a hero.

"Then, this meeting is over." Queen Isabella rose from her seat and waved her hand in dismissal. "We shall reconvene again in a few days."

Alaric, Irena and Navi all rose and left the meeting chamber.

Ambrose straightened to his full height, but Gideon shot to his feet before he had a chance to say or do anything. "How dare you embarrass me like that," he snapped. "Why do you insist on blowing this situation with the rifts out of proportion? There's no danger to anyone. You are causing fear over nothing."

That did it. Darius would not let his brother underhand his mentor. People were dying, and neither Gideon nor his mother would do anything to acknowledge that.

Darius raised his hand; light flashed around Nyx, who yelped in alarm. He had cast another web around her to make sure she couldn't run off. He didn't have time to go chasing after her and knew she would try escaping again at the first opportunity.

Darius stormed out of the antechamber and into the meeting hall. "A darkling attacked me today. If not for Ambrose, I would be dead now. When are you going to do something about this problem?"

Gideon gave a harsh laugh. "Of course you would defend the old fool here. You would say anything to increase his agenda."

"Agenda? Are you out of your bloody mind?" Darius didn't care about repercussions. Gideon was out of line, and he knew it.

"Watch your tongue, brother," Gideon warned. "I sent you to retrieve something important, not for you to go gallivanting off with the old man. I grow weary of the two of you coming to the council with endless problems. It's tiresome."

"Why are you so determined to ignore this problem?" Darius retorted. "People are dying, and the veil is breaking. If it fails, all of Erthea will be destroyed. A true leader would help his people, not condemn them to death."

"You are not a leader, brother," Gideon scoffed. "No, you are woodsman who spends his days chasing sprites around."

Darius' blood boiled. "You —" Power flared between his fingers, and he clenched his hand into a fist. Spirits, why now? He rarely ever lost control of his powers, but Gideon always seemed to set him off. He wasn't like Nyx. He had been trained from a young age to keep his power under control.

Ambrose put a firm hand on his shoulder. "Perhaps you should fetch the mind whisperer."

Darius stared at his mentor, incredulous. "But—"

Go, boy, Ambrose said. *Arguing with your brother will only cause you more problems. Besides, I'm sure Nyx is anxious for this to be over with. And we don't need her trying to escape, which no doubt she will.*

Darius hissed out a breath and stormed off. He clenched both hands, and static rippled over his fingers. What was wrong with him? He took several deep breaths to calm himself. Still, his power and the darker side of it ached to get out. Darius pushed it back and locked it away where he always kept it deep inside himself. Just because he didn't act like a Valeran didn't mean he did not have the power and darkness which came with his family name.

He had to get this over with. Ambrose was right about one thing: as soon as he delivered Nyx, he would be able to get back to more important matters like solving the darkling problem.

CHAPTER 9

Nyx gritted her teeth. No matter what she did, the bracelet wouldn't come loose. When she made a run for the exit something blocked her way again. Another invisible wall of energy. Curse that druid!

She had seen enough of the argument between Gideon and Darius to know she didn't want to meet the other Valeran brother. She had to leave or the gods only knew what they would do with her.

Nor did she believe the nonsense Darius had told her about suppressing her power to keep her alive. Why would he do such a thing? It made no sense to her. If he wanted to help, he wouldn't have brought her before his brother in the first place.

Like it or not, she needed her curse. Without a sword or her power, she wouldn't be able to defend herself.

Come off! She gave the bracelet another tug.

Still, it wouldn't move.

Come off! Nyx screamed inside her mind and power pulsed inside her. Good gods, her power was still there. That meant she could still access it — or at least she hoped she could.

Darius came back in, his face like thunder. "Don't answer back to my brother. It won't do any good. Come on." He motioned for her to follow. "Let's get this over with. I have other things to take care of. Stopping the darklings is more important than wasting time here."

Nyx opened her mouth to berate him for whatever magic he had used on her. She hesitated. He sounded genuine about wanting to stop the darkling problem. She hadn't expected that. Maybe there was some good in him.

Maybe.

Curse it. There would be no escaping now, even if she did try to run. Nyx should have tried harder and gotten away earlier. No point in what-ifs now. She would have to face her fate and come face-to-face with the fae prince.

Nyx stomped in beside him. Perhaps it was better to get this over and done with. At least she would know what she was up against and whatever the prince had planned for her. Then she would make her escape and get back to the lower realm before it was too late.

Queen Isabella came back into the room and gasped when she caught sight of Nyx. "Who is this filthy creature, and why have you brought her here?" She covered her nose and mouth in disgust. "Is it someone you rescued from the woods?"

Nyx gritted her teeth, bit back a retort and glanced at her bedraggled clothing. She might be a little dirty, but it was not as if she had had a chance to bathe or change into anything else. She couldn't even remember the last time she had eaten.

"Here is the mind whisperer." Darius motioned to her. "This is Nyx Ashwood."

"Holy spirits, this is her?" Gideon's lip curled. "You could have cleaned her up beforehand."

Darius crossed his arms. "You wanted us here at once."

Nyx's stomach dropped, and her wings drooped. She felt a hideous, filthy thing compared to their ridiculous beauty. Her dark pink hair flashed with a riot of colour as it always did when she fought to keep her emotions under control.

Bow, Darius told her in thought. *If you don't show them any respect, it will only make things worse.*

She snorted and glared at the druid. *Respect has to be earned. I don't bow to anyone. He's not my prince and* – She clenched her hands behind her back so no one would see them.

Gideon came over and stared at her, expectant.

His energy felt different from Darius. Cold, dark and seductive. This man got what he wanted. No matter the cost.

Nyx gasped as Gideon raised his hand. Faint words of power whispered on the air. Energy pulsed against her skin, beating her limbs, demanding she bow.

Nyx found herself hitting the floor face-first. Bastards!

Gideon knelt and pulled her head up by her hair. "Scruffy little thing, aren't you?" He forced her to look up and meet his icy gaze.

His energy washed over her like icy water, sliding across her skin. Nyx shivered without meaning to. *Get away from me!* Her magic pulsed at the edge of her mind, but it didn't reverberate through her body like usual. Something held it back – her bracelet. The barrier tingled against her skin forcing her power back.

"Is that it? You're not even going to resist me?" Gideon scoffed, and an evil grin spread across his face. "I expected more from the mind whisperer given the legends I've heard about your kind. Most of them were fierce and fought with their minds. After all the boasting Harland did about you, I'm disappointed. Perhaps you don't have any real power at all, do you?"

Stop! She screamed and willed her curse to rear up and slam into him. Why wouldn't it work? Had the druid suppressed her power that much? Nyx remembered the band he had placed on her earlier that morning to prevent her from escaping. That had been supposed to block her power. Instead, her magic had burned straight through it as if it meant nothing. What had he used on her bracelet to hold her power back so much? It didn't matter. She wanted it gone. She wanted to hit this awful prince with the full strength of her power. Real power. Oh, she might not be cursed, but she did have power. That much she had realised today when she had lost control.

But Gideon didn't stop; his power held her in place. This was dark magic. All the stories about the Archdruid and how he forced people to bow before him were true. How long would he keep her down like this? What did he want from her? For her to show him her power?

Then she remembered what Darius had told her. He had said to keep her mouth shut and her power hidden if she wanted to stay alive. She also knew her power might not even work against Gideon as it didn't work against his brother. He might be immune as well.

Think. Stay alive. Nyx had escaped death once today already, and she did not want to have to face it again so soon.

She would not be forced to cower like some snivelling dog. The pressure increased as she forced her limbs into a sitting position. Even if she couldn't use her power, she wouldn't be forced to endure this any longer.

"You have strength, but it feels much weaker than I thought," Gideon observed. "How is this the infamous girl we heard so many stories about?"

"Don't know what you heard, but it isn't true," Nyx growled. "I don't have any power. I am a thief, nothing more." Pain throbbed through her head like a hammer hitting an anvil.

"So you don't hear thoughts?" Gideon raised an eyebrow and still refused to relinquish his hold on her.

Nyx hesitated. Should she lie or admit the truth?

Darius shot her a look. *Do not tell him the true extent of your abilities.*

It made her wonder what the druid was playing at. Did he have his own agenda? Perhaps. Only time would tell.

Nyx snorted. "If I could, don't you think I would have escaped by now?" She shot Darius a look, daring him to speak up and tell Gideon the truth. Now would be the perfect opportunity to do just that.

Queen Isabella came over. Nyx made a move to get up, but her body refused to comply. "Release her, my son. I want to look at her."

The pressure pounding against her lessened but didn't fade. Nyx scrambled up, and Queen Isabella circled around her, her gaze scrutinising everything. Energy crackled against Nyx's skin. The queen's power felt like ice, but not as aggressive or forceful as her son's. "We haven't encountered a mind whisperer in a generation. If she does have power, it is minimal at best. I sense nothing from her." She gave a derisive snort. "Throw her back in the gutter where she belongs. I do not like vermin within my palace walls."

Nyx's power continued to rage beneath the surface. It surged through her body and burned its way down her arm to where the leather band encased her wrist. It wanted to get out and demanded to be let loose, but whatever magic the druid had used held it back.

"Are you sure you brought the right person back?" Gideon demanded of Darius. "Her power is average at best. The reports stated her powers were strong, that she could influence others. Where is the mind whisperer I heard all the tales about?"

"You told me to fetch the mind whisperer. That is what I did. She was the only one to be found in the disgusting tavern." Darius raised his chin and crossed his arms. "I only did as instructed. It's not my fault she doesn't have any power. Perhaps the slave owner exaggerated about what she can do. Mind whisperers have been gone for so long, even if some of their bloodlines did exist, it's probably weak at best."

"What is your lineage, girl?" Queen Isabella demanded.

"My what?"

Isabella sighed and rolled her eyes. "I mean, where are you from? Who were your parents?" she demanded. "If there are other mind whisperers out there, we need to know about them. One of your parents must have been a mind whisperer to have passed the gift onto you."

"She came from a gutter, no doubt." Gideon laughed.

Nyx hesitated and wondered how much she should reveal about her past. No doubt they would mock her even more. "I am a foundling. I lived in Joriam with the couple who took me in after they purchased me from the slave market." She would not mention Harland's name again for fear of seeing his spirit.

"Where were you found?" Gideon sneered.

"Under a tree." She glowered at him. Just because she had to keep her mouth shut and her power reined in didn't mean she had to completely hide her disdain for him.

The doors to the meeting hall burst open as a man wearing a long white robe etched with silver strode in. A silver crown adorned his head and looked like it had been carved out of leaves.

Nyx instinctively bowed her head. She didn't need her powers to tell her who this man was. It was ingrained in everyone. Power hit her hard and made her head pound like a heavy drum. Anyone could sense the aura of the Archdruid. It was how he reminded people of his reach, his influence and his absolute power.

Fergus Valeran towered over his wife. His dark blonde hair fell past his shoulders, his body was all rippling muscle. Odd. He looked only a decade older than his two sons. Nyx guessed if you could live for centuries perhaps age wasn't an issue.

A woman trailed in alongside him. Dark hair fell past the shoulders of her red velvet gown. Her cool grey eyes took everything in. Her face looked more striking than pretty. Nyx knew she must be Darius' mother given the resemblance between them. Her magic crackled over Nyx's skin, icy and colder than Gideon's magic.

Nyx shivered. This woman's energy had a touch of death to it.

"I heard you found a mind whisperer. Is it true?" Fergus demanded. "Where is it? Have you killed them already? You should have informed me sooner. If that infernal Magickind still exists, we could have another realm war on our hands."

Nyx would have thought the Archdruid would have been glad of that. He seemed to delight in raging war against any race. But that made her wonder: were there still mind whisperers out there? She must have come from somewhere before she ended up in slavery. Yet she had no memory from before that time. Perhaps something awful had happened to her and her mind had blocked it out.

Both Gideon and his mother lost their smug looks. The Archdruid commanded everyone, even them, it seemed.

Nyx thought she caught a flash of disdain from Isabella which was soon replaced by a smile. "Husband, you should have sent word of your arrival." Isabella touched her face. "I agree. Kill the girl before she has a chance to breed and create more of her unnatural kind." Queen Isabella sneered. "To let her live is to put us all in danger."

Nyx glanced towards the door. Would they kill her? She had been sentenced to death once already. The Archdruid's form of death would probably be even worse than being burned on a pyre. But how could she escape?

Fergus ignored Isabella as if she wasn't there. "Well?"

"Darius brought back this mind whisperer." Gideon motioned towards Nyx. "But her power is minimal. She's no use to anyone."

Fergus flicked his dark gaze towards her.

Nyx winced as his senses roamed over her, like a clap of thunder, hard and fast. *Leave me alone. Gods, make this stop.*

"You are right. I don't sense much power from her at all." Fergus frowned. "How can a mind whisperer still exist? My father wiped them out decades ago, and I made sure to destroy any stragglers early in my reign. Are there more of you, girl?"

Nyx gritted her teeth, from the pain of his energy and to stop her mouth from falling open. The Archdruid didn't sense her full power? How was that possible? The Archdruid was the most powerful person on Erthea. How had Darius pulled one over on him? True, Darius had power, but nothing like his father's. Darius' mother's magic scanned her as well. Nyx shivered and took a step back. Gods, she wanted to run.

Maybe she should just do that. Run and take her chances. It didn't matter if they struck her down. She wanted to get away from these people once and for all. They couldn't harm her or use her for her power then.

"Are you incapable of speech?" the Archdruid demanded.

"No. I don't know if there are any others left. I was a foundling and didn't even know I was a mind whisperer." Nyx finally found her voice. Gods, she couldn't believe she had spoken to the Archdruid himself. This had to be a dream. One that she hoped she would wake up from and find herself back at the tavern. This day had been nothing but a nightmare since Harland's death, and she longed for it to be over with

Fergus scrutinised her a moment longer. "Just kill her and be done with it. I won't have a mind whisperer wandering around. We all know how dangerous her kind were back during the great wars." He turned to Gideon. "Why did you have her brought here? If you knew of her existence, you should have had her killed. I thought I taught you better than that, boy."

"I thought —" Gideon winced as Fergus struck him across the head.

"You never think, do you? What if she had true power? She would be a danger to everyone in Andovia."

Her heart lurched. Would they kill her because of her abilities? She didn't think that was why Gideon had sent his brother to fetch her. If he wanted her dead, he could have just sent an assassin to do the job.

The Archdruid's power continued to thrash against her. Her head throbbed from the pain of it. How did anyone stand being around this man? She had thought Ambrose's energy had been powerful, but this felt overwhelming.

Nyx half hoped Darius might have done something. He knew how overwhelmed she got, but he did nothing. He stood there unmoving and kept his gaze on the floor. She had known he wouldn't be on her side even though he claimed to have been trying to help her by suppressing her power. Perhaps all he had done was bought her a little more time before they killed her.

"Perhaps you should keep her around for a while and see if her powers develop," Darius' mother spoke up. Her voice sounded rich and sophisticated—nothing like the lilting, melodic voice of the queen.

Queen Isabella's lip curled. "The girl is useless. Like I said, send her to the slave islands. That's about the only thing she'd be good for. They should at least get a few days' work out of her before she expires." She laughed, and her laughter sounded like music. How could someone so beautiful be so cruel? Were all the fae like this?

Slave islands? She knew what the that meant: weeks of hard

labour, little food and living in awful conditions. It would mean certain death. No one lasted long there.

Maybe that would be a better fate than being stuck here.

"Do not be so sure. Perhaps her powers need time to manifest," the woman remarked.

Nyx collapsed to her knees. The force of the Archdruid and Darius' mother's powers were too much.

It will be alright, Darius told her.

Nyx blinked back tears, ashamed at her own weakness. Why had he said that? He had made it clear he cared nothing about what happened to her.

Gideon whispered something to his father that Nyx could not hear. The Archdruid's expression darkened. "You killed Harland? He was one of my best slave traders. Excellent at weeding out miscreant fae and other undesirable Magickind. How could you have killed him?"

Nyx flinched as his power whipped against her.

Someone please help me. She wanted her curse to come back, to help the way it always did.

"She has some skill with the blade," Darius spoke up. "Harland had injuries. Perhaps she stabbed him."

What? The druid knew full well Harland's body had not had any stab wounds. He had had bruising and bleeding. She also noticed he hadn't outright lied. Perhaps he couldn't lie to his father. Interesting. Nyx frowned at him then dropped her gaze to the floor.

"Perhaps we should give it some time," Darius' mother suggested. "See if her powers emerge. If she is the one the prophecy speaks of, we need her in our grasp."

Isabella glowered at the other woman. "How could you suggest such a thing, Mercury? What if she is a descendant of the dark queen? She could have been sent by the resistance to murder us all."

Mercury laughed. "The resistance is nothing but a bunch of fools. They have no real power and will never be a threat to any of us."

Fergus scoffed. "There's nothing remarkable about her. Kill her and be done with it." He raised his hand, and an invisible force pulled Nyx to her feet.

She gasped as energy tightened around her throat, choking her. Gods, she couldn't fight this. Even if she had full access to her power, there was no fighting the Archdruid.

"I'm sure we can find some use for her that doesn't involve her going to the slave islands." Mercury put a hand on Fergus' shoulder. "Darius, you need a servant. Why don't you make use of her? Train her up a bit. You're always putting yourself in unnecessary danger." She arched an eyebrow at her son. "If she does not prove useful, bind her powers and keep her as a servant until she expires." Mercury turned to Gideon. "Unless you want her."

Fergus glowered at his other wife. "She is a mind whisperer. Have you forgotten what they did during the great wars? They almost overthrew my father and ended the Valeran dynasty."

"Look at her." Mercury gestured towards Nyx. "She's only a girl. She's no threat to anyone. See how pathetic and weak she is." She leaned closer and spoke to Fergus in thought, *If she does have power, perhaps we can harness it. She could become a valuable asset — one that we should keep on our side. Imagine the possibilities if she could harness her power. You would then have one of her kind under your control.*

Nyx looked away; afraid Mercury might realise she had overheard her. She didn't hear anything from the Archdruid. His mind remained hidden behind a wall of impenetrable energy. Good. She did not want to hear any more about what they had planned for her. This had turned out far worse than she could have imagined. Darius had warned her they might want to harness her powers. She shuddered to think of what they might force her to do if they did discover how powerful she was.

Gideon snorted. "She is not fit to be my servant. Let the little bastard have her. She's worthless."

Isabella cackled. "Why would the little bastard need protection? His life has no value."

Nyx caught the way the queen said "bastard." She didn't like Darius and would be glad to get rid of him.

Mercury's jaw ticked. "We all have enemies. We can't afford not to be careful any longer— even you know that, Isabella."

"You, perhaps, but not I." Isabella glowered at Mercury.

"Fine, do as you will with the girl. If you can't make use of her, bind her powers at once." Fergus waved his hand in dismissal. "Come, wife, we have things to discuss."

"Wait." Nyx couldn't believe the words coming out of her mouth. She scrambled up and rose to her full height. All eyes in the room turned onto her. "If I prove to be a good servant to the druid, I want my freedom."

"Who are you to bargain for such a thing?" Isabella scoffed. "I should have you whipped for your insolence."

Nyx, be quiet, Darius snapped.

Nyx held up her hand. "Begging your pardon, but I'm not your subject. I wasn't born in your realm, and Harland's death was self-defence. Under the laws of the lower realm, I demand to be released if I serve my penance." She knew the laws of the lower realm well enough. Harland had taught them to her in case she ever got arrested. He had always said, "If a good thief knows the law, they can work their way around it."

"You are still a fae and—" Isabella protested.

Fergus held a hand to silence his wife. "You are still a slave and subject to my laws, girl. Unless someone buys you, you will remain the property of my son." Nyx's heart sank. "If she doesn't prove useful over the next few weeks, I want her dead." Fergus swept out of the room.

Nyx knew one way or another she was stuck here unless she found a way to escape.

CHAPTER 10

Darius breathed a sigh of relief once his father and stepmother finally left the council hall. Thank the spirits that was over with, though it hadn't gone as he had expected. How had he ended up with Nyx as his servant? Darius might have wanted to keep her power a secret, but that didn't mean he wanted to be stuck with her.

Gideon gave Nyx a scrutinising look. "Perhaps you do have power and are hiding it somehow. I will train you as well. Come to my chamber one evening. I'll send for you." With that, he left too.

Nyx glowered after the elder Valeran brother; her hands clenched into fists. She had looked afraid earlier but now fear seemed to have given way to anger.

"You have courage, girl. I will say that," Mercury remarked.

Nyx didn't wilt under his mother's steely gaze. "I know how to get what I want." Nyx raised her chin. "Even around powerful people. What gives you the right to treat people this way?"

"Nyx," Darius warned. His mother might not be in such a strong position of authority as the Archdruid, but still her power was not to be underestimated. Why couldn't Nyx keep her mouth shut like he had told her? Did she have a death wish?

Darius couldn't believe Nyx had stood up to the Archdruid the way she had. He didn't know whether to be impressed or horrified. No one challenged the Archdruid. His father had killed people for lesser offences than that. Fergus must have been in an amicable mood for a change. Darius had expected his father to kill her on the spot and he probably would have if Mercury had not intervened.

Mercury chuckled. "Lose your defiance, little sewer rat. You might be a good thief, but on these islands you are nothing. You're worth even less than the dirt on my son's boots." Her lips twisted into a grim smile. "I can treat people any way I wish. I am the wife of the Archdruid. Who are you? A queen? A highborn lady? No. You are nothing."

Darius winced. Anger flared up in him at what Nyx had to endure. He might find Nyx irritating, but he felt sorry for her. Others would have gone mad or been broken by the Archdruid's full power, but she hadn't and Darius had to admire her for that. Nyx gritted her teeth then opened her mouth to speak again, but Darius cut her off. "Mother."

"It's good to see you." His mother gave him a stiff embrace.

Darius returned her embrace. Although he loved her, he doubted the feeling was reciprocated. Mercury loved power. It was why she allied herself with the Archdruid. Who else had more power than him?

Darius opened his mouth to speak and send Nyx away, then he closed it. He couldn't tell her to leave. She would run off and he doubted his web would slow her down forever. She was too strong to be contained.

"Mother, I don't need a servant."

"Would you rather your brother had her?" Mercury arched a perfect eyebrow. "I suspect she has power but is somehow hiding it. You are lucky your father did not sense it, or he would have killed her. Imagine what your brother would do if he could harness her abilities."

Darius shuddered at the thought. No, he didn't want Gideon using her. That was why he had repressed her power. But that didn't mean he wanted to be stuck with her. Still, she was safer with Ambrose than here with Gideon. After all, his mentor would know what to do.

"Come, let's walk. I haven't seen you in weeks." Mercury took hold of his arm.

"Mother, I have to get back to Ambrose," Darius protested.

"I'm sure that old fool can spare you for a few moments."

"He's not a fool."

Mercury cackled. "You think too well of people, my son."

Darius glanced back at Nyx. *You'd better come with us,* he told her.

Nyx glowered at him. *It's not like I have a choice, do I?* She trailed a few paces behind them.

Darius conjured a ward so Nyx would not hear them. As much as he wanted to get back to Eldara, Darius knew he had to indulge his mother for a little while.

"I do wish you would move back to the palace. It's much safer for you here than living on Eldara," Mercury remarked. "How you stand living among all those trees and those fae I will never understand."

Darius snorted. "I'm stifled here. The court is your world, not mine. Besides, I like living among the other druids, and having different fae around does not bother me."

Mercury scowled. "It would be nice to have my children by my side. Your brother and sister are at Trewa because your father feels it's safer for them there. I never get to see any of you."

Darius bit back a laugh. Blaise and Flora weren't allowed to stay here because Isabella refused to have them on the islands. She hated having Fergus' other children paraded in front of her. If anything happened to Gideon, any of Fergus' other three children could become his heir, and the queen knew it. Darius only got to stay because he was born here. Mercury had refused to send him away no matter what the queen said.

"How long are you staying this time?" Darius asked. His parents were always gone for months, travelling from realm to realm. Some of the courtiers often travelled with them whilst those loyal to Isabella remained here. When he was younger, he had been dragged along with them and stayed in the care of a nursemaid or any druid who was available to care for him.

"A month or two perhaps." Mercury shrugged. "You know your father never likes staying here for long. Who can blame him when he is forced to contend with that pointy-eared harlot?"

"Mother!" Darius winced. "You know you can't talk about the queen like that. She is still his wife. Besides, your feud with Isabella is your business. I want no part of it."

"I am his wife too, dear boy," Mercury snapped. "I do wish your father would see reason and annul his marriage to that fae whore."

There would be no point in telling his mother to watch her tongue. She would never listen, and she considered herself far beyond Isabella's power. Isabella feared Fergus too much to ever go up against Mercury directly. It was one of the many reasons why he had chosen to leave Avenia and live on Eldara with the other druids.

Darius decided to change the subject. "Do you know anything about the rifts and the darklings?"

Mercury waved a hand in dismissal. "I do not, nor do I see why it's a problem. Evil spirits come and go all the time."

"Yes, but people are being killed. The veil is breaking, and you of all people should know the danger that poses to the rest of Erthea."

Mercury laughed. "The veil between the worlds has been there since Erthea came into being. Nothing can break it. Rifts are bound to occur at some point."

"But how else would you explain the rifts? They are not natural. Spirits like the dark things are not meant to walk in this world." Darius sighed in frustration. "How can that not bother you? It isn't right, and you know it."

Mercury had taught him sorcery and about how the spirit world worked. He didn't like to use such magic and preferred to stick to the elemental magic used by the druids. The druids believed in spirits, both good and bad, rather than any gods. The magic that controlled and used spirits was forbidden by them as it went against nature itself. Anything that did that was not the druid way.

"Rifts do happen, especially if someone is using dark magic to summon spirits."

"Who would do that and why?" He frowned at her. "You haven't been practising anything, have you? If you caused this problem, I want to know about it." He had considered the possibility of this being his mother's doing. No one on Erthea could control spirits or had the knowledge of them the way she did. Although Darius couldn't figure out why she would do such a thing. "Did Father put you up to it?"

Mercury glowered at him. "How dare you accuse me of such a thing! No, neither of us had anything to do with it. Even if we did, would you go against us?"

I go up against you all the time. That's why I joined the resistance and do everything I can to help them. Darius kept his thoughts to himself. He hoped to the spirits his parents never found out about his affiliation with the resistance or the work he did with them. They would punish him no doubt, but it didn't matter. Helping others was much more important.

Darius hesitated. "I would have to, yes. You know how I feel about Father and his dark magic."

Mercury gave a humorous laugh. "You sound so self-righteous, my boy. This is the world you belong in and the legacy from which you were born. You have that same darkness inside of you no matter how much you try to fight it."

Darius shivered. "Do you know anything about the rifts or not? You may not care about the problem, but I will do everything I can to stop it." He scrutinised her gaze. He knew her in some ways better than he knew his father, and if she tried to lie to him, he would know.

Mercury shrugged. "It could be any number of reasons. Even so, it's foolish of you to be wasting time on this. You're second in line, you should be with your father and I." She shook her head. "Instead, you waste time running around in the forest with the other druids. I thought I taught you better than that."

"I joined the Guard to help people. I do more good out there than I could ever do at court." Darius kissed his mother on the cheek. "Now if you'll excuse me, I have to go." He needed to get home or else he risked being stuck here with her even longer.

She scowled at him. "That's it? You only have a few moments for your mother?"

He rubbed the back of his neck. "I'm tired. It's been a long couple of days venturing into the lower realm and back. I need to return home. I'll visit you again before you and Father leave."

Mercury hmphed. "See that you do. It would be nice to spend some time together for once."

"We could spend more time together if you didn't follow Father everywhere."

She chuckled. "Who else would keep him in line? His harlot? No, I think not." She hesitated as she turned to leave. "I may not know what is causing the rifts, but be careful, boy. If the tear in the veil is unnatural, you will be dealing with some very dark magic. Magic that is best left well enough alone."

Mercury turned and trailed off in the opposite direction.

"Why do you think I stay away from you and Father so much?" he muttered under his breath. "Your magic is best left well enough alone." He rubbed his chin. He needed to get home but at the same time he wanted to investigate the matter further to find out more information about the darklings. That would have to wait till the morning. He had to talk to Ambrose first.

"Are we done here now?" Darius spun around and found Nyx sitting on a bench. He had almost forgotten she was there. "Can we leave?" She stopped tugging at her bracelet. "I think I've learnt enough about your family for one day."

He sighed. "Neither of us is happy with this arrangement, so let's try to make the best of it, shall we?"

Nyx scowled. "I still don't understand why you —"

Darius held up a hand to silence her. "It's been a long day, let's go."

Darius used a transportation ring to transfer them over to Eldara.

Nyx gasped when they appeared in the middle of the forest. The trees dwarfed above them so high they disappeared into the clouds.

"Welcome to Eldara, the druid isle," Darius said.

Despite it being nightfall, lights sparkled all over the trees. Sprites danced overhead and more lights twinkled as seeds blew in the wind.

"This is...magical," Nyx breathed.

"Now you know why I like living here instead of at the palace." Darius took in the familiar scents of trees and grass. Being here felt like true freedom. "Ambrose said you can live with us, so this is your home now too." Weariness washed over him. It had been a long couple of days since leaving home for her village and rescuing her from execution that morning. They both needed rest.

Nyx gasped when a hoard of glowing lights swirled around her head. She waved her arm to shoo them away. "What are they doing?"

"They're spirits. It's alright, they won't hurt you. Spirits are everywhere here since the veil between the worlds is thinner at this point on Erthea."

"Is that why you refer to spirits all the time the way others do gods?" Nyx flinched. "Why are they touching me? I don't like it."

"They do that to anyone they consider a good soul. Druids don't worship any gods; we believe in following our own path. Spirits are part of life and death, that's why we respect them."

"No doubt your father thinks he's a god. What do these things want?"

Darius bit his lip to stop making a remark about his father. "They must like you." Darius couldn't imagine why. "I know you're not happy about this arrangement, but let's make the best of it, shall we?"

Nyx tugged the bracelet and yanked it off. "Fine."

"Ambrose's house isn't far." He trudged ahead. "You can have some food and rest when we get there. I thought you would be glad for that."

Nyx didn't answer. It took him a few moments to realise her presence had retreated.

Nyx was gone.

CHAPTER 11

Nyx bolted the moment Darius' back was turned. She had no idea whether the bracelet would help her or not since her powers gave off so much energy, but she didn't want to risk that strange invisible barrier appearing again and blocking her way. She had to get out of there and find a way back to the lower realm before anything else went wrong.

Those strange, coloured lights — or spirits as the druid called them — had freed her and healed her injuries, including her damaged wing. Nyx had to admit it felt a lot better not being covered in bruises and scrapes. Her wing no longer ached either, which she was grateful for as she ran past the sky-scraping trees.

More lights danced around Nyx's head. Were those spirits too? She didn't have time to find out. Why was this place so full of lights? Back in her forest in Joriam it had been pitch black at night and the perfect place to hide away. The land there had been much easier to navigate. Here, she couldn't hide anywhere. Plus, she had no idea how to get out of this realm. The only way she had seen to travel was by airship, dragon, or through those circles the druids had used.

Nyx had no idea how those rings worked or where to find a ship. She would have to use everything within her power to get off the island by herself. She had never flown long distances before and didn't know if she even could do so. First, Nyx needed to find somewhere to hide and take cover for the night.

She flapped her wings and rose off the ground. Once high enough, she grabbed onto a tree and swung up into the branches.

Climbing was one thing she was good at. The branches were thick and sturdy, so she knew they would hold her weight.

When she got high enough, she would have a good view of which direction to go in. Maybe she could rest here for tonight and leave at dawn. She didn't like the idea of trying to navigate her way in the dark. At least during daylight she would be able to see better and decide what the best course of action would be. Despite the healing she had from the spirits, weariness washed over her. Nyx had never used her power as much as she had today. It had drained her strength, and she needed some sleep.

Nyx climbed higher. Good gods, how high did the tree go? The tree limbs rose into the heavens. But she could not stop, she would not become a slave to that druid or anyone else. She might not like her abilities, but they were hers, and she would not let anyone else use them for their own gain.

"Climb, little Nyxie; there's nowhere to hide." Harland stood on the branch above her. "I will always find you."

She shivered as Harland appeared before her. Not again. Nyx's hands slipped, and she yelped as her fingers slid from the branch that she had been reaching for. She gripped the tree and flapped her wings to gain some momentum. Her grip tightened as she scrambled up onto the heavy limb. Nyx glowered at Harland. "You can't be here. You're dead." She couldn't believe he had appeared again. She had hoped seeing him earlier that morning had just been her imagination. Yet he had come back to haunt her once more.

"Dead, but not gone. I'll always be here to haunt you. You belong to me, girl."

"I belong to no one, least of all you." She took a few deep breaths, flapped her wings and grabbed onto another branch. "You lied to me all these years by making me think I'm cursed. You never wanted me to know I had magic, did you?"

"You can't run. And what difference would it have made if you had known? You're a slave and still belong to me. You always will, even in death."

Her hands clenched into fists. Would it have made any difference if she had known the extent of her magic? Perhaps it would have given her the courage to turn against him sooner. Nyx had always planned to run away and find freedom with her sisters. That hadn't changed because she had been dragged to the upper realm and forced to become a servant to one of the Valeran brothers.

I might not be able to get away from you, but I can ignore you. Nyx imagined a protective grove of trees around her, just as she had done last night when the druid and his friends had been looking for her in the woods back in her realm. Light flashed around her, but for some reason the grove wouldn't appear as it had before. Odd, she always retreated to that place of safety whenever she needed to escape from something. It was what kept her going through over the years of dealing with Harland's abuse. Nyx couldn't understand why it wouldn't work. Perhaps it was because she felt so exhausted.

Why wouldn't Harland leave her alone? Was it because this place was full of spirits? Maybe not. She had seen him earlier that day before they even came to Andovia.

"Killer, you can't run." Harland reappeared on the branch above.

Nyx growled. "Go away." She shifted up onto the next branch. Gods, it took a lot longer climbing these trees than the ones she climbed back in her forest. She had to move faster. What would make Harland go away? Nyx didn't dare use her magic or the druid would sense her.

"It won't take long for everyone here to see you for the monster you are" Harland goaded. "Why don't you jump? It is a quicker and much more painless death than you would have found on the pyre."

"Why? So, I can be with you?" She sneered. "You're the monster, not me." She stepped along the length of the branch and took to the air so she could get to a higher point.

"I never killed anyone," Harland snapped. "I always knew you were dangerous. That's why you were my favourite girl. No one could outdo my little Nyxie." Nyx pulled down a large branch that snapped when she threw it at Harland. It passed straight through him. "You won't get rid of me that easily." He laughed.

Nyx ignored him and climbed higher. In the distance loomed more trees in every direction, their thick canopies blocking out any sign of an escape route.

Ignore him. You will never get anywhere if you keep talking to him.

"Don't think you can run from me so easily, girl." Harland grabbed onto her wrist and heat seared her skin.

Nyx bit back a scream. If she made too much noise the druid would hear her and drag her back. How on Erthea was he physically touching her? His fingers felt solid and real.

"You will never escape me. I owned you in life. I will have you again in death."

Tears stung her eyes. *Get away from me!* Energy flared through her, and it was enough to make Harland retreat. Nyx scrambled onto another branch and clutched her burning hand. Ripping off a piece of her tunic, she wrapped it around her palm. Nyx put her head between her hands and sighed. There had to be a way to make Harland leave her alone.

Something thunked onto the branch beside her.

The druid?

She lowered her hands. A large winged fae stood there, its fangs gleamed and its eyes shone an eerie yellow.

Not the druid. Now what? Could she never be left alone?

"Who are you?" Nyx scrambled up. She didn't want to risk being attacked whilst in a vulnerable position. Her senses screamed of danger.

"I am merely a servant of the darkness. You are a clever girl to climb so high." He lunged at her.

Nyx jumped back. "Look, I don't want any trouble. I just want to be left alone." She reached for the familiar weight of her sword. Of course, it wasn't there. She lost it sometime the night before, and it had been left behind back in Joriam.

The strange fae swiped at her. "The prophecy will never come to pass."

"What is this stupid prophecy about?" she demanded. "Because I'm not part of it. All of you are mad."

He lunged again, his claws grazing her neck.

No, don't! Power whirled up from deep inside her. Energy reverberated from her eyes into his, knocking Nyx backwards. She screamed as the blast sent her falling.

Nyx flapped her wings but fell too fast for it to make any difference. Wind roared past her. Nyx crashed from one giant leaf to another, screaming as she descended. She squeezed her eyes shut and braced herself for the inevitable impact. She landed with a thud and strong arms wrapped around her.

"This is becoming a bad habit."

Her eyes flew open. "Druid? Watch out!"

Her attacker and two more like it appeared. Good gods, what were these creatures? Why were they so determined to kill her?

"Give us the girl," one of them said. "She can't be allowed to live. We will never allow another mind whisperer to take power. She will bring about the dark age."

"The darkness is already upon us," Darius snapped. "You are fools if you can't see that." He dropped Nyx to the ground and lightning sparked between his fingers.

Nyx landed with a thunk. "Help me," she hissed at one of the beasts. Nyx had no idea if her power would work. If it had, the victim usually became protective towards her and did whatever she commanded. It was one of the few things she liked about her abilities. It came in handy at times like this.

"What are you doing?" Darius hissed at her.

Running away.

Her assailant lunged for Darius whilst the other two fae came at her.

Darius raised his hand and hit the fae with a lightning bolt.

Her assailant dodged another bolt.

Nyx remained on the ground, too weak to move. She guessed using her power so much today had taken its toll. She had never used her influence to this extent before.

"You used your power on him," Darius groaned. "Didn't you listen to anything we told you?"

"I didn't have a choice. They were trying to kill me," she snapped. "Stop being so judgemental. You know I can't control it."

"This Sluagh is now under your control – but I think you know that, don't you?" Darius demanded. "You have no idea how dangerous this is. You're turning people into your slaves."

"Oh, don't be ridiculous, druid. It wears off, and he's just helping me to escape." Nyx stood then wished she hadn't. The world around her spun, so she dropped to her knees again. "Tell me about the prophecy. Why do they want me dead?" Good gods, how would she escape when she couldn't stand?

"The prophecy talks of an age of darkness that will engulf all of Erthea," Darius answered. "Two fae will rise and meet on the coming battlefield, surrounded by darkness. But it's unclear if the two chosen will stop this darkness or bring it about."

The Sluagh lunged for Darius again. "Both the chosen must die or all fae will be forced to obey their will."

Nyx swallowed the bile in her throat. "What does that have to do with me?"

"You're the first mind whisperer in a generation. Some races say one of the chosen will wield great power with their mind," Darius said. "Will you get this thing to back off? I came to take you home with me."

"Home?" She scoffed. "I don't have a home anymore. No thanks to you." Nyx slumped forward and rested her head against the cold hard ground. Darkness threatened to pull her under, but she wouldn't give in to it. "Why did you save me from... your brother?"

"Because it's safer this way. With Ambrose, you can learn to control your gift. My brother would force you to use your power for awful things." Darius raised his hand and hit the Sluagh with a fireball. The creature screamed in agony as his body erupted in flame. He then fired on the other two Sluagh and killed them both.

Darius sighed and lifted Nyx into his arms. "Can I please stop having to save you now? I'm exhausted, and this is getting tiresome."

Nyx managed to scowl. "Your fault..." Her head slumped forward as she finally gave in to exhaustion, and let the darkness drag her under.

CHAPTER 12

Darius sighed. His body weary with exhaustion. Nyx had slumped into unconsciousness in his arms. She would need to rest for a while. It surprised him she hadn't collapsed long before now. That must mean she had high resistance when it came to using her power to influence others more than once in a day.

He trekked back through the forest, his mind racing. How had those Sluagh known about her? Ambrose had warned him attacks against her were possible, but Darius hadn't expected them so soon. Her power must have attracted them to her, but he had thought the Sluagh were long gone from these islands, banished early on in his father's reign.

It shocked him how Nyx had used her influence on the Sluagh, especially as she had lost control twice now in just under a day. It had to be well past midnight now. Running through the woods in search of her hadn't been very enjoyable and tracking her hadn't been easy. Darius had no idea how she had managed to escape detection for the last couple of hours. Maybe she used her power to shield herself without even knowing it. After all, Nyx must have some control even if she didn't realise it.

Darius decided against waking her. It was better if she rested and stayed quiet for once. He noted a piece of tattered cloth around her palm. She'd injured herself.

Nyx mumbled something and wriggled in his arms.

He considered stopping to draw a circle to transport them to the house, but he would have to put her down to do so. He didn't want to risk her running again if she woke up. So, he continued on foot. Ambrose's house loomed ahead, perched on the branches of a great tree. Darius took the platform up and walked into the sitting room.

Warmth greeted him as a fire crackled in the hearth. A fur rug covered the wooden floor, and a table with chairs and two large divans all made from dryad wood took up the space. A bookcase housing rows of books and other objects stood on the other side of the cosy room. It was a world away from the Crystal Palace and felt like a true home in a way that place never had.

Ambrose rose from his chair as Darius brought Nyx closer to the fire. "You were gone a long time. I feared you had been detained at the palace." His brow furrowed at the sight of Nyx. "Is she hurt?"

"She ran off and got attacked by a few Sluagh. She used her power to influence one." Darius sighed. "I had to kill them. Holy spirits, why do I have to be saddled with her?"

"Because she is safer here with us than anywhere else. Good, we can't have them coming after her again or being left under her influence," Ambrose said. "She will need to rest now. You look exhausted too, boy."

"I know keeping the extent of her power hidden is the right thing to do, but she's the most infuriating person I've ever met," he grumbled. "She won't stop trying to run away."

Ambrose chuckled and called out, "Ada?"

A small, wrinkled woman with leathery skin that looked like bark came in. "Aye, master?" Her beady eyes widened when she saw Darius. Darius forced a weak smile at the Brownie. "You're home, boy." Ada beamed. "About time too. You been getting up to mischief?" She came over and pinched his cheek. She always liked fussing over him.

"I've been busy," Darius replied. "But it's good to be back. I hope I won't have to leave again for a while."

"By the great mother, what happened to that wee girl?" Ada motioned towards Nyx. "Is she injured? Should I fetch healing supplies?"

"We had an eventful day. It's a long story," Darius said.

"Let's get her nice bath. I'll have one drawn up for both of yer. Ya look a state, my boy."

Darius wanted to protest. He wanted nothing more than to go to bed and sleep for a week. But he knew it was best not to argue with Ada. She meant well, and he adored her.

Darius left Nyx on the chair and headed to his room. It looked just as he'd left it with its bark-covered walls. He had a map of the entire upper realm hanging on one wall with the rest of the room occupied by a bed, a table and a bookcase filled with neatly organised books and other objects. The rest of the room had a couple of trunks filled with weapons. He dropped his cloak and pack on the foot of the bed, kicked off his boots and slumped onto the rich red covers. He'd closed his eyes for a few moments then take a bath.

He was asleep before his head even touched the pillow.

Darius woke to the sound of screaming. *Argh, what now?* It felt like only moments since he had fallen asleep. He rubbed his eyes and yawned as he dragged himself off the bed. He guessed Nyx must have woken up. Sunlight streamed in through the open window, and a cool breeze blew in. He must have slept more than a few moments then.

What was Nyx screaming about now? Ambrose's house was heavily warded so he doubted anything could have broken in to attack her unless another darkling had emerged.

He sighed and rushed down the hall to find Nyx in the hallway pointing a fire poker at Ada. "What's going on?" Darius demanded, and all trace of exhaustion vanished from his body. He couldn't believe Nyx was threatening Ada of all people. What could the Brownie have done wrong?

"This thing just attacked me." Nyx motioned towards Ada.

Ada turned pale and had her hands raised in surrender. "It was just a misunderstanding, my boy. Tell her I mean no harm."

"Nyx, this is Ada. She's Ambrose's house Brownie. She's not a threat to anyone."

"What's a Brownie?" Nyx glowered at him. "She was touching me. You can't expect me not to defend myself."

"She's fae like you, now put the poker down."

"She attacked me," Nyx insisted.

"I only came to tend to your injury," Ada said. "Your hand is burned, and I came to put some salve on it."

"Nyx, no one in this house will harm you. Now, please put the poker down."

Nyx lowered the poker. "Where am I?"

"Ambrose's house. You passed out last night, so I brought you here and left you in your room to rest."

Her eyes narrowed. "I have a room?"

"Yes, you didn't think I'd lock you in a cell, did you?"

"That wouldn't surprise me. You said I'm a danger to everyone around me."

"As I said, no one here is going to hurt you. Locking you away wouldn't do any good. You're not a prisoner."

Nyx scoffed. "We'll see about that."

"Come along, miss." Ada took the poker from Nyx's grasp. "I ran a bath for you. I'll help you dress, then you can have some breakfast." Ada gave Nyx a gentle push in the direction of her room.

To his relief, Nyx went along with her.

After Darius had washed and dressed in a dark tunic and clean trousers, he pulled a green jerkin over the tunic and made sure his sword and crossbow were ready for when he left. He headed down to the dining chamber. A large table took up most of the space surrounded by six chairs. A tablecloth covered the dark oak wood and plates of food covered the entire length of the table. Ada always made more food than they could eat despite Ambrose's objections. She often gave the leftover food to those less fortunate.

Ambrose already sat at the head of the table with a book open beside him.

Darius' mouth watered at the sight of the small feast. He couldn't remember the last time he had eaten. Yesterday he hadn't been able to get a single decent meal and made do with the small provisions he had taken with him when he left to go and find Nyx.

"I heard you had a commotion with Nyx," Ambrose remarked. "Is everything alright? Did she try escaping again? I did set up a few wards last night, but I thought she would be too exhausted to run again."

"It was a misunderstanding." Darius slumped into his seat. "Are you sure having her here is a good idea? She's insufferable. I know she needs our help, but…" He sighed in exasperation. "I can't have her as my servant."

"Would you rather your father or brother have her?" Ambrose arched an eyebrow.

"No, but she's… she will keep trying to run away. And we have more important problems to deal with, like the darklings." Darius poured himself some tea. "I thought I might head out to spirit grove and see what the spirits can tell me."

"Good idea. Take Nyx with you."

Darius gaped at his mentor. "But… you're supposed to be helping her control her powers."

"Of course, but I want to see what the spirits know about her."

"The spirits in the forest came around her last night," Darius said. "The Sluagh knew who she was too and thought she was part of the prophecy."

"That came much sooner than expected." Ambrose spread jam over his toast. "After you've been to the grove, you'll get back to your usual duties."

"What am I going to do with Nyx? I can't perform my duties if I have to worry about her running off." He would never get any work done if he had to keep chasing her.

"Make good use of her then. Show her the forest, teach her your range of duties."

Darius scowled. "I don't have time for that. She won't like anything about the forest or anything we stand for. She will cause more harm than good with her powers." He reminded himself to look up mental blocks and see how his father had given him such a strong one. Once he knew what to do, he would place one on the other guards and anyone else who might be at risk from her powers, like Ada. "I know we need to help her get her powers under control, but perhaps it is too dangerous to have her here. She will put innocent lives at risk. Nyx can barely control herself, let alone her abilities. What if she somehow enslaves people?" Darius doubted her spelled bracelet would rein her power in forever. Sooner or later it would seep through. Her magic was like a dam waiting to burst and it would destroy everything in its wake.

"If she is part of the prophecy, she might be able to help us fix the rift in the veil before it's too late. Nyx is your servant. You have to have her with you."

Darius repressed a sigh. He didn't want or need a servant. Living at the palace and travelling with his parents he'd always been surrounded by servants and hated it. It offered him no privacy or independence. The last thing he wanted was to have Nyx in tow wherever he went.

"She will never agree to do anything I ask of her — you've seen how stubborn she is. Why can't she stay with you?" he asked. "You can keep an eye on her and teach her at the same time."

"Alas, I'm not immune to her powers. But I will do what I can to help her." Ambrose sipped his tea. "She is your responsibility."

Darius groaned. "You're not afraid she will use her influence on you, are you?" He had known Ambrose for most of his life, and the other druid never seemed to be afraid of anything.

Ambrose chuckled. "Blessed spirits, no. I'm certain I can shield myself from that. She might have been a thief, but that's only because she's never had the chance to be anything else. See what she can do. You may find her more useful than you thought."

Darius glanced over at the empty seat opposite his. "Where is she?" He had expected Nyx to come down by now. What was taking so long? "Ada?"

The Brownie scurried in, face flustered. "Aye, boy?"

"Will Nyx be joining us?" Ambrose asked. "I thought she would be hungry after everything she had to endure yesterday."

"Aye, master. I've just been tending to her."

"If you want to stop her from running away, give her a reason to stay." Ambrose took a bite of his toast.

Darius slumped back in his seat. "Like what? She wants freedom more than anything." He doubted she would ever truly have that. Perhaps not even after she learnt how to control her powers.

"There's no reason why she can't have that here. I won't have her treated like a slave – that goes against everything we have been fighting for."

"Isn't there a spell I could use to stop her from running away?" Darius persisted. "I already cast a web around her, but she breaks through anything I use against her."

"That doesn't surprise me. Try not to use spells on her. That will only make her despise us further."

Someone stomped in. Darius' mouth fell open when he realised it was Nyx herself.

Her long hair now looked bright and glossy in its shade of pink, and she wore a long red tunic dress, dark hose and boots.

"Morning." Ambrose gave her a bright smile as Nyx sat down. "How are you feeling?"

Darius couldn't believe how different she looked. Her long hair fell past her shoulders in a thick plait. If it weren't for her scowl, he might not have recognised her.

"Don't she clean up well?" Ada beamed. "Pretty thing, ain't she?"

"Indeed." Ambrose gave an approving nod.

"Stop gawking at me, druid." Nyx shot Darius a glare. "Have you never seen a girl before?"

Darius closed his mouth. "You look…so clean." He knew he sounded pathetic and wondered what had come over him.

"I'm not always covered in dirt," she retorted. "I do know how to bathe; thank you." She frowned at all the food. Her stomach grumbled in response. "Am I allowed to eat this?"

Ambrose chuckled. "Of course, we won't starve you, my dear."

Nyx frowned at them. "So, what will I be doing then? Getting attacked by more hideous fae?" She picked up a piece of bread and gave a tentative bite as if she expected it to be poison.

"They're called Sluagh, and they used to live in the wilds on Migara. They're not the friendliest."

"Used to? Were they extinct like mind whisperers are supposed to be?" Nyx snorted. "Why would they want to kill me? I haven't done anything to them."

"A lot of fae were wiped out during the great wars," Darius explained. "Some of them are thought to be extinct while others were… forced into servitude." He couldn't deny the fact that both his father and many of the archdruids who had come before him had forced many races, especially fae, into slavery. Any race who had been viewed as a threat or who didn't fall in line with the Archdruid's rule met the same fate. If they couldn't be useful as slaves, they were exterminated.

"Oh, that does not surprise me. I was sold as a slave and forced to work for…a horrible man for the past few years. I know how the world works, druid." All colour drained from Nyx's face. "Why is your father married to a fae queen then if he enslaves races? I don't understand." Nyx piled more food onto her plate. "If he despises fae so much why did he marry and have a child with one? I can't imagine the Archdruid being forced into anything."

"Because the fae and druids are close kindred. An alliance with the Archdruid was the perfect match for both Isabella and Fergus. Isabella is a Silvan, and even though they are fae, they don't consider themselves as such. They think of themselves as the first race and see other kinds of fae as lesser races. They can trace their history back to before the dark times and have been in power since time unknown," Ambrose answered. "One thing you need to prepare yourself for while living in these lands is prejudice from the other races. Even the ice elves consider themselves superior to others and are close allies of the Silvans."

Darius kept his mouth shut. He had never understood why his father had married Isabella since he despised the woman. Sometimes he wondered why he didn't just annul the marriage, but that would probably cause Fergus more problems than solutions.

"I grew up in a human tribe; I know how to deal with prejudice." Nyx scowled. "Try being a fae among humans. They always said I was an unholy thing. They worship their own gods, but they believe in the nonsense the Archdruid spouts about certain races being unnatural."

"Darius told you about the prophecy, yes?" Ambrose asked.

"Yes, I don't believe it. And neither does he."

"I never said that," Darius insisted.

"Yes, you did. You said prophecies could be interpreted in different ways. Plus, I'm good at reading people." She took another bite of toast. "What does the prophecy have to do with me, anyway? I don't see how I could be part of it. I'm no one important."

"It doesn't matter what I believe. People have a way of making prophecies come true. And they think you're part of it."

"I'm a nobody. I can't even control my curse."

"Your curse, as you put it, makes you very desirable." Ambrose sipped his tea. "Later we'll get started on more tests."

Nyx scowled. "Why? I already told you how it works."

"And I've been on the receiving end of it," Darius added which earned him another glare from Nyx.

"We still don't know the full extent. There may be more to her abilities than we know. But first I wanted to ask you, where did you come from before you ended up in Joriam?"

Nyx shrugged. "I don't know. I don't remember anything before I ended up with Harland."

Ambrose frowned. "How old were you then?"

"Around age ten, I think. Someone found me wandering around in the forest, and that's how I ended up in the slave market."

Darius furrowed his brow. She had been old enough to have some memories of her life before. It seemed odd she didn't remember anything, unless something terrible happened and her mind had blocked it out.

"Whilst you are here, perhaps we can find out where you came from. We will get to work on testing your powers later today. First, you're going to be working with Darius whilst he performs his usual duties in the Forest Guard."

After breakfast, Darius motioned for Nyx to come with him. They took the platform out of the treehouse and down into the forest below.

She crossed her arms. "Is this my new role now? Following you around?"

"This wasn't my choice, believe me. We're headed into the forest to talk to spirits."

Nyx scoffed. "You speak to spirits? Why?"

"You will find out when we get there."

"Wait, this won't involve seeing the spirits of people we knew, will it?"

"No, these are different spirits. Let's go."

Darius just hoped the spirits wouldn't block him from entering the grove again after bringing Nyx there.

CHAPTER 13

Nyx didn't know what to expect as she traipsed after the druid. She did like all the trees here. They fascinated her. All of them were enormous, and their energy washed over her like cool water. Minds buzzed at the edge of her senses, but she couldn't make out the thoughts clearly. It felt refreshing. More sprites danced overhead. They didn't bother her as much this morning. This place felt so different compared to the tiny forest back home in Joriam, so alive and vibrant with energy. She had never imagined a place like this could exist.

Darius looked different too. Nyx had been afraid of Ada at first but decided she didn't mind the strange woman after spending some time with her. She hadn't sensed any threat from her. Nyx didn't like having her hair combed so much.

Still, she had liked the clothes Ada had given her. Nyx had no idea where Ada had got the clothes from or how they fit her so well. Perhaps brownies could create clothes from magic. Nyx was so used to wearing the same thing all the time that it felt odd wearing different clothes. Her old clothes had been rough, woollen and homespun. These felt soft and comfortable, unlike anything she had worn before. Ada had tried to get her to wear a dress, but Nyx had been disgusted by the idea. She never wore dresses. They were such cumbersome things, and she had never liked them. They were even worse for flying.

"Why are there so many spirits here?" Nyx asked. "Is it because the veil is broken?" Fear coiled in her chest. What if she saw

Harland's spirit again? Nyx wondered if she should ask the druid about that, then decided against it. She distrusted him enough already and didn't want to give him something else to use against her. He would probably say it was a sign of a guilty conscience. She did feel guilty over Harland's death, but she knew she was not the one responsible for it. Nyx hadn't killed him — wouldn't she remember if she had?

Trees stretched out as far as the eye could see, their heavy leaves hanging down like green curtains and their blue and brown branches reaching towards the heavens. More lights swirled about, even as slivers of sunlight crept in through the heavy canopy.

Leaves crunched under her feet, and the foliage grew denser. Branches snagged her hair and clothes. "Druid, where are we?" She stopped when they stepped out into a clearing. Trees circled all around, their canopy a blanket of darkness overhead. Green orbs of light danced around, and a strange energy washed over her senses.

"What is this place?" She didn't hear any thoughts but knew there was something here.

"This is the spirit grove. The veil is thin, and druids come here to commune with our ancestors and the spirits around us. It's a special place — sacred." Darius set his sword and bowed down outside the circle of trees. "No one can carry weapons here. Whatever you do, do not insult anyone."

Nyx snorted. Even she could feel the importance of this place. *Then why did you bring me here?* It felt almost wrong to say anything, like breaking the silence would be a crime.

Spirits help and provide answers. I need to know what they can tell me about the darklings, Darius replied and motioned her over. "Come sit with me." Darius sat on the ground and crossed his legs.

Nyx hesitated and slumped down beside him. Energy pulsed underneath her as Darius raised his hand. Lines of glowing energy appeared. "These are earth lines," Darius explained. "Natural veins of magic that runs through Erthea itself. They are the lifeblood of this world. Without them, Erthea would cease to exist." The green orbs whizzed faster and a few zipped around their heads. "If you ever need energy, this is a good way to get it. But only use it in times of dire need. Those who take energy when they don't need it go against nature itself and that would be considered dark magic."

Nyx reached out and yelped when energy sparked against her

fingers.

Darius chuckled. "Not like that." The lines faded.

She scowled at him.

Darius closed his eyes, and the green orbs came nearer. His mental shield dropped, and she winced as the feel of his power washed over her senses. She realised he must somehow be opening himself up to the energy around them.

Nyx wondered if she should do the same and spotted his sword a few feet away. She could grab it and kill him. There would be nothing to stop her from escaping then. Nyx scrambled up, and the orbs of light zipped around her. She bit back a cry of alarm.

"Nyx?" someone whispered her name.

Good gods, had Harland followed her here? Panic flooded through her, but it didn't sound like him. Who else would call her? She didn't know anyone else who had passed onto the spirit world. No one of importance anyway.

"Nyx?" The voice grew louder.

Darius grabbed hold of her hand. "Sit and listen."

"But—" If Harland found her here, he might try to kill her again, then the druid would see it. That would only confirm his suspicions about her and make matters worse. Somehow Nyx doubted the druid would bother helping her get rid of Harland's spirit.

"Nothing will hurt you. Sit." Darius motioned to the ground next to him.

Nyx slumped onto the ground but didn't relax. She scanned every direction, bracing herself for Harland to appear. What would he try to do this time? Why couldn't he just move on and leave her alone?

"Nyx?" the voice came again, but it didn't sound like Harland. Or maybe that was a trick.

The green orbs spun faster until they expanded into dozens of more orbs. What were those things doing?

Nyx let out a breath she hadn't known she had been holding.

"Welcome, Darius of the druids. And Nyx, child of the fae," a voice said.

Darius bowed his head in respect. Nyx did the same. She didn't want to risk offending anyone, especially not any spirits. She had already seen what kind of power Harland now had in spirit form. If the spirits here had been powerful in life, Nyx dreaded to think how strong they would be in death.

"Why have you come here?" the voices asked.

Darius spoke up. "To ask for your help. People are dying, and dark things keep coming forth. I need to know how to fix this."

"The veil between the worlds grows thin," the voices chorused. "Those thought to be lost from this world shall once again walk free."

"But why?" Darius persisted. "Who is causing it? How do we close the rifts?"

At least he seemed to be asking the right questions for once. Nyx wanted to know all of those things herself.

"The veil grows thin," the voices chorused again.

Nyx repressed a sigh. *I thought you said they gave answers.*

They do, but they're usually cryptic or hard to understand, Darius replied. *That's why we have to listen closely to everything they say or we might miss some key information.*

Nyx rolled her eyes. "Who or what is fracturing the veil?" She had never liked cryptic messages. It was better to get to the point instead of running around in circles.

"Darkness is coming. It waits and hides behind the shadow. Only two can stop it," the voices whispered.

"Does this have to do with the prophecy then? Is that coming to pass?" Darius asked.

Wonderful, they were talking of that damned prophecy again.

The glowing lights whizzed even faster. Nyx's head spun at the dizzying sight.

"Welcome home, child of the fae," a voice whispered in her ear. "You have been gone for too long."

"What?" Nyx gasped and made a move to get up. "Who said that?"

Listen with your mind, Darius told her. *Everyone hears different messages. Listen to what the spirits have to tell you. You might learn more than you think.*

Messages? Why would anything here give her a message, except for maybe Harland.

Nyx tried to settle down again. *Who's there? Harland, if that's you, go away!*

No evil can enter here, a voice said. *You have come home.*

Come home? Nyx furrowed her brow. *What do you mean? This place isn't my home.*

You have come home...

Nyx hesitated. She couldn't remember anything about the time before she had been with Harland, nor had he or Mama Habrid known much about it. All she had been told was she had been left under an ash tree. Ash trees were rare in the lower realm, and some of the tribe claimed the tree had appeared out of nowhere.

Odd, she hadn't thought of that in years.

Nyx closed her eyes and her power pulsed through her. She was always aware of it. Most of the time she blocked it out or ignored it as best she could. This time she let her power flow free just as Darius did. Her power didn't affect him, and it felt somehow natural.

Everything felt open in this place, as if walls and boundaries didn't exist.

"Nyx?" the voice called louder this time. "Come to me."

Where are you? she asked. *Who are you?*

"Come to me…"

Light blinded her, and Nyx found herself standing in front of a massive tree. Golden light danced around its branches. Power pulsed and washed over her like sunlight.

The grove faded, and Darius stood beside her.

"What are you doing here?" Nyx scowled at him. "Did you use some kind of magic on me? Because that's rude, druid. You have no right to invade someone's mind."

"No, I didn't do anything. You invade people's minds all the time." He shrugged. "I heard the voice too. I just followed what I heard. Our minds must have somehow merged."

Nyx opened her mouth to protest and realised he had a point. She did invade people's thoughts without even meaning to most of the time. She had never thought of it as rude or invasive, though. It wasn't like she could stop her power from overhearing people's thoughts or whatever they were feeling.

"Okay, so what's happening?"

"I'm not sure. We…"

Nyx stopped listening to him and reached out for the tree.

"Don't." Darius grabbed hold of her arm. Her fingers glided over the solid bark. "You are not supposed to touch it."

"I know this place…"

He frowned. "How?"

"I don't know." She searched her mind but had no recollection of ever being here. "It's like a memory from a dream. Yet I've never been here."

"This is the tree of life. The source of all magic," Darius breathed. "This place is sacred and protected. Even my father isn't allowed to come here. I dread to think what he would try to do if he could access this place."

Nyx frowned. "Doesn't he know it exists?"

Darius gave a harsh laugh. "Oh, he knows. But every Archdruid has been barred from this place for centuries now. One of my ancestors tried to use the magic here once, the results were unimaginable."

"Why are we here?"

A woman walked around the tree. She was beautiful with pale skin and long raven hair. Her purple gown looked to be made from silk and had gold streaks across it. Sprites danced around her.

"Welcome, Nyx." The woman gave her a warm smile, and Darius bowed his head in respect. He seemed to know who she was, at least.

"Do we know each other?" Nyx furrowed her brow.

"I summoned you both here," the woman said.

Who is she, druid?

She is the Great Guardian. The protector of this place. She is the one who told me I had to find you.

Nyx narrowed her eyes. *You said Gideon –*

Gideon knew about you, but she's the one who said you were important.

And the Great Guardian is?

The Guardian of the tree of life. She is considered a protector of the fae. She rarely interferes, Darius explained. *She's good at giving cryptic messages. Don't disrespect her, I beg you.*

I'm not stupid, druid. Nyx knew this woman had a lot of power, and she was not about to disrespect her in any way.

Darius fell to one knee. "You called us, Guardian."

Nyx bowed her head. She didn't want to disrespect this woman. Power flowed from the Great Guardian like waves crashing against rock. Somehow, Nyx didn't feel overwhelmed by it.

"I have summoned you because you are tasked with stopping the darkness creeping over these islands," the Guardian said. "You must repair the rift in the veil or it will fall, and unspeakable things will come through."

"How do we do that?" Nyx asked. "Can we have some clear answers, please? I don't understand all of this cryptic nonsense."

Darius gave her a look. *I said don't disrespect her.*

"I'm not, druid," she hissed and gave him a shove.

"You must learn to work together," the Great Guardian held out her hand, and a butterfly flew into it. The butterfly's wings sparkled with orbs of light. "If you do not…" The light on the butterfly's wings went out, and the creature turned to dust. "This will happen to many on Erthea."

Nyx gasped. She couldn't believe that beautiful thing had withered away. "But how can we stop it? I'm no hero. Back in Joriam, I was little more than a slave." She glowered at Darius.

"I never said you were a slave," he protested.

"You must learn to work together," the Great Guardian said once more.

"I'm not part of the prophecy," Darius pointed out.

"Neither am I for that matter." Nyx crossed her arms. "There's nothing special about me. I just want to be left alone to lead a normal life somewhere where I'm not treated as a slave."

"Prophecy can be interpreted in many ways. Find who lurks in the shadows."

Light then blinded them. Nyx opened her eyes and found herself back in the spirit grove. "I thought you said we'd find answers here."

"I think we did." Darius scrambled up. "She said to find whoever is working in the shadows. So, someone must be using the darklings. We have to find out who."

Nyx rubbed her now aching temples. "How are we going to do that? You don't even know where to begin, do you?"

Darius opened his mouth then closed it again. "We will have to figure out that part ourselves. What else did the Guardian say to you?"

Nyx hesitated and wondered if she should tell him or not. "Not much. She called me a child of the fae."

"She didn't tell you anything else? Like about where you might have come from?"

Nyx shook her head. "No. So let's focus on fixing the problem with the rifts, shall we?"

CHAPTER 14

"Do you really think we can work together, druid?" Nyx demanded as she trailed behind him. "That would imply trust — and I don't trust you."

"I don't trust you either. I sensed you were about use my weapons against me earlier." Darius retrieved his weapons off the ground where he'd left them. "What stopped you?"

She shook her head. "I'm guessing that Guardian." Nyx crossed her arms. "You never once mentioned her when I asked you why you came to get me. I thought Gideon was the only one who wanted me. Now it turns out she does too. Who asked you first?"

He shrugged. "I wasn't sure you would believe me." He had considered telling her about the Great Guardian but decided against it. "Gideon asked me to find you right after I left the spirit grove a couple of days ago. I went there seeking answers about the rifts."

"Why does she think I can help?" Nyx frowned. "I can't control my powers, and like you said, I'm a criminal. Why would she consider me important?"

"Have you ever considered that you might be destined for something more than thievery?" Darius had no idea why the Great Guardian thought Nyx might be important, but he couldn't deny her wisdom. If she thought Nyx was important then she probably was. The Guardian never got things wrong.

"Of course I have. I never wanted to steal. Sometimes people just do what they must to survive."

Darius could not argue with that. He might have been born of privilege being the son of the Archdruid, but he had done what he had to do to survive. "Agreed but we need to learn to trust each other."

She crossed her arms. "Trust must be earned, druid."

"Must you keep calling me that? There are dozens of druids on this island. I'm not the only one in existence."

"Would you prefer prince then? And yes, I will continue calling you druid because that's what you are."

Darius snorted. "I'm no prince, and no, I wouldn't. Trust works both ways. If you help me find who is trying to bring down the veil, I'll ask my brother to grant you your freedom." Darius had no idea how he would convince Gideon to do so. Even if he somehow managed to prove Nyx was innocent, she was still a mind whisperer and a fae of unknown origin. That still made her a threat in the eyes of the court and to the Archdruid. There was little chance of her managing to gain her freedom unless she ran away or he used the help of his resistance contacts to smuggle her away. He would worry about that later.

"That's not good enough. I never asked to be dragged into this," she snapped. "I just want to go home to my sisters. They need me. If I don't return, they will be sold, and the gods only know where they will end up this time. They'll probably end up with someone far worse than Harland."

"Would you leave to be with your sisters if you knew you could help save the world?"

Nyx hesitated. "This isn't my homeland, it's yours."

"If the veil falls, your realm will be just as badly affected as Andovia. Come on, I still have work to do."

They headed away from the grove and through the woods. Shafts of sunlight splintered through the heavy canopy of leaves overhead. More sprites zoomed above their heads and the faint ringing of bells carried on the air.

"Are there only trees on this island? Nyx asked.

"Mostly, but I want to show you something else first." Darius stopped when they reached the clearing and headed up a steep cliff. The canopy parted, giving way to open sky and lush green grass.

"Ambrose said something about you being in the Forest Guard. Aren't you supposed to be doing that?"

"I'm about to. One of my duties is patrolling the forest." Darius grabbed her arm when she stumbled.

"This isn't the forest, druid." She shoved his hand away. "Or did you bring me up here for something else?"

He chuckled, shook his head and whistled.

Nyx put her hands on her hips. "Now what are you doing?"

"Just wait." He whistled again.

A shadow swept down towards them from the outcrop of tiny floating islands. Massive wings stretched out as it glided down to Darius. It was a massive creature with scales the colour of moonlight and piercing golden eyes. The creature roared as it landed beside Darius.

"Is that a…?" Nyx gasped and took a step back.

"A dragon, yes." Darius patted the dragon's snout. "This is Sirin. She's mine. I've had her since she was a hatchling. The island is too vast to patrol from the ground — the Varden patrol most of the forest. I help to patrol the skies, so we'll be doing it from the air. Let's go."

"Wait, you want me to climb on that?" Nyx's mouth fell open. "That's not going to happen. I can fly fine by myself." She motioned to her wings that flashed with a riot of colour.

"Sirin won't hurt you." Darius scrambled onto the dragon's back. "You won't be able to fly around with us all day, and I doubt you could keep up with her speed. Climb on. "

"Oh, I'm not getting on that thing." She raised her hands in protest. "She looks like she's about to eat me."

He chuckled. "She doesn't eat people. Although she will attack anyone she views as a threat to me. Come up." He held a hand out for her. "It's safe. You won't fall off. I've been flying around on dragons since I was a child."

"But she's big and…"

"And we are wasting time. I have to go out to where the first rift opened up. Either that or I'll send you back to Ambrose for more tests." Darius knew how much his mentor wanted to test Nyx's powers further. Although he would like to be present to see what would happen, he had to keep track of the rifts as well as check for any darklings that might have come through. Even if the high council refused to acknowledge the problem didn't mean it would go away.

113

One way or another, he would convince them of the danger. He only hoped more people wouldn't have to die before that happened.

Nyx sighed and took hold of his outstretched hand. Darius pulled her up onto Sirin's back. "Are you sure this is safe?" Nyx clutched his coat. "Because if we fall out of the sky, I may kill you myself."

"I wouldn't make idle threats like that if I were you." Darius clicked his heels, signalling for Sirin to take off.

Sirin flapped her massive bat-like wings and took flight.

Nyx let out a startled cry of alarm as Sirin rose higher until they were over the heavy canopy of trees. The great trees loomed below them, their curtains of green flapping in the breeze and their branches creaking and groaning. They glided along.

Darius glanced behind him and realised Nyx had her eyes shut. "You can look now." He laughed. "Besides, I don't know why you're so afraid. You fly."

"Yes, I fly using my wings and my body, not the wings of a strange beast." She narrowed her eyes and scowled at him. "I could push you off this dragon."

He did laugh then. "You could, but Sirin would save me. Or I would use magic to make myself float as I did with you yesterday."

Around them were dozens of much smaller islands and outcrops of land, including Doringa, where the Dragon Guard was stationed. The might of the Archdruid's army was scattered all over these islands.

"When did the first rift open up?" Nyx asked as her grip around his waist loosened.

"About five days ago. More are opening all the time." Darius leaned left, so Sirin banked that way and they glided around the northern-most point of Eldara.

"Then why did you and Ambrose come to Joriam?"

"You know why I came – because of the Great Guardian. Ambrose came to the lower realm to track the rift and see if the veil was torn any further down there," Darius replied. "He didn't come to find you. We have to track how far the veil is cracking so we can attempt to find something that might slow down the break."

Sirin's senses hummed at the edge of his mind as though they were one being. Darius had grown up training with the Dragon Guard and had a special bond with Sirin. He could call her when they were separated over long distances, and she could commune with him through her mind as well. Fergus might only see dragons for their strength and ability to enforce military might, but Darius knew they were much more special. Sirin glided lower as they descended and reached the north peak of Eldara. Trees and hills surrounded them. Below them stood several houses, some in the trees like Ambrose's villa and others on the ground.

"What's that glowing wood that the houses are made from?" Nyx asked. "They look so… strange. Is it some kind of ward?" The houses shimmered with a faint blue and green hue.

"No, wards are always invisible. It's called Ashwood, made from the wood of a rare ash tree. The wood can change colour depending on the season. Ash trees usually only grow here on Eldara and the Andovian islands."

"How could one have ended up in the lower realm then?"

Darius shrugged. "One would have to have been planted there as a sapling. Or sent there. It's harder for them to grow outside of this realm. They need magic to survive on and a land rich with natural energy. That's more difficult to find in the lower realm." That made Darius even more curious about Nyx's past. He guided Sirin towards the ground where they landed with a thump. Darius climbed down and patted Sirin's head. "Good girl."

Nyx slid down the side of the dragon. "Phew, I never thought I would be glad to be on solid ground again." She breathed a sigh of relief. "I hope flying around on her won't be a habit, druid. I thought I was supposed to be your servant? Shouldn't I be doing household chores or something? I could have stayed back at Ambrose's house and helped Ada. I'm used to menial tasks."

Darius grimaced at the word servant. He didn't know what Nyx was yet. Not a servant as such, just someone he would have to put up with — at least until she got control over her powers. "I don't think Ada would appreciate the help. She hates anyone interfering with her kitchen, and Ambrose insisted I take you with me. We'll have to figure this out as we go along."

Darius had no place for a servant in his life, and still didn't know what he would do with her if he had to take her everywhere with him. What if she found out about his connections to the resistance? Had Ambrose even thought about that? He would have to speak to his mentor about that later. Why Ambrose thought Nyx would be safer with him Darius couldn't fathom. She was much more likely to get in danger whilst he was on patrol than if she stayed with Ambrose himself. Although he supposed Ambrose couldn't take her to council meetings, and it would be much safer if she stayed away from the Crystal Palace altogether.

"Now where are we going?" Nyx asked as they trailed away from Sirin towards a large building made of grey stones. The roof was thatched, and smoke rose from the chimney. "I thought we were looking for a rift? This doesn't look anything like the one I saw yesterday."

Darius repressed a sigh. "Do you always ask so many questions?" Her constant questioning would irritate him to no end. How was he supposed to get any work done? "This is the Forest Guardhouse. I'm here to find out if there are any more reports. All guards come here to get orders and to pass on any relevant news about what they've heard or seen around the island. I have to report into my general."

"Aren't you in charge here?" Nyx raised an eyebrow. "I mean, you are the son of the Archdruid. How could anyone rank higher than you?"

Darius did sigh then. "I don't use my family name to work my way through the ranks. I am a Captain. Everything I do I earn on my own merit and not because of my father. So, come along and stop asking questions." He turned away from her and pushed open the door to the guardhouse.

He stepped inside. A wooden board with pieces of parchment pinned to it took up one side of the wall. A large fireplace sat on the far side of the room along with a large desk. Behind it sat a dark-haired man with long grey hair and a weathered face. He wore the usual forest green tunic of the guard and looked up as Darius walked over. "About time you came back out here," the dark-haired man said. "You've been gone longer than expected, Valeran."

"General Killian." Darius gave him a nod. "Sorry to be away for so long I had other matters to take care of." He shot a glance towards Nyx as she trailed in behind him. "Any more signs of rifts?"

"Not yet, but the one that opened up last has grown in size."

Darius gritted his teeth. He had feared that might happen and muttered an oath. He should have been here working on the problem instead of wasting so much time looking for Nyx in the lower realm.

"Who is the girl?" General Killian arched an eyebrow at Nyx.

"This is Nyx. She is working with me under Ambrose's orders." He knew she wouldn't appreciate him calling her a servant and the fewer people who knew about her powers, the better. Besides, the general never questioned Ambrose's advice. "Do you have any other duties for me? If not, Ambrose wants me focused on finding a way to stop the rift from spreading."

Nyx's eyes widened, but she didn't say anything. For that, he was grateful.

Killian steepled his fingers. "This rift is a danger to all of us. Stopping this threat is your priority. My orders are for you to find a way to close it and quickly. If you need extra men let me know and they will be assigned to you."

Darius nodded to the other druid as they passed out of the guardhouse.

A few minutes later, they stopped at the edge of the village. Green smoke emanated from the rift.

"Can you do something to close it?" Nyx motioned towards it.

He shook his head. "Don't you think we've been trying? Sealing the veil isn't so simple. It takes powerful, dark energy to break and even more power to re-seal it." Nothing they had tried so far had had any effect.

Darius cast his senses out and scanned the rift. He coughed at the toxic fumes that emanated from it. Darius crouched and ran his fingers over the earth.

"What are you doing?" Nyx frowned.

"See what you can feel."

Darkness, old and black, washed over his senses. The question was, who had punched a hole through the veil and why?

CHAPTER 15

Nyx took a step back as Darius examined the rift. The toxic green fumes made her chest ache. Worse still was the energy that hit her: cold and eerie, like death itself.

"What do you sense?" Darius asked. "Focus on the rift and see what your senses tell you."

"That I want to get out of here." She coughed and drew further back.

"Use your senses. It's a good way of learning to control your gift."

She opened her mouth to insist her power was not a gift then closed it again. Nyx hesitated, then let her power roam free. The icy energy intensified. She took another step back. "I don't like this." She shivered. "It's cold —"

"Killer," Harland's voice whispered in her ear.

Nyx jumped and spun around but found no one there. Good gods, had he followed her again? Would the druid see him? She scanned the entire area, still expecting to find him. No one appeared. Gods, why did he have to haunt her again? Why did it have to be with the druid around? She had no idea what Darius would do if he spotted the spirit. He might insist it was a sign of her guilt and tell Ambrose not to teach her how to control her powers. Maybe they would lock her up then or send her to the slave islands. She couldn't decide which was a worse fate.

Nyx forced herself to focus again and waited. More energy struck her.

She knew she should be looking and planning her escape, yet she couldn't deny this was important. What was she supposed to find anyway? Her power allowed her to hear thoughts and influence people. What good would that do against evil spirits and other creatures coming from beyond the veil?

"I don't feel anything except cold," she said after a few moments. "What do you expect me to sense? The killer?"

"The only killer here is you, my Nyxie," Harland's voice came again.

Nyx glanced around, still expecting to see Harland there. Nothing.

Darius frowned at her. "You are sensing something, though, aren't you?"

Sensing? No, just hearing the voice of the spirit who won't leave me alone.

Nyx decided to ignore him. "No… I don't like this place." She tucked a lock of hair behind her ear. "Can… Can spirits hurt people? Even the spirits of humans?"

Darius nodded. "Yes, if they choose to."

"Can you banish them?"

"Sometimes, but darklings are different. They are controlled by something that gives them more power."

"Like what? You must have a theory about who might be behind this. Could it be an enemy of your father?" Nyx had no doubt the Archdruid had dozens of enemies. Entire races of Magickind despised him and everything he stood for.

Darius shrugged. "I don't know enough about this problem yet to have any idea who or what might be causing it. A tear in the veil like this has never happened before."

"I still don't understand why your Guardian thinks I can somehow help with this problem. What am I supposed to do?"

"Darius?" another voice called, and Lucien emerged from the tree line.

Darius strolled off, leaving Nyx alone by the rift. She knelt, placing her hands on the ground. Below, a rock fell away into an empty chasm of darkness. She shivered as more iciness washed over her. Nyx half expected to see Harland down there or shadows moving around.

"Jump, girl. You know you'll be with me soon enough," Harland hissed. "There's no point fighting it. Jump in, and you won't have to endure the suffering of your curse any longer."

"Go away," Nyx muttered under her breath. "I am not going to join you in death. Leave me alone." Despite how hard controlling her power had been over the years, she had never contemplated suicide. Her sisters had always kept her going. They made her fight even harder.

Nyx closed her eyes and focused on the familiar grove of trees in her mind. The grove of glowing trees flashed through her head, and she stopped for a moment. For the first time she noticed the glowing blue hue on the tree trunks, just like she had seen on the houses earlier. Odd, she had never wondered why they glowed before. The grove in her mind had always been a sanctuary, a place to retreat to when she needed to escape from the rest of the world. She had a vague memory of someone telling her to go into that place whenever she needed to be safe but didn't know who had said it.

The trees around her expanded, their branches twisting and stretching around her, forming a protective cage so that nothing could get through. The fresh scent of leaves and grass surrounded her. Then the sound of screaming pierced the air.

Her eyes flew open again, and her protective grove vanished before her eyes. Good gods, who was it? Their fear made her heart pound.

The screaming drowned out the buzzing sounds she got from the other druids. The sound grew louder. Nyx covered her ears, but that did nothing to stop it.

The druid and Lucien were still talking, but she couldn't make out what they were saying.

Help me! The words thrummed through her mind.

Where was it coming from?

She rose and moved away from the rift, but the scream didn't cease. Nyx gritted her teeth. Fine, she would find the person, if only to quiet them. Her temples throbbed with the onslaught of a headache.

She opened her mouth to call out for the druid then decided against it. His questions would only interfere with her concentration.

Nyx hurried past the rows of houses as the scream grew louder. Several people sent curious glances her way.

Help me! The voice came again. *Someone, please.*

Where are you? Nyx thought and scanned another row of cottages. More minds buzzed inside. She ran faster; more houses rushed past. The screaming person had to be around here somewhere.

Nyx stopped to catch her breath, and the iciness washed over her once more. The same coldness she had felt yesterday when the darkling attacked.

A shadow passed over her as someone swooped down. "Nyx." Ranelle gave her a bright smile. "It's good to see you. How do you like —?"

"Quiet," Nyx snapped and waved a hand at the other girl.

Nyx? someone else called out to her.

The druid.

She repressed a sigh. Why couldn't these people let her concentrate? She couldn't find whoever was in danger if she kept getting interrupted. She had had this problem before when she had searched for her intended targets whenever Harland told her someone important would be passing through the village or in one of the neighbouring villages.

Darius? Ranelle called. *Nyx is with me. I think she might be running away again. You should come over here and help. I don't want her using her powers on me.*

"I'm not running away, and I won't use my powers on you," Nyx ground out. "I'm trying to find—"

The screaming filled her mind again.

Stop, please stop…

"Find what?" Ranelle asked. "Nyx, what's wrong?"

Nyx brushed off her concern and bolted for the nearest house. Inside stood nothing but an empty stove and a dirty flagstone floor. Pots and pans covered the entire kitchen and herbs hung from the wooden rafters.

No, this wasn't the right place.

Damn Ranelle for distracting her.

Darius bounded over, his long cloak billowing behind him. "Nyx? Are you—?"

She glowered at him. "Shut up!" Nyx clutched her head as another wave of screaming deafened her. "Darkling…"

Darius' eyes narrowed. "Where?"

Nyx shook her head. The screaming grew so loud she couldn't form words any longer. The screams and the sounds of people's thoughts blended together. Darius caught hold of her arm. All at once, the world quietened.

Nyx blew out a breath. "Someone is being attacked — I think I know where they are."

Lucien came over too. "Is it the darkling? Can you sense it?"

Ranelle frowned at him. "No one asked for your help, Wolfsbane."

"Oh quiet down, dragon." Lucien waved his hand in dismissal. "No one asked for your opinion either."

"Concentrate." Darius relinquished his grip. "Focus on the voice."

The noise flooded back in, hard and fast. Nyx clenched her hands into fists. *Where are you?* She demanded of the screaming voice. Nyx felt herself falling as she closed her eyes. Gods, she needed to stop the screaming.

"Rae, take to the air," Darius told her. "Luc, scout the area and see what you can find. Follow your senses and see if there is any sign of the darkling."

Ranelle spread her large bat-like wings and shot into the sky while Lucien took off in the opposite direction in a blur of movement.

Nyx motioned for the druid to follow and took off running. She made it to the tree line when all at once the screams stopped, her mind quieted to the drone of nearby thoughts. The fear and desperation were gone, evaporated as if they had never existed.

"I — I can't hear it anymore," Nyx remarked.

Darius halted beside her. "You don't sense the darkling anymore?"

Ambrose appeared in a flash of light. "Where's the darkling?"

Nyx guessed Darius must have called him for help. How did Ambrose appear and disappear so easily? Some other magic, no doubt. She would be sure to question the older druid about it later.

"I sensed it." She ran a hand through her long hair. "But it's gone now." She rubbed her aching temples.

"Perhaps the darkling claimed its next victim," Darius mused. "They are becoming much bolder. A few days ago, the attacks were limited to night. How are they moving around in the daylight? Unless they aren't as immune as we first thought."

"Nyx, I need you to concentrate," Ambrose said.

She groaned, her mind still reeling. She wanted nothing more than to go somewhere quiet and recover from what she had endured. "What? I don't hear the screaming anymore." Nor did she want to hear it again. Nyx hadn't thought she would have to feel people dying while she was here. She didn't know what she had expected, not that at least.

"Close your eyes and focus." Ambrose motioned with his staff.

Nyx gaped at him. "Focus? In the midst of all this chaos? There's too much noise."

"Learning to focus on one thing is the first step to control. Close your eyes and focus. Quieten your mind."

Nyx scowled and closed her eyes. "How do I do that?" Silence didn't exist inside her mind. It never had, not unless she went into her grove sanctuary, but she wasn't about to do that in front of these people. Domnu insisted she disappeared when she had done that around her before. Nyx didn't want to test the theory to see if it was true.

"Turn your thoughts inward. Focus on the place where you feel safe and calm. Try to imagine that place."

Safe? Nyx didn't know anywhere that had ever felt safe to her in the physical world. The only peace she had ever found was using the drug Nilanda. Reluctantly, she pictured her grove with trees surrounding her. They formed a protective ring that could shield her from anything. Voices still buzzed around her like annoying insects, but the sound lessened to an extent.

"When you get to that place, concentrate on what you want to find," Ambrose told her.

Nyx bit back a curse. She did not want to come face-to-face with the darkling again. "How do I do that?" Nyx frowned. "What do you want me to find?" She knew the screaming person had to be dead now. Why else would they have gone quiet?

"Concentrate on the source of the screams you heard. The idea is to focus on that one thing without lowering whatever boundaries you already have to protect yourself from getting overwhelmed."

Boundaries? She had nothing to keep her power at bay unless she put on that bracelet or touched the druid. Nothing aside from Nilanda or staying away from people kept her power at a bearable level. She had tried wine and other things, but nothing helped.

Nyx had no idea how to find the screaming person. She almost opened her eyes. "I don't know how."

"Use your instincts. You can control your power. It's a matter of finding it." Ambrose's energy moved closer to her, his magic a faint hum against her mind. "Darius mentioned you were a thief. How did you use your power to find people?"

She furrowed her brow. "I knew who would be easy targets and what they were carrying." Nyx was glad she had her eyes closed. She didn't want to see their judgemental gazes. Thievery had only been a way to survive and feed her sisters.

Nyx turned her thoughts away from her sisters and focused on the screaming person. *Where are you?* More thoughts buzzed around her mind. *Come on, where are you?* The trees moved closer; their branches curled around each other tighter.

"I can't find it," she grumbled. "What if they're already gone? It's probably too late."

"Strong emotions leave behind remnants. It's just a matter of finding them."

Nyx decided to concentrate on her breathing instead. She always did that when the noise became too much for her.

In and out. Calming breaths helped – Domnu had taught her that.

Help me, please. The voice came as barely more than a whisper.

Where are you? Nyx demanded. *I can't find you unless you tell me where you are.*

An image of a house between a group of trees came to her. Nyx opened her eyes and shot to her feet. "I know where they are — but I don't know how to get there." She hadn't been here long enough to know the layout of the land. Plus, the wild energy of this place made it hard for her to pinpoint the exact location.

"We can find it faster if we fly." Darius whistled, and Sirin swooped down. "Let's go."

CHAPTER 16

Darius winced as Nyx gripped onto him, hard. He ignored the uncomfortable feeling. He kept his senses on alert as they scoured the treeline and rows of different houses. "Anything look familiar?" Darius sensed a few druids below but no sign of the darkling. He couldn't be sure if the creature would still be around. Today had made him realise just how little they knew about them.

What if they could move in daylight now? They would be able to kill more people than he had anticipated. Dozens of people could die. Darius dreaded to think of how many people it would take before the high council finally decided to take this threat seriously.

Nyx furrowed her brow. "No, nothing. Maybe I saw the wrong place or…"

"It's no use second-guessing yourself. First instincts are usually right." The wind rushed past as he guided Sirin lower. He reached out for the elements and used them to scan for any trace of the darkling. Nothing. No disturbance at all, but then darklings were hard to detect. Darius almost wished he had Nyx's sensitivity to them so it would be easier to find them. "Maybe you should try again."

"I sense the living, not the dead. Is there even a chance the person I heard is still alive?"

Darius hesitated. He hoped they were still alive, but Eldara was the second largest island. They could be anywhere. Given how strong Nyx's abilities were they might not even be on this island but one of the surrounding islands. There was no way to tell how far her power expanded.

"Nyx, was the person you sensed on this island or somewhere else?"

"I'm not like you, druid. I can't give you exact answers."

Darius didn't doubt she could do it, but it would take time and practice. He couldn't expect her to master her abilities in one day. "Describe what it looked like. Tell me everything you can remember."

Nyx bit her lip. "A small house — more like a wooden shack. There are a couple of dead trees outside it."

"Anything else?"

Nyx shrugged. "It's not like the houses I've seen on Eldara. More…derelict."

Darius' mind raced as he tried to decide the best way to help her find their intended quarry.

Ambrose had asked Nyx earlier how she found her usual victims. Maybe getting her to act like a thief was the way to get her power to work.

"If this was a victim you were about to rob, how would you find them?" Darius asked.

"I don't have victims, druid." She glowered at him and crossed her arms. "You asked me not to judge you, so do not judge me for the crimes I have done in order to survive."

He sighed. Thievery still affected people in a bad way. Coins she had stolen for herself would have left others penniless. He decided against mentioning that; antagonising her would only make her more resistant.

"Can you show me what you saw?" Darius turned as best he could to face her.

Nyx frowned. "How am I supposed to do that?"

"If I lower my mental shield, you should be able to project the image to me." He held out his hand to her. "Try to picture it in your mind."

"Your power suppresses mine. How would that work?"

"It should work. I can read surface thoughts when I choose to."

Nyx grasped his hand. Darius closed his eyes and the image of a shack flashed through his mind. He gulped. "I know where that is and it's not one of the main islands." Dread formed in his stomach.

"Where is it then?"

126

"Doringa." He left it at that. Telling her it was an island where slaves were kept wouldn't sit so well with her. Better to wait until they got there. "It's in the lower realm."

A small group of islands existed beneath the lands of Andovia. The slave islands, as some called them. Most of the fae avoided going there unless they were those who worked with slavery.

Darius signalled to Sirin to change course. The dragon banked left. His heart pounded and disgust twisted in his gut. He hated going to the slave islands. People there were treated as little more than chattel. All races had the right to be free – despite what his father decreed. He knew Nyx wouldn't be pleased at going there either, but they had no choice. They had to keep track of any potential rifts.

"This is pretty barren compared to what I saw on Eldara and Avenia," Nyx remarked as Doringa came into view. "What is this place? Is this where poor folk live?"

"Something like that."

Doringa was a harsh place and one of the larger islands in the lower realm. It consisted mainly of fields to grow crops in. Crops didn't grow as well in the upper realm due to the altitude and high winds. Plus, they had more flowing water down here.

Sirin's wings grazed the water as they neared the island. Another much larger dragon loomed overhead and charged towards them.

Unlike Sirin's silver skin, this dragon was all black with glowing red eyes. A ridgeback. Darius recognised the Dragon Guard's favoured beast.

"Who goes there?" The rider astride the ridgeback called out. The man's armour gleamed like bright silver fire, and he aimed his staff at Sirin. "No one is permitted on Doringa."

"I'm Darius Valeran, a Captain in the Forest Guard."

The guard guided his ridgeback closer; the two dragons circled each other. Sirin let out another cry, warning the ridgeback not to come any closer.

"Who is your companion?" the guard demanded.

Darius' jaw clenched. "A servant. And who are you to question me?" He forced himself to put on his Archdruid façade. The Archdruid answered to no one and nor did his sons. At least that was what his mother had told him. Darius didn't like to use his family name to lord it over everyone, but it did prove useful at times.

The guard lowered his staff. "Very well, my lord. I will escort you to the island."

Nyx scoffed at the words "my lord".

Darius waved his hand. "Return to your post. I can find my own way there." He urged Sirin onward. "Perhaps next time you will have the sense not to get in my way."

His dragon gave another screech then surged away. Darius couldn't blame her for wanting to get away from the ridgeback. He didn't like the beasts either; they were trained until they were broken, until they had no spirit left in them. It was one of the reasons why he had adopted Sirin due to her size and gentle nature and why he had refused to join the Dragon Guard.

As they came close to land, Nyx gasped. Below, people dressed in little more than rags tended to their fields. A few glances came their way, then people averted their gazes. Some looked as soulless as the ridgeback. "These are slaves, aren't they?" Nyx hissed in his ear. "Good gods."

Darius sighed. "Yes, this is one of the many slave islands. And before you say anything, yes, I disapprove of it. But like it or not, this is the way things are." He guided Sirin down to where a row of small shacks stood then dismounted.

Nyx jumped down beside him and rubbed her legs. A guard glanced their way then raised his fist to his chest.

"We won't be long, girl." He patted Sirin's head. Darius sent his senses out once more. No sign of the darkling, but that didn't mean there weren't nearby. He motioned for Nyx to follow him.

Neither of them said anything as they scanned the different houses. No one dared to look their way either. Most of the shacks all looked the same, wooden and roughly made, like they wouldn't survive a strong storm.

They moved past the first row and away from the field.

"I still don't understand this," Nyx hissed. "Why is the Archdruid imprisoning fae when he is married to one?"

"Look at them." Darius motioned to the workers. "What's different about them compared to the other fae you have seen so far?"

Nyx frowned. "They… they have wings and pointed ears."

"Exactly. These are Andovians — an old race of fae which Silvans despise," Darius explained. "But I know someone here who might be able to help us."

"You're friends with slaves now too?" Nyx scoffed. "You are full of surprises, druid." She shook her head. "Nothing about you or these lands makes sense to me."

"Yes, I am." Darius raised his chin. He wasn't about to defend himself to anyone, least of all her. He hesitated as they moved away from the fields and approached another row of shacks.

These were in better condition and could almost pass for a rural village. If Darius introduced Nyx to his friend, he would be showing her weakness, one she could use against him. He could have forced her to stay with Sirin, but she might have made another escape attempt. Besides, he needed her to identify the person she had sensed and to track the darkling if it was still somewhere nearby.

Darius approached the last house in the row and knocked.

After a few moments, the door opened, and a man with green hair emerged. "Darius. Good to see you, my boy." He clapped Darius on the back. Pointed ears stuck out of his long teal hair and blue wings trailed behind his bony back like pieces of broken leaves.

"Nolan." Darius gave him a grim smile. "We are looking for someone who we think may be in trouble. Maybe you can help us find them." *Nyx, can you see if you can sense the person you heard earlier?*

Nyx didn't acknowledge she had heard him.

He sighed. Darius would have to work on forming a mental link with her so they could communicate more easily.

Nolan's smile faded. "Who?" He eyed Nyx. "Why is she here? You know how dangerous this place is for outsiders."

"I'm not a threat to anyone." Nyx crossed her arms.

"She's… here to help. We are looking for someone who —"

Nyx pushed past Darius. "Come on, druid." She took off running.

Darius and Nolan glanced at each other before they both hurried after her.

"Who is the girl?" Nolan puffed as he struggled to keep up. "You've never brought her with you before. She looks like one of my people except she doesn't have pointed ears."

"It's a long story." Darius picked up the pace so he didn't lose sight of her. For all he knew, she might be making a run for it again.

This would be the perfect place to escape from, and she could fly after all.

Darius stopped at Nyx's side where she stood and stared at a small shack. This was the place she had shown him earlier.

"They're inside, I can sense them." Nyx craned her head towards the house. "They are still afraid, but I think they're still alive."

"Is the darkling still inside?" Darius frowned, and Nyx shrugged. "Nolan, who lives here?"

Nolan paled. "Lyon. Oh, by the mother, no."

Darius rushed inside the house. On the floor lay a young man, his wings splayed around him. His eyes flickered. Darius knelt and placed a hand on him. Dark magic hit his senses. Marks were etched on the man's neck where claws had dug in. "He's still alive," Darius gasped.

The room contained little more than a straw mattress and a few dirty blankets and, in the far corner, a wooden stool and a few cooking pots. That didn't surprise him as all of the slaves on the island were not allowed to keep personal possessions.

"What happened to him?" Nolan asked, face etched with concern. "How did you know he was in trouble?"

"A darkling attacked him — a spirit," Nyx answered and came over to Darius' side. "Can you help him, druid?"

Darius shrugged. He had never felt magic this dark before. "I will do my best, but I think we need to get him to Eldara. Ambrose is better equipped to deal with this than I am."

"We can't carry him back. I doubt Sirin will be able to hold three people." Nyx shook her head.

"She's right. He looks too weak to be carried by a dragon," Nolan remarked. "But we can't keep him here either. Radek kills any slave who falls ill."

"Who's Radek?" Nyx frowned.

"The commander in charge of this island." Darius' lip curled. Spirits, he hated Radek with a passion and did not want to run into him either. "We'll do what we can to help him," Darius assured his friend. "Help me carry him to his bed." Darius and Nolan heaved Lyon up and dragged him over to a mat in the corner. "Nolan, do you have any herbs and potions that we might be able to use?"

Darius and his contacts smuggled such things out here whenever they could. He even spelled the items to camouflage themselves so they could be hidden from the guard's prying eyes.

Nolan shook his head. "No, Radek has his guards doing weekly checks. They confiscated what meagre supplies we had. Darius, you know what they'll do if they find Lyon here. Can't you transport him somewhere else?"

Darius sighed. "No, transportation spells don't work here on this island. My brother put spells in place to ensure no slaves could use the rings to escape."

Gideon had insisted it was to stop slaves from escaping but Darius knew better than that. Gideon didn't want anyone getting supplies onto the island and helping slaves. Gideon always did everything he could to thwart the resistance's attempts to help people. It also meant no one from the resistance could come and go from the island either. Their old escape plans had all been ruined.

One way or another, they had to find a way to save Lyon before it was too late.

CHAPTER 17

Nyx paced up and down the narrow length of the shack whilst Darius chanted strange words over Lyon. Light flashed from the druid's hand, and he continued to cast different spells. She knew how to be patient from her days on the streets stealing coins, but she hated standing around feeling useless. She needed to do something. Anything. Nolan had gone off to see if he could find anything left over from his secret stash of supplies that had been smuggled onto the island.

Nyx sighed. "Is it working?"

"No. This magic is unlike anything I've dealt with. I have no idea if any of my spells will work."

"Can't Ambrose help?" Judging by how powerful the elder druid was, she thought he would be able to heal anyone. She didn't know enough about druid magic yet to understand how it worked.

"Maybe, but it would be easier if he were here." Darius rose.

Nyx couldn't get too close to the man without the iciness from the dark magic overwhelming her. "Can't he fly here? Or transport using those circles that you druids keep drawing?"

Darius shook his head. "The commander forbade Ambrose from coming here. He didn't like Ambrose helping the slaves. I'm only allowed here because I am a Valeran."

"Why wouldn't —" Nyx shut her mouth. No, no one helped slaves. She knew that from experience. Slaves were cheap labour and used throughout the lower realm and beyond. Most people considered slaves dispensable too since there were always more to come by.

Harland had kept her and her sisters fed and sheltered so he could profit from their abilities. Nyx had only ever thought of her curse as a means to an end, a way of surviving and eventually escaping from Harland. She might have a chance to escape whilst she was here. She had eyed possible escape routes. Escaping here might be easier than getting off Eldara. She had considered taking Sirin but decided against it. Darius probably had a way to call the dragon back so that wouldn't work. It didn't look like there were any boats around either. How did these people get around if they had to transport slaves somewhere? Or more likely they didn't move them. Ships came to bring people and no one ever left.

The iciness crept over her again, overpowering the constant buzz of thoughts. Was the darkling still nearby? If so, maybe she should go and look for it. It would give her a good excuse to look for an escape route. Escape would take time and planning – that much she already knew. So, she had better get started.

"I sense something," Nyx said. "The darkling maybe. I'll go scout around and see if it's still here." She would not ask his permission. Nyx might be a servant, but she wouldn't ask him for anything. Her pride wouldn't let her. Nor did she want to stand around feeling useless.

Darius narrowed his eyes. "I can't leave Lyon."

"I'm not suggesting you do." She crossed her arms. "I can go and look. You do not have to come with me." Nyx needed to do something or she would lose her mind, or more likely lose control of her power.

"And what if it attacks you? There are no other routes off the island except by dragon. Sirin only takes commands from me — so don't think of trying to escape whilst you're here."

"You said I wasn't a prisoner, yet you treat me like one." Nyx gritted her teeth. "I'm not running away. I want to find the darkling because its energy is almost as annoying as being subjected to everyone's thoughts." Her fists clenched. "I can't be around people for too long, druid. Or would you like a repeat of yesterday?"

Darius shook his head. "Doringa isn't somewhere you can roam around. There are guards everywhere. I can guarantee one of them will stop to question you."

"How else can we find the darkling? If I can track it, maybe you can banish it."

He sighed. "Fine, but stay close. And, for the love of the spirits, don't use your powers on the guards or draw any unnecessary attention to yourself. If you get overwhelmed, use your bracelet."

"I may never wear that again. Also, don't defile what few possessions I have. That was a gift." Nyx turned and hurried out.

She took a deep breath and sensed someone coming towards her. Nolan.

It didn't take long for her to become accustomed to seeing someone's energy.

Darius stepped outside. "Nolan, would you mind accompanying Nyx? Make sure she doesn't get lost and keep her out of trouble if you can."

Are you out of your mind? Nyx snapped and switched to talking in thought so Nolan wouldn't overhear her. *What if he gets attacked by the darkling? I'm not going to be responsible for someone else's life.* She had no idea what she would do if Harland appeared and tried to kill her again.

Darius arched an eyebrow at her. *It wouldn't be safe if you were alone.*

Nyx frowned as Nolan came closer. There was something odd about him. Energy hummed somewhere deep inside him, but it somehow lay beyond reach. *He's bound,* Nyx realised. No one here would be allowed to have magic. She had heard of such tales and always thought they had been an exaggeration. How had they managed to bind entire races?

Nyx reminded herself not to be surprised by anything. This place fell under the rule of the Archdruid after all.

How will sending me off with someone powerless help? She glowered at the druid. *I can move around quicker on my own.*

You're getting better at communicating in thought. His smile only infuriated her further.

She scowled at him. *Answer me, druid.*

Darius rolled his eyes. *You will draw less attention that way.*

Right. She scoffed and headed out.

Nolan trailed after her. "Unusual for Darius to have a servant. He despises such things."

"How do you know I'm a servant? I'm just a slave like you." Her lip curled in disgust.

Nolan gave a hearty laugh. "Darius would never have a slave. He despises slavery as much as every slave on this island does. No, you must be either a servant or an apprentice, although the latter seems unlikely. The fae court would never allow anyone like you to become an apprentice."

Nyx narrowed her eyes. "Lucky me then. I am sorry you have to come with me. No offence, but I prefer to be alone." His energy didn't bother her since it was restrained and his mind sounded unusually quiet, but how could she look around with someone following her?

"Even more unusual to see a winged fae roaming free. Can you fly?"

Nyx ignored him. She didn't have time for idle chatter. Iciness washed over her once more. That darkling had to be somewhere around here. She had to find it and get a sense of what it was.

"Do —?" Nolan began.

"Quiet. I have an evil spirit to find. Then I can help the druid." Nyx sprinted off in the opposite direction. The iciness intensified. "Where are you?"

No sign of anything.

She didn't know how to focus her power. Instinct didn't tell her what to do either.

Nyx hurried along the trail, dirt crunching underneath her boots. *Where are you?*

"Looking for me, Nyxie?" Harland's spirit emerged from behind a tree. "You didn't think I would stay gone for long, did you? Look at you, trying to act like a hero." He gave a harsh laugh. "These people won't be fooled by you for long. They will soon see what a little rat you are. So stop trying to pretend you can help them. No one can help the people on this island. They were born slaves and will die that way. They are as worthless as dirt."

Oh, good gods, not now.

"Go away," she hissed. "You are not welcome here." Nyx knew she had to find a way to get rid of him once and for all, even if it meant telling the druid about him.

"I told you you'd soon be joining me."

Nyx furrowed her brow. "What do you mean?"

Harland laughed and leaned back against the tree. "You'll find out soon enough." With that, he vanished.

Nolan puffed as he jogged to keep up with her. "Wait. There are other dangers on this island apart from the—"

A man rounded the corner. His long hair was wild about his shoulders and his eyes were dark, almost black. Sharp claws covered his hands.

What now?

Redcap, a voice whispered in her mind. Odd, was she hearing someone's thoughts? She didn't think so. It sounded like her own inner voice. Nyx had no idea what it meant.

Blood must have blood. The creature wore a cap on its head that had gone brown – was that blood on it?

"Back away slowly," Nolan told her.

"I'm not about to let a tasty morsel get away," the Redcap said, and lunged for her.

Nyx dodged his swipe, spun and kicked out. Her foot missed its intended target.

Darius had warned her not to use her influence on anyone. She would have to make do without a sword.

I don't have time for this. Nyx kicked the Redcap away before its claws had the chance to make contact with her skin.

He used his other hand to make a grab for her again. His claws passed inches from her throat.

Nyx grabbed his wrist to stop him and power slammed through her before she had time to react. The energy reverberated through her into the Redcap. The force of it made him stumble backwards. The Redcap screamed, clutching his head.

"What the?" Nyx gasped and fell to one knee. Not again. She couldn't believe she'd lost control of her power. She hadn't wanted to use it. She had only wanted to make him stop.

"By the spirits, you're a soul seer," Nolan breathed.

The Redcap screeched as if in agony. Nyx had never seen anyone react to her power that way before. "What's... what's wrong with him?" She scrambled up.

"You projected onto him."

"I did what?" The druid had not mentioned anything about projecting— whatever that meant. "What is a soul seer?" Nyx hated how everyone seemed to know more about her powers than she did. She had to get Ambrose to start teaching her and get this damned magic under control.

"Your magic can cause great suffering when you choose to project your emotions onto others. Your influence can bend someone to your will and make them suffer depending on your intentions," Nolan explained. "A soul seer is an old term for what they now call a mind whisperer. Incredible. I thought everyone with that gift had been wiped out a generation ago."

"My intention was to get him away from me," she growled. "I didn't mean to do anything to him." The druid would scold her for this no doubt. "How do I undo it?"

Nolan furrowed his brow. "That's difficult. How well versed are you in your powers?"

"Not much, judging by him." She inclined her head towards the Redcap. "How do you know so much about my curse?"

"Curse?" Nolan's frown deepened. "You were born with an incredible gift. You should be proud of that."

"I wouldn't call my power a gift, would you?"

"Of course. A talent such as yours is rare. I know of soul seers, but I don't know everything about them."

Nyx's heart sank. Why couldn't anyone teach her to control her curse?

The Redcap slumped to the ground, unmoving. His screams had ceased.

Nyx grimaced, bending to roll the Redcap over. Glassy eyes stared back at her, and a trickle of blood dripped from its nose. "Oh, gods." Nyx put her hand over her mouth. "He's dead. How can he be dead?" Gods, she couldn't believe her powers had killed someone. Had Harland died this way?

Had Harland known this would happen? He must have known about the attack given his snide remarks. Only now she had sent someone else to death instead of going there herself. How much more blood would she have on her hands before she got her power under control?

"What are you doing?" Armed men swarmed in around her and raised their weapons, and Nyx wondered how she would get out of this one.

This can't be good. Nyx took a step back and raised her hands in surrender. Why had she not sensed them coming? She always sensed people approaching.

No thoughts came from their minds; she realised it must be because they were shielded like the druid. Darius had been right to warn her about them. Her influence would not work on them either.

How would she explain this to them? If they realised what she had done, Gideon would find out the true extent of what her power could do.

"I am the servant of Lord Darius Valeran. I was…running an errand for him." Nyx hated how pathetic she sounded. She didn't even know if she had gotten Darius' title right.

A tall, dark-haired man who appeared to be the leader scoffed at that. "You expect me to believe that? You are trespassing here on this island."

"Lord Darius is here. Didn't any of you see him arrive on his dragon?" Nyx put her hands on her hips. "There's nothing to see here." Nyx hoped she wouldn't be signing her own death warrant, but acting authoritative worked for the druid, so perhaps it would work for her as well. None of these men would want to risk Darius' ire since he was the Archdruid's son.

The dark-haired guard stepped forward and pointed a staff at her chest. "Explain yourself right now or you will die, girl."

Panic whirled in her chest and her heart pounded so hard she thought it might break through her rib cage. Gods, she had to do something before she risked losing control of her power once more. Only this time, it would cause her death and not to any of these men.

"If you don't believe me, I will call Lord Darius out here then." Nyx didn't know what else to say or do. She had been Darius' servant for less than a day and although she didn't want to admit it, she needed his help.

CHAPTER 18

"Why is nothing working?" Darius said, more to himself since he doubted Lyon could hear him. He got up from where he had been crouched on the floor and paced up and down. There had to be some way to drain the dark magic out of Lyon's body. He just needed to find the right way.

Have you tried a cleansing spell? Ambrose asked, breaking him out of his racing thoughts. *Try one of the more powerful ones that you learnt from your parents. That should be more effective.*

Yes, I tried. Darius gritted his teeth. *It didn't have any effect.* His mind continued to race with more spells, many of which he had already tried. Darius searched his memories for something he had learnt from his parents. As well as teaching him how to use high magic, they had also taught him how to reverse its effects. His mother had always been insistent about that in case anything ever went wrong.

How are you getting along with Nyx? How is she controlling her powers?

She has...gone off to look for the darkling. He didn't mention the fact that he was glad to have her out of the way for a while.

You let her go off alone? What were you thinking? Ambrose sounded incredulous. *What if she loses control again? I thought you had more sense than that, boy. You know how unpredictable her powers are. You have to keep her strength a secret. Letting her roam around on her own, you might as well be announcing her to the entire upper realm.*

Her powers won't work on the guards, Darius pointed out. *I can't be with her every minute of every day. I'm trying to save an innocent life here. Isn't helping Lyon more important?*

They will still arrest her if she loses control. Go and help her, Ambrose insisted. *Now.*

What about Lyon? I can't leave him, Darius protested. *There isn't anyone else here who can watch him. Nolan went with Nyx.*

Help Nyx then come back to help him.

Darius could not believe what his mentor was suggesting. Saving an innocent life always came first, at least that was what Ambrose had always taught him. Why did Nyx come before that? Even if she was somehow a part of the prophecy and could help fix the tear in the veil, he was not about to let this man die.

I could use your help here, Darius snapped. *Is there no other way you could get here? Use a glamour spell if you must. The ones I showed you that were taught to me by my mother should be enough to shield you from the guards.*

Um, druid, I have a slight problem, Nyx's voice rang through his mind.

Darius' head throbbed from having to maintain a mental link with two people. One he could do, but two at the same time proved impossible. Ambrose's presence all but disappeared from his mind.

He sighed. *What is it?* He should have known Nyx would get into trouble. *Did you find the darkling?* If she had managed to find it, he would have to go and help her.

No, a Redcap, and now he's dead. I'm in trouble. There are guards here, and they say they're going to arrest me. What should I do? I can't hear any of their thoughts, and I'm trying really hard not to use my powers.

Darius clenched his jaw. *A Redcap? I can't leave you alone for one moment, can I?*

Nolan needs your help. The guards are threatening to arrest him for killing another fae. So, come out here. Unless you want me to use my powers?

He rubbed his aching temples. By the spirits, what had he done to deserve being stuck with her? The Great Guardian must have lost her mind to think they could work together. *How did the Redcap die?* He groaned. *You killed it, didn't you? Please tell me I'm wrong.*

Darius? Ambrose called out, but his voice sounded far away. Overwhelmed by Nyx's presence, no doubt.

I'm on my way. Darius flinched as pain stabbed through his head as he ended the connection with Nyx. *Nyx is in trouble. Again,* he told his mentor. *She should stay on the island away from anyone until someone can teach her how to control her powers.*

What about the infected victim?

Darius groaned. *I can't leave Lyon to die to go and rescue Nyx. The guards have Nyx and Nolan.*

Don't risk Nyx using her powers on them. The guards will kill her— if Gideon and your father don't find out how powerful she is first. Ambrose's voice grew urgent. *Go and help her.*

But what about Lyon? Can't you come here and help him?

Put Lyon under a stasis spell. It might slow down the rate of infection. And no, I can't come there. You know Radek would arrest me for trespassing.

I'll do what I can. Darius ended the connection and stood. He raised his hand and muttered the words of a spell. He had no idea how long helping Nyx would take. Light pulsed from his hand and Lyon groaned. He hoped the stasis spell would slow down the dark magic inside his body. Darius cast his senses out again. At least the dark magic had stopped moving.

He hurried outside. Holy spirits, what had he done to deserve Nyx? She had been nothing but a thorn in his side since he had laid eyes on her. He had only agreed to let her search for the darkling so he could concentrate on helping Lyon. Her pacing had distracted him along with the feel of her energy. She was like a conduit.

People sent curious glances his way as he ran past the houses and up the hill.

Darius gasped for breath when he finally reached the top. To his surprise, Nyx and Nolan still stood surrounded by Radek and three other men. They each had the dark armour and red cloaks of the Dragon Guard. Wonderful, it had to be Radek himself. How he despised the man who enjoyed making others suffer.

"What's going on?" Darius forced his face to become impassive and stopped panting for breath. He took in the sight of the Redcap on the ground: yet another fae thought to have been banished from these lands a generation ago.

"These two killed this strange creature." Radek, a tan-skinned man with long black hair, sneered. He motioned to the body of the Redcap. "What have I told you about bringing outsiders to my island, Valeran?"

"We didn't kill anyone." Nyx raised her chin. "We found him like this. Something else must have killed him."

Radek snorted. "I'm sure a few lashes will loosen your tongue. Take —"

"Wait." Darius stepped in front of the commander. "This girl is my servant. She and Nolan were running an errand on my orders."

Radek's sneer turned sinister. "You have a servant now?" He scoffed. "A scrawny girl at that. I'm sure you could do so much better. If you need a more hard-working and durable slave, I'm sure one could be found for you." He motioned to one of his men who heaved the Redcap up. The fae's glassy eyes were empty. "Does this look natural to you?"

"It looks like he has been infected the same way as another man I'm here to help." Darius didn't flinch at the sight. He had seen more corpses than he cared to remember. It would take more than that to bother him.

Radek's smile faded. "You're here helping slaves again? I warned you —"

"No, I'm investigating to find out what is killing these people. Another slave has already been attacked and infected with dark magic."

"That's not my concern." Radek shook his head. "My only concern is keeping this island in order. Which I can't do if people keep interfering —"

"I sent my servant to look for what might have attacked the man I'm treating," Darius cut him off. "If there's a killer on the loose on these islands, you should be concerned. It could go after the guards too and kill hundreds of slaves– faster than you can bring any more here."

"Who is this killer? And how are they killing?" Radek demanded. "Why have I not been informed of this?" His hands clenched into fists. "I outrank you, so I should be informed of anything that might be a potential threat to my —"

Darius almost lost his façade but took it in stride. "Because my father doesn't want panic spreading. Only those in his close circle know the truth. And no, you don't outrank me. I am the son of the Archdruid and brother to the fae prince. You are little more than a lowly foot soldier. Now, release my servant. I have more important matters to deal with than you."

Nyx's eyes widened, and for a moment, she looked almost impressed. Then her usual scowl returned.

"But — but I have a right to know," Radek snapped. "I am the general here, and I oversee this entire island. Archdruid son or not, you are only a Captain."

"Take it up with my father then." Darius pushed past the commander and grabbed Nyx's arm. "I'm taking possession of the body too. All you're doing is preventing my servant from carrying out her duties."

Radek's jaw tightened. "Don't give me orders, boy. I still outrank you."

"I'm part of the Forest Guard, not the Dragon Guard. Like I said, take your grievances up with my father. Or should I call him here and tell him how you're interrupting my duties?" Darius knew Radek would never want him to call Fergus here, not over such a petty matter or else he would be stripped of rank and made a laughingstock. His father had killed men over less if they displeased him.

Radek's mouth opened and closed like a fish. His face turned bright red.

"Give me a hand with the body, would you?" Darius motioned to the other guards. "Bring it back to the village."

"This is your problem, deal with it. One dead slave is not my concern."

Darius gritted his teeth. "It will be when hundreds start dying."

Radek and his men marched off.

Darius waited until they were out of sight before he blew out a breath. "Holy spirits, I can't leave you alone for a moment, can I?"

"I was looking for the darkling. He attacked me." Nyx pointed at the Redcap's body

"She is telling the truth," Nolan agreed. "She has little control over her power. You can't scold her for that. Besides, it's no loss. You know how vicious Redcaps are."

Redcaps had been another kind of fae thought to be long extinct. Redcaps were not usually slaves either, so it seemed unusual to find one here on one of the slave islands. They were vicious killers, so naturally Fergus had recruited them as warriors until they had turned against him.

Darius sighed. "I'll call Sirin and get her to take you back to the island."

"I came here to help with the darkling problem. Let me do that," Nyx protested. "If people didn't keep trying to kill me, this wouldn't be an issue."

Darius muttered the word for fire. It wasn't his strongest element, but a ball of flame appeared in his hand. He tossed it at the body and it turned to ash.

Nyx gasped. "Why… why did you do that?"

"We don't have time to bury him, and the other fae would scavenge his remains. We have to get Lyon some help. I think the only way to do that is by getting him back to Eldara."

"You said yourself, we can't do that unless you fly him back."

Darius shook his head. "He's not well enough to fly. Doing so might make him worse than he already is." Darius paced back and forth once again. "There has to be another way we can get him back there. Nolan, are you sure none of the tunnels we used are still accessible?" The tunnels were not the fastest route back to Eldara, but they might be one of the safest. Darius knew most of them had either collapsed or been filled in by the Dragon Guard.

"Yes, all of them collapsed when the guard caught one of our last raids on the island. There is no possible way to use them to escape from here now, not unless you have crystals that could grow a new tunnel," Nolan replied. "Why can't you use magic to transport back to the island? You must have learnt things from your parents to transport from one realm to another."

Darius didn't want to go anywhere near some of the dark magic that his parents used. Creating portals took time and required a lot of energy – energy that didn't exist here on this island. His mind raced with possibilities. He didn't have any crystals that he could use to grow new tunnels. Even if he did it would take too long to construct a usable tunnel and to drag Lyon back to Eldara.

"I don't have the power to use some of the things that my parents use to transport between different realms." Darius resumed pacing.

"Come on, druid; there must be something you can do. You have magic, don't you?"

"As do you," Nolan pointed out to Nyx.

"My magic can't help the situation. All it does is cause trouble." Nyx shuddered. "Good gods, I don't want anyone else dying because of me."

"Of course you can help. You are still fae, and your powers are unbound." Nolan frowned. "I know you didn't mean to kill the Redcap, but it's just as well you did. If you had not, it would have killed us both."

Darius shook his head. "Nyx isn't trained in magic. It's safer if she doesn't use it." He didn't want Nyx using any magic again. "I can't risk anyone else coming here either or it will cause another scene with Radek." He motioned for Nyx and Nolan to follow him. "Come on. We need to get back to Lyon."

They trailed back towards the shack. He had hoped getting out of there for a while would have cleared his mind enough for him to find a solution, but it hadn't.

"Can't you use those transportation circles somewhere off the island?" Nyx suggested as they approached Lyon's shack. "Like somewhere in the air or on the water?"

Darius rubbed his chin. "I don't know. It's usually cast upon something substantial. Air and water aren't soluble, but runes may be cast upon it. It might be worth a try. Nolan, go inside and keep an eye on Lyon. If he gets any worse, call for Nyx in your mind – she should hear you." Nolan nodded and headed inside. "Nyx, let's go."

Darius and Nyx headed off in the opposite direction, past several shacks and the watchful eyes of the guards and the other slaves.

"Where are we going?" Nyx asked.

"To test your theory and to see if I can create a transportation circle somewhere off the island."

She arched an eyebrow. "So I'm helpful then?"

Darius opened his mouth to deny it then nodded. "Maybe." He left it at that. He didn't want her to think she was too helpful. Darius still didn't like the idea of working with her, but he would have to find a way to endure it. The Great Guardian was not one to get things wrong.

Darius pulled out a stylus — a marker used to draw magical symbols with — and traced each rune for a transportation circle.

Nyx frowned. "How do you know it will work?"

"I'll test it first." Darius knew he couldn't risk sending anyone through unless it was safe. He still didn't know how far Gideon's magic expanded. It might cover more than just the land on the island itself.

He picked up a rock and tossed it into the glowing circle. The stone passed through and dropped into the sea with a loud thunk. The glowing runes fizzled out.

"Damn it, whatever magic my brother used extends around the island," he groaned.

"Could I do it?"

Darius frowned at her. "What?"

"Cast a circle. Nolan says I have magic, so maybe I should cast it."

"You don't have any training. There's no telling what your magic might do."

"Then show me. I'm a fast learner. I can do it."

Darius hesitated. He didn't want to give Nyx the perfect way to escape, but they were running out of time. They had to figure out a way to save Lyon before he succumbed to the dark magic coursing through his veins.

"It can't be that hard. You draw them, and then you step into it, right?" Nyx arched an eyebrow.

Darius shook his head. "It may look easy to use, but it's all about timing and precision. Any number of things could go wrong." He rattled things off using his fingers. "Weather conditions, energy, location — all of these things come into play."

"Show me what to do."

Darius' mind raced. Everything in him told him this was a bad idea. But what other choice did they have? "How do I know you won't use the circle to escape?"

Nyx scoffed. "Where would I go?"

"Back to Joriam. You said you want to be back with your sisters more than anything."

"I — I do, but I won't. Not this time." Nyx shook her head. "I want to help."

Darius didn't believe her, but decided he had no choice. He pulled a spare stylus out of his tunic and gave it to her. She drew a couple of symbols as he had done and gasped when glowing lines appeared then fizzled out. "Not bad," he observed. "Try again. You have to be accurate."

"How can I? I feel the energy here wiping away mine." Wait, Nolan is calling me." She touched the side of her head. "He said guards are on their way. They found Lyon and are saying he is poisoned. Poisoned or infectious slaves are burned. Good gods, are they going to kill him?"

Darius muttered an oath. He had suspected Radek might interfere again. He hadn't expected it to be so soon. Spirits curse him!

"We need to get out there." He grabbed her arm. "Let's go and follow my lead."

Together they ran back towards the shacks. Darius checked inside the one Lyon had been left in and found both he and Nolan were already gone.

"What are we going to do?" Nyx asked.

"We are leaving." Darius whistled for Sirin.

Her mouth fell open. "What? We can't leave. Lyon needs our help, and Nolan could be put to death if we don't do something."

"Nyx, I chose to trust you when I taught you those runes. Now I'm asking you to trust me, can you do that?" Darius gave her a severe look. Nyx hesitated, then nodded. "Good, now we have to leave." Sirin swooped down and landed beside him. Darius scrambled up onto her back, and Nyx reluctantly climbed on behind him.

Sirin screeched and spread her wings as she took flight once more. Cold air hit their faces as the dragon rose higher above the island.

"Okay, you asked me to trust you. So, what do we do now?" Nyx demanded. "We can't just leave both of them behind to die."

"Agreed and we're not going to. Are you confident you can cast that circle?"

"Yes. What are you planning, druid?"

"I have a plan, but it's mad."

Nyx chuckled. "I already think you're mad, so that doesn't surprise me. Whatever it is, I am on board. What you need me to do?"

"I need you to be the one to open the circle. I will go and fetch Nolan and Lyon with Sirin and fly them back towards you. Do you think you can do that?" Darius asked her. "It has to be a big circle, large enough for us to fly through. I'll drop you off down here." He motioned to the cliff below them. "You can hide there."

"But what are you going to do? How can you get to Nolan? He says the guards already have him."

"Let me worry about that. Hide under the cliff. The guards may come searching for us again." He quickly cast a glamour over her.

Nyx flinched as the magic flashed over her body. "Are you sure you can help them?"

Darius hesitated. Nolan was his contact in the resistance on Doringa. He couldn't afford to lose someone so valuable, let alone a friend. Nolan had done nothing wrong but help him. He didn't deserve to die. "I will do everything I can to help him," he promised. "Now go."

Nyx spread her wings and jumped from the dragon with a small cry of alarm as she flew towards the cliff. Then, she disappeared from view.

Sirin. Darius reached out to his dragon with his mind. *Hurry.*

They flew off towards the keep where most of the Dragon Guard were stationed. It loomed below a giant building of dark stone meant to intimidate and withstand any attack. Darius' mind raced as they flew. Darius felt glad he had only given Nyx symbols for a single-use transportation circle. It could only be used once and would never work again. It could be used over longer distances and required a lot more energy, but given Nyx's strength, he didn't doubt she could do it.

Nolan, where are you? Darius reached out for his friend in thought, but he didn't spot any sign of Nolan below. It had always been harder to talk to Nolan mind to mind because he had no active magic, which made for a weak mental path to each other.

No reply came.

Darius heightened his senses and scanned the area below. He activated the glamour around himself then activated the runes he had inked onto Sirin's skin so it would shield them from view and from the guards' senses.

Nolan, where are you? Darius called again.

You're breaking my concentration, druid, Nyx grumbled.

He sighed. *I can't find Nolan or Lyon.*

They are close to a large stone building.

That must mean the keep. Right where he had planned to make his diversion. They must have used a transportation circle. Radek could never have moved or dragged Lyon's body away so fast. *Thanks. How can you sense them so far away?*

I can sense every mind on this island.

Be ready. He cut off the connection to Nyx and urged Sirin onward.

148

A few moments later, a mass of guards dragging along the body came into view.

Damn Radek. He did not know when to leave well enough alone.

Stay quiet, girl, he told his dragon.

Sirin swooped lower and circled the guards. Darius knew he could end up in big trouble for this. He sensed the energy of another dragon nearby. Untamed, unbroken, and hot with fury.

Perfect.

Darius guided Sirin around. *I must be out of my mind.*

His father would kill him if he found out his involvement. That was why he had made a show of him and Nyx leaving earlier so there would be witnesses. As far as the Dragon Guard was concerned, he and Nyx had already gone.

Darius had always had an affinity for Dragonkind. He kept it secret even from his parents. Ambrose had been training him to become a dragon sorcerer which allowed him to communicate with Dragonkind and withstand their fire.

Can you hear me? Darius reached for the other dragon's mind.

It took time to be able to communicate with them. Some didn't know how to communicate with words. It had taken him months to teach Sirin how to speak in the common tongue with her mind.

I hear you, the dragon growled.

Why are you talking to him? Sirin sounded irritated. *He's angry. We should leave him be.*

Hush, Sirin. Darius focused on the other dragon. *Would you like the chance to be free?*

The dragon's anger turned to curiosity. *You will help me?*

Only if you agree to help me, Darius said. *I need you to serve as a distraction.* He guided Sirin over to the cage.

The ridgeback roared. It might not see them because of the glamour, but it still felt their minds. *What do you need?*

If I release you, I need you to swoop down and distract the guards approaching the keep so I can grab two prisoners. You can't kill them. Agreed?

Sirin scoffed. *You feel his hatred. He should not be trusted.*

Agreed. The ridgeback clawed at the bars of his cage. *Free me.*

Think about this for a moment, Sirin said. *Imagine how he'll wreak havoc if he goes free.*

Everyone deserves to be free. Darius raised his hands and said words in the ancient dragon tongue.

The door burst open and the ridgeback shot up into the sky. Its roars echoed around them as the ridgeback flew over the keep. He and Sirin flew close behind. The guards fired their staff weapons the moment they caught sight of the dragon.

Nyx, are you ready?

And waiting. Hurry up, I can't keep hovering in one place. She sounded impatient.

Is the circle big enough for us to fly through?

I think so. I spread it out over a wide area.

Good. I'll be with you soon.

Darius urged Sirin down as the ridgeback surged at the guards, knocking them to the ground and thrashing out with its tail.

I told you not to hurt them, Darius snapped.

They deserve nothing less.

Nolan took cover by the fallen stretcher on which Lyon lay.

The ridgeback sent plumes of fire at the guards. They raised their shields. Darius hoped it would be enough to keep them safe. He didn't want anyone to die because of him.

Sirin swooped lower and circled around. Darius waved his hand and conjured a protective ward. *Nolan, if you can hear me stay close to Lyon.* The runes took a moment to set, then the ward flared to life.

Nolan ducked lower, using his body to shield Lyon.

Down, Sirin! Sirin circled around. *Nolan, hold on.*

I can't see you!

Dragon, keep firing at them! Darius grabbed hold of Nolan and pulled him onto Sirin's back as the ridgeback pounded the shield with fire, masking their escape. Together he and Nolan yanked Lyon up too. *Sirin, get us back to Nyx.* Darius glanced over at the ridgeback that still pummelled the guards with flame.

You're free. You leave them! Darius called out as Sirin rose above the chaos.

I will have revenge.

Darius held out his hand and gripped the ridgeback with his magic. *I said leave them,* he commanded. *Leave now or they will capture you again.*

The ridgeback roared then took to the air. *I won't forget this,* the dragon growled and soared into the distance.

"How is this possible?" Nolan clung to Darius as they struggled to keep hold of Lyon's body between them.

"I couldn't leave you to die," Darius replied. "Now we have to get somewhere safe. I hope the guards were fooled when that shield burst."

Nyx, are you ready?

I'm ready. She sounded impatient.

"Are you flying us to Eldara?" Nolan asked.

Darius shook his head. "No, that's too risky." He hoped the place he had in mind would be safe.

The cliff came into view, and Sirin swooped down. Nyx hovered underneath the ledge. The runes glittered in a vast circle.

Darius' mouth fell open. The circle shimmered with crackling green fire. How had she done it?

Nyx spread her wings and flew over to them. The runes flared with more powers than he could have imagined along with other symbols he had never seen before.

Nyx waved then flew over and clambered onto Sirin's back. Sirin buckled under the weight of her four passengers. Then Sirin dove into the growing circle and light exploded around them.

Darius closed his eyes and braced himself for whatever came next.

One thing went through his mind. What were those runes Nyx had cast? And how had she known them?

CHAPTER 19

Nyx screamed as Sirin landed with a thud. She fell from the dragon's back and hit the ground, hard. The air left her lungs in a whoosh. Nolan fell too, and Darius struggled to keep hold of Lyon.

"Did it work?" Nyx scrambled up and checked herself over for any sign of injuries. She found none.

Nolan got up and he and Darius eased Lyon down. Sirin huffed at them.

"Sorry, girl," Darius told her. "And yes, Nyx, it worked."

The keep and the rest of Doringa had vanished. Instead, grass spread out before them in a large field.

"Where are we?" Nyx brushed the dirt off her arms.

"Migara. How did you know how to draw those runes?" Darius frowned at her.

"What runes?" She had hoped he wouldn't notice those extra symbols that she had drawn in the circle.

Darius rolled his eyes. "Those strange ones you made. I thought you had never been trained in magic?"

"I haven't been."

"Then how did you know what to use?"

"I don't know," Nyx admitted. And that was true. She had no idea what those symbols meant. They had popped into her head and somehow felt right. If only the druid hadn't noticed.

"You must know," Darius insisted. "How else could you have known what they did?"

"Shouldn't we focus on helping him?" She motioned towards Lyon.

Lucien appeared in a blur of light. "You called?"

"I did. Nyx and I smuggled two slaves away from Doringa." He struggled to keep hold of Lyon. "We need to put him somewhere safe."

"You're smuggling slaves in daylight now. Have you gone mad?" Lucien scoffed.

"We didn't have a choice. Lyon was attacked by a darkling and Radek was going to put both him and Nolan to death."

Lucien came over and lifted Lyon into his arms as if he weighed nothing. "I'll take him to Alaric's. The healing house would draw too much attention." Lucien inclined his head for them to follow him and trailed off. "Come, Nolan. We'll find you somewhere safe to stay." Nolan trailed after Lucien.

"How did you know those symbols?" Darius hissed at her as they trudged through the field after Luc.

"I already said I don't know." She scowled at him. "I have no idea what they even mean."

"And you expect me to believe that?"

"Believe whatever you like, druid. I don't know how those symbols came to me."

Darius didn't look convinced and stalked ahead in silence.

Nyx held back and realised this was a chance to flee. The opportunity she had been waiting for. Where would she go? Even if she made it back to Joriam somehow, there was nothing left for her there. Would her sisters even be there? She knew Habrid would sell them as soon as she got the chance. She sighed. Freedom would come when she had a decent escape plan in place. Flying off now would do no good. Nyx needed supplies and money ready, along with a destination in mind.

Up ahead stood a sizeable stone-built house with a spiral tower and ivy covering the walls. The place looked a world away from the splendour of Avenia and the sweeping forests of Eldara.

Lucien headed up the steps and carried Lyon inside.

Energy crackled against Nyx's skin as she ran to keep up with the druid. "Now, where are we?"

"Alaric lives here."

More energy washed over her. The very air crackled with static.

Darius led her into a large sitting room. Books were everywhere along with shelves covered in crystals and strange devices Nyx had never seen before. Some had sparks flying around them.

"Alaric lives here?" Nyx whispered.

Darius nodded. "He likes collecting technology from other races. Some of these are ancient. Others are Silvan technology."

Lucien carried Lyon into a room with a large fourposter bed in the centre.

Alaric himself came in. "You're putting us at risk with your antics, Darius."

Darius glared at him. "I wasn't about to let him die; this is the first victim we found still alive."

"Still, there are other ways of helping slaves."

"The resistance can't get anywhere near Doringa. Our usual methods would never have worked."

Nyx slipped back into the sitting room. She had already guessed Darius worked with the resistance. Maybe her first impression of him had been wrong. She would never have thought a Valeran would be involved with the resistance, much less save slaves.

Nyx felt out of place. What was she supposed to do? She knew nothing about magic and couldn't be of any help to them.

Lucien came in and eyed her. "Looking for something?"

She gritted her teeth. He thought she was looking around to steal something! In truth, Nyx hadn't stolen anything from either here or Ambrose's house or people would notice. Besides, there was no need to steal. Ambrose had already given her clothes and a belly full of food that morning.

"I thought it would be best if I stayed out the druid's way." Nyx crossed her arms. "Aside from sensing darklings, I can't be of much help."

"I heard you and Darius arguing. He says you used strange runes he'd never seen before. Is that true?"

Nyx hesitated then told him what had happened on Doringa and how they had escaped. Nothing inside her warned her not to trust Lucien even if she did still feel a little wary of him. There would be no point in hiding it since the druid had already seen what she had done.

"And these symbols just came to you?" Lucien frowned. "How did you know what they meant?"

"I felt it somehow."

"Has this happened before?"

Nyx bit her lip and shrugged. "Things come to me sometimes. I guess that is because of my powers."

"You think you picked up on someone else's thoughts?"

Nyx shook her head. "No. I don't think so. They just come to me."

"Has Ambrose tested you yet?"

"Only on the ship yesterday. There was no time last night." She didn't elaborate further.

"Ambrose will be here soon. In the meantime, do you want to make yourself useful?"

She furrowed her brow. "Useful how?" She wanted that more than anything. Then again, she reminded herself not to get too attached to this place. She would only stay here for as long as she had to. These islands were not her home, and these people weren't her friends. Not really. Nyx had to remember that.

"I need to run some tests on Lyon and I could use a hand. Would you like to help?"

"I'm not a healer." She played with the long strands of her plait.

"It's a few experiments. Alaric will do the actual healing." Lucien turned then hesitated. "Can I trust you not breathe a word of this to anyone?"

Nyx nodded. "I know how to keep a secret. So yes, you can. I promise I won't tell anyone you're working with the resistance."

Lucien's eyes widened. "How…?"

"It's not that hard to figure out after everything I saw on Doringa."

Lucien sighed. "I keep telling Darius to be more careful. Him being a Valeran won't protect him if his father finds out what we've been doing."

Nyx followed Lucien into another room. This one had books arranged in neat piles or lined up on shelves with jars, crystals and coloured vials.

Liquid bubbled and boiled around tubes. Nyx's mouth fell open at the sight. "What is this place?"

"I call it my alchemy room. Alchemy is a dying art, but I love to experiment." Lucien beamed. "Alaric is the only one who would let me have a place like this. Experimenting with magic from other races is forbidden. I would be put to death if anyone caught me."

"What do you need me for?" Nyx stared around the room in awe. She couldn't even pretend to know what any of these things were for.

"I took some of Lyon's blood. Look." He pulled a small vial of blood out. "Do you see anything unusual in it?"

Nyx peered into the container. "No. It just looks like blood."

"Look closer."

The druid had mentioned that Luc had enhanced senses and could see and hear things other people couldn't. She still didn't know what Lucien expected her to see. Nyx narrowed her eyes and waited and gasped when green wisps of light appeared. "That looks like the rift smoke."

"Exactly. Now I need a way to separate the blood and the dark magic affecting him."

"How?"

"That's the question, fairy. I'll get to work on a potion. I may need help mixing the ingredients."

"I'll help. At least it gives me something to do. I still don't see how I can be a servant when I'm not qualified to help with half the things the druid does," Nyx grumbled. "I can't even do chores since Ada insists on doing everything. I don't know how to fit into this place."

"I'm a shifter who shouldn't even have magic, so I know what it's like to not fit in. That's why Alaric trains me in secret. Perhaps you can learn some magic too."

Nyx scoffed at that. "I doubt anyone would let me – would they?" She had never thought about learning to use magic. It had never been a possibility for her before now.

"It's a harsh world we live in, and given everything that happened, I'd say you need to learn to use everything at your disposal." Lucien grabbed a couple of jars from a shelf behind him.

"I don't know if I can use magic," Nyx admitted. "Other than hearing thoughts and using my influence on people."

"From what I've heard, all mind whisperers could use magic and cast spells. You may have those abilities too."

Nyx didn't know whether to be intrigued or terrified by that possibility. She didn't want to get her hopes up. The chance of her learning magic was slim, and she still intended to leave.

The way Lucien and the druid talked made it sound like she would be here for a while. Planning her escape route would take some time, but that didn't mean she would stay. She had to get back to Joriam to save her sisters.

"The only way to find out is to test it." Lucien pulled an empty jar from the shelf and threw it towards her.

"Hey!" Nyx raised her hands to shield herself from a blow that never came. She lowered her hand to find the jar hovering mid-air. "What the?"

"See. You do have another ability." Lucien grinned.

"I'm not — I can't do that." The roaring in her ears intensified, then the jar dropped to the floor with a thud.

"You can move things with your mind. You've done it before, haven't you?"

Nyx hesitated, and her mind raced. Strange things had happened before, but she'd always put it down to her curse or brushed it aside. "Maybe."

"That could be the thing we need. Come here and see if you can move the magic out of the blood." He motioned to the vial.

Nyx moved closer. "I can't — I don't know how to." Levitating that jar had been an accident.

"Magic works based on instinct and emotion. It's all a matter of controlling your emotions — or so Alaric says. It's how I learned to control my inner beast and change forms. Concentrate."

Nyx narrowed her eyes and willed the glowing green energy to move.

Nothing happened.

"See, it doesn't work. How do you know the jar floating wasn't... Something else?" She glanced around, half expecting to see Harland. Nyx prayed he wouldn't appear again. She had no idea how she would explain his presence to anyone if they saw him.

"Like what?" Lucien raised an eyebrow.

She shrugged. "I just don't see how I can move smoke." She motioned to the smoke and gasped when it appeared between her fingers. "Gods! What... what do I do?"

"Incredible."

The smoke curled between her fingers in between orbs of dancing light. "What do I do with it?"

"Here." Lucien grabbed the fallen jar from the floor. "Release the energy in this."

Nyx motioned with her fingers and energy shot into the jar. Lucien then slammed the lid over it. She breathed a sigh of relief.

Gods, she hoped she never had to do that again. Her heart pounded in her ears. She had been afraid the magic would somehow infect her.

"You might be what we need to save Lyon. Let's go." Lucien motioned for her to follow him.

Nyx played with the end of her long plait as she followed Lucien back to the room where Ambrose, Alaric and the druid stood around Lyon's bedside. She hadn't realised Ambrose was there too.

"I think we can find a way to save the slave," Lucien announced as he rushed in.

All eyes fell on them.

"A potion?" Alaric arched an eyebrow.

"No, Nyx can move things." Lucien beamed. "She moved the magic from the blood sample I took."

Nyx shifted from foot to foot as their gazes turned on her.

"You never mentioned that," Darius remarked.

"I didn't know." Nyx scowled at him.

"That's not surprising. Many soul seers could move things with their mind," Ambrose said. "I doubt you could move it out of Lyon. It's poisoning his entire body. It will take more than removing the dark magic to save him now."

"We could still use the spell I mentioned," Darius said.

Ambrose shot him a warning look. "No, that spell is too dangerous."

"Maybe Nyx and Darius could combine their abilities," Lucien suggested. "I have a potion that could create a mind link that I'm desperate to try."

Alaric scowled. "How many times do I have to tell you not to test your concoctions on people?"

Lucien blanched. "How else will I know if they work or not?"

Alaric sighed. "Spirits, help me. The answer is no."

"Because I'm willing to try," Nyx surprised herself by speaking up. "Shouldn't we try everything? I – I'd like to help."

It wouldn't make up for everything she had done, but it was a start.

"I know I can do it," Darius insisted.

"The spell you want to use is high magic and dangerous." Ambrose rubbed his temples. "What if you lose control? Worse, what if you both lose control?"

Nyx frowned. The druid lost control of his powers too? She found that impossible to believe. He seemed so calm and in complete control of his magic from what she had seen. Unlike her powers, which acted like a raging storm.

Ambrose sighed again. "Fine, but we'll have to wait until nightfall. You two will need to be prepared. Go to the great library and dig up everything you can about the spell. In the meantime, I will prepare a circle for you. We will have to somehow keep your powers shielded. Spirits help us all if anyone senses it." He shook his head. "I sometimes wonder why I agreed to mentor you, boy. You'll be the death of me."

"You agreed because I wanted to learn to be a true druid and not like my father." Darius gave Ambrose's shoulder a squeeze. "Don't worry; we'll be ready."

Nyx wondered what she had gotten herself into.

CHAPTER 20

They reappeared outside an ornate marble building with sweeping pillars and giant statues of griffons that stood on either side of the double doors.

"What is this place?" Nyx's eyes went wide with wonder.

"It's the great library," Darius explained. "Everyone who studies magic uses the knowledge here. They have records dating back centuries. I need to check on the spell I plan to use and see if Ranelle has found anything else during her research about the tear in the veil and the darklings."

Nyx gasped when they headed inside. "It's a real library." Shelves stretched from floor-to-ceiling with rows upon rows of ancient tomes. Everything inside the great library was made from white marble. It had a cold, icy beauty to it as light shone in through an ornate domed ceiling.

"I said great library. Why so shocked?"

"I've dreamt of visiting a place like this." Nyx beamed.

"You can read?" Darius arched an eyebrow.

"Of course I can read." She glowered at him. "Har — he made sure I could read. He always said an illiterate thief is a lousy one."

Good, at least he wouldn't have to worry about teaching her that skill.

Ranelle herself appeared. "Darius, I didn't expect you to stop by so soon." She glanced over at Nyx. "Is everything alright?"

Darius scanned the great library with his mind and sensed other people nearby. He conjured a ward so no one would be able to overhear them but still motioned Ranelle into a private antechamber. This was a much smaller room with only a table, a couple of chairs inside and a scattering of books on the shelves that weren't available to the public.

"I need help with the spell — it's a healing spell that involves high magic. It removes all dark magic, and it's one my parents taught me."

Ranelle's eyes widened. "I know the one you mean. We have lots of books on high magic. Why do you need to know about that spell?" She frowned. "You are not thinking of using it, are you?"

Darius then told her about what happened on Doringa and how they needed to save Lyon. He watched Nyx perusing the different shelves in the next room. "I need everything you have about that spell," Darius told Ranelle. "Have you found anything else about the tear in the veil?"

Ranelle shook her head. "There is no record of the veil tearing before, or about how it could have happened. None I found anyway." Ranelle glanced around, uneasy. "You know everything here is tightly controlled. Everything is the way they say it must be."

Darius scowled. Yes, he knew full well. No one could question their laws or their history since the Silvans insisted they were the first race. Any race that came afterwards was irrelevant.

"Do you really think that spell is the only way to save Lyon?" Ranelle added. "You know what happens when you use high magic."

"Keep your voice down," he hissed. "I don't want Nyx to know how I struggle with high magic. She already knows about my involvement in the resistance." That was bad enough. He didn't want to give her any more leverage against him.

"Why not? She's one of us now, isn't she?"

Darius gaped at his friend. "You can't be serious. She's a killer, and we barely know her. She will run the first chance she gets."

"Not if we convince her to join our cause. There hasn't been a mind whisperer in a generation. We can't afford to lose her." Ranelle pulled several books down from the shelf and laid them out on the table. "She reminds me a little of myself when I first came here."

Darius scoffed. "She's nothing like you. You're not a killer."

"We all do what we must to survive, Valeran." Ranelle pulled a few more books down.

Darius hesitated. "Lucien says I should use Nyx to help during the spell." He still could not believe he had suggested such a thing. "Luc thinks he can give us a potion to get into Lyon's mind and while I cast the spell, she can move the inflicting magic."

Ranelle gave a harsh laugh. "And you're willing to listen to what Wolfsbane has to say?"

"Why do you hate him so much? We are supposed to be different and not let age-old prejudices get in the way." That was one of the things he enjoyed about the resistance: no one looked down on other races like the Silvans did.

"Because he's so irritating and self-righteous. Besides, you are quick to judge Nyx even though we don't know what happened in the tavern that night."

"Lucien is still our friend. And Nyx is different. We don't even know her."

Ranelle shook her head. "Exactly. And Lucien is your friend, not mine. The hatred between our races runs too deep for that." She paused. "Why can't you just go into Lyon's mind? Or Nyx, given she's a mind whisperer? I don't see why you need a potion to do it."

"Nyx is too untrained — it's going to be hard enough showing her what to do." Darius sat down and opened the first book. "Going into someone's mind takes a lot of energy for me. I need all my strength to make the spell work."

"I'll see if I can find something to help with that." Ranelle tapped her chin and hurried off.

Darius held his hand over the book. The pages moved on their own as he scoured the information in each different volume.

"What are you doing?" Nyx gasped as she entered the room.

"Scanning each book. It's quicker to use magic. It saves me hours of research."

"But how?"

He sighed and ran a hand through his long hair. "I can use my mind. It's something my mother taught me. It makes learning easier, but it requires more energy than most spells."

Nyx slumped into a seat opposite him. "I still don't know where those symbols came from."

"Draw them on a piece of paper. Maybe Ranelle can figure out what they mean." He had to focus on the spell and what they would do that night. Still, he wondered what those symbols meant and how she knew them.

"If I'm going to be working with you shouldn't I learn magic too?"

Darius dropped the book he had been holding and gaped at her. "What?"

"I don't know anything about magic, and it's a way of life for you. If I'm going to be stuck following you around all the time, don't you think I should know this stuff?" Nyx rested her chin on her fist. "You could be injured, and I wouldn't know how to help, would I?"

Darius frowned at her. "I thought you were desperate to escape?"

"If I'm going to be stuck with you, then I should get something worthwhile from it. I don't like feeling helpless, druid."

Darius sighed. "That's not my decision to make. Ask Ambrose." Although he knew full well, Ambrose would agree she needed to learn magic to keep herself safe. If he did, Ambrose could be the one who dealt with her, not him. Darius didn't have the time or patience to teach her.

Nyx furrowed her brow. "I'm supposed to be your servant, aren't I?"

"In reality, no. I don't want or need a servant."

"Why not learn to be friends then?" Ranelle suggested as she entered the antechamber. "You have so few of them. Aside from me, that is." Her nose wrinkled. "And I suppose Wolfsbane."

"Friends?" Nyx laughed. "How could we ever be that? He doesn't even like me."

Darius opened his mouth to protest then closed it again. "I don't trust you. There's a difference."

"I never killed anyone." She crossed her arms.

"I have the perfect solution for you too." Ranelle pulled a book down and whipped it open on the table in front of them. "A mind-to-mind sharing."

Darius put a hand over his eyes. "You can't be serious."

Nyx leaned forward; brow furrowed. "What's it for?"

"You two can share your knowledge with each other. It's a good way of building trust."

"It's more than that." Darius shot to his feet and gripped the edge of the table. "It's also bloody dangerous. I can't believe you're even suggesting it." He thought Ranelle had gone mad. Mind sharing was high magic and dangerous at that. They could get lost in each other's minds or both could go insane, overwhelmed by the other person's memories until they became catatonic.

"It's the perfect way for Nyx to learn about magic. At least she'd know what to do during the spell. Thus, it would only be limited. You control it and —"

Darius snapped the book shut. "No, it's too risky, and we both need our energy for the spell." He scowled at Ranelle. "Don't you have a library to oversee?"

Ranelle glared at him. "You asked for help. Don't get angry at me because you didn't like my suggestion." She stalked off without saying another word.

Darius pinched the bridge of his nose.

"You need to work on your people skills, druid."

Darius gave her a withering look then slumped back into his seat. "Just draw those symbols." He waved his hand and some ink and parchment appeared. Darius turned his attention back to the book that mentioned the spell he needed and read through it.

Minutes passed with the sound of Nyx scribbling away. The scratching of the quill grated his nerves. Darius looked up to ask her how many symbols she needed to draw and gasped. Nyx had covered several different sheets of parchment with odd-looking runes.

"What are these?" Darius grabbed one and examined it. The symbols looked beyond anything he had seen before. Nyx continued scratching more symbols out and didn't look up. "Nyx?"

Still, she ignored him.

"Nyx?" He rose and grabbed her arm.

She jumped. "What?"

"What are these?"

"You said to draw the symbols."

"This is more than the symbols you drew on the transport circle. What are they? I've not seen them before."

She shrugged. "How should I know?"

He shook his head. "You must have learnt these somewhere."

"If I did, I don't remember it. I don't even remember what happened the other night at the tavern."

"We will figure this out. One way or another."

The rest of the day passed in a blur of getting ready and trying to prevent Lyon from getting worse. Darius hated having to wait until nightfall, but it gave them time to prepare the circle.

Nyx paced up and down the length of Ambrose's sitting room. "Are you sure we can do this?"

"I've told you what you need to do and we're as ready as we can be," Ambrose replied.

"Maybe we should have tried that mind sharing spell, like Ranelle suggested." Nyx slumped back in her chair.

Ambrose shook his head. "I doubt it would work given Darius' immunity to your power."

Darius had been relieved when Ambrose dismissed the mind sharing idea. He didn't want to share his innermost memories with anyone, much less a stranger.

"The moon is up," Darius observed. "We should get going."

The three of them transported over to Migara where Ambrose had set up a large circle. Alaric carried Lyon into the centre of it. Nyx trailed behind, and Darius knew she must be nervous.

"Just relax," he told her.

"You said the spell you're casting is dangerous. I've barely begun using magic." She played with the end of her long plait.

"That's not true. You've been using magic all your life. Now you're using it in a different way."

"Lyon is very weak," Alaric told them. "I feel we might be too —"

"I have the potion ready," Lucien interrupted his mentor and held out two vials.

Darius took one then handed the other one to Nyx.

"Drink these, and it will lead you into Lyon's mind. It will only last half an hour. Maybe less. So you'll need to be quick," Lucien told them.

"Are you sure this will work?" Nyx frowned at the vial, dubious.

"I know it will. I tested it myself." Lucien nodded.

Darius pulled the cork from the vial and gulped down its contents. Its acrid taste burned his throat.

Nyx gulped hers down too before they both fell into unconsciousness.

165

The circle faded, and Darius found himself surrounded by darkness. He had never had much experience with going into people's minds. He knew how to read people's surface thoughts if he chose but going deep into someone's mind took a lot of energy and he had never liked to do such a thing anyway, it felt like a violation.

Darius stopped and stared. Had the potion worked?

"Nyx?" he called out. "Are you here?"

The darkness around him whirled then turned into a riot of colour until he found himself standing inside a long hallway.

"Good, you're here, druid. Finally. I thought I'd be stuck here by myself." Nyx strolled over to him. "This place looks strange. What are all these doors?"

Are you both in? Ambrose's voice echoed around them.

Yes, we are. At least I think we are. Darius frowned. He hadn't expected to see a hallway.

Nyx went over to one of the doors and a rush of images flashed by. She slammed it shut again. "What was that?"

"I think we are here because of your power. Those were Lyon's memories." He sighed. Darius had feared this would happen. Her power was active even here. "Your power is allowing you to access his thoughts and memories. That isn't what we came for. We need to find the dark magic and eradicate it."

"You know I can't control it. I didn't expect us to end up here. I was hoping for somewhere... pleasant." She rubbed her arms. "How do we find the poison? This is a maze."

Darius cast his senses out. A chill ran over him. "We may not see the magic. It feels like it's all around us."

"How am I supposed to move the poison if I can't see it?"

"You're sensitive to dark energy. I have to begin the spell here." Darius took a deep breath.

"But Ambrose said we would be somewhere neutral, not in the depths of his mind."

"Ambrose, a slight change of plan. It seems Nyx's power took us deeper into Lyon's mind than we expected," Darius said. "Should we continue?" They waited, but no response came. "Ambrose?"

Still nothing.

"Why isn't he answering?" Nyx glanced around, uneasy.

"I don't know. I'll have to do the spell without him."

"They were supposed to guide us and—" Nyx paled.

"Nyx, not everything works out as intended. I have cast spells by myself for most of my life." Darius took another deep breath. The words didn't come for him. He had always feared using high magic in case he lost control. Using it often brought out a darker side of his powers.

"Poisoned body and soul, shall once again be whole," he chanted.

Bolts of lightning flashed over the walls of the hallway as his power flowed through.

Nyx flinched. "You sure this is safe, druid?"

"Relax. The spell can't harm us. We are only connected to Lyon through our minds." He chanted the spell again. "Nyx, use your senses. See if you can trace the poison."

The intensity of the lightning grew brighter.

Nyx closed her eyes, and he felt her power flow to life. Darius chanted the spell once more. The lightning shot in every direction, bursting doors apart.

Power rose through him like an uncontrollable storm. He gasped, and the doors around them flashed in and out of existence. He said the spell one more time and energy intensified. One by one, the doors exploded and winked out.

Darius sank to his knees. He couldn't control it.

Lyon's life force was fading, and his heartbeat slowed.

"Druid, he's dying. I need to move the poison." Nyx raised her hands which flared with a green light.

They were too late.

His power flared at the edge of his senses. No, Lyon couldn't die. Darius would not let that happen. He let his power go, ordering it to heal Lyon and hold his spirit there.

"Druid, what are you doing?" Nyx's voice sounded far away now.

Darius ignored her. He couldn't stop. Part of him didn't want to either.

"Druid!" Nyx came over and gripped his shoulder.

The landscape around them shifted in a blur of colour. Dizziness rolled through him until they appeared surrounded by enormous trees. Golden leaves fluttered around them, and the branches creaked and groaned, forming a protective circle.

Darius blinked. "What… Where are we?" He couldn't tell if they were inside his mind or he'd woken up and been sent somewhere else.

"Strange, I've never brought anyone here before. We must be in my mind now." Nyx strode over to him.

"But how? What did you do?" Darius scrambled up. "Where is this place?"

"Lyon is dying, and we couldn't stop it. You kept using magic to revive him."

He sighed and looked away. Darius lost control again. Worse still it had been in front of her.

"You struggle with controlling high magic, don't you?"

"Yes," he growled. "It's a good thing you stopped me. There, you've seen my biggest weakness. Satisfied?"

"No. I'm not going to judge you if that's what you're thinking." Darius frowned at her. "You're not?"

"Everyone struggles with something, druid. I know better than anyone what it's like to have something inside you that you can't control." Nyx crossed her arms. "Maybe now you won't be so quick to judge me."

Darius fell silent. Too ashamed to look at her again. His friends knew of his struggle, but they had rarely seen it. Not like this. He hated admitting to having such a fatal flaw.

"I've been learning high magic for most of my life," he said after a few moments. "It's part of my nature too in a way. All druids can access it — some more than others. It's potent, and my family can use it in ways others can't. That's why... that's why it's easy to give in and let the power take control."

"Is that why your father is so awful?" Nyx came and sat beside him.

Darius shook his head. "I don't know. But that same temptation runs through me too. It's why I don't use high magic unless I have to. Ambrose is gifted with the ability to control it but... I'm not sure I ever will be." He ran his fingers through a pile of leaves, surprised to find how solid they felt. "What is this place?"

Nyx shrugged. "It's special. I always come here when I need to feel safe. Sometimes it feels like my body comes too. No one can find or harm me here."

"It feels so real. How long have you been coming here?"

"Forever, I suppose. I don't remember anything about my life before I got sold to Harland. I was around ten at the time."

"You really don't remember what happened at the tavern?" He had suspected she had lied before, but now he couldn't be so sure.

Nyx shook her head. "No. It's a blur. I remember you and your friends looking for me, then Traveller died and after that… everything is a blur." Her hands clenched into fists. "Harland was dead when I woke up. I don't know what happened before that." Her shoulders slumped. "I wanted to save Lyon. I wanted to know I'd done something good for once."

"He was dead the moment the darkling attacked him. One thing you have to learn is we're not gods. We can't save everyone." Darius glanced around. He decided he liked this place. It felt calm and safe — a haven in the chaos of the outside world.

"How do we get back to our bodies?" Nyx rested her hands on her knees. "I always open my eyes when I want to go back, but you're here too."

"The answers about you must be locked away in your mind somewhere. We'll figure them out together."

Nyx closed her eyes and Darius did the same. He willed himself back to his body.

Nothing happened.

Oh no. Had something gone wrong?

"Nyx? What —?"

Nyx gasped as the forest burst into flames around them. Screaming and a faraway voice calling out was the last thing he heard before blackness swallowed him.

Darius' eyes flew open as he came back to himself inside the circle.

Nyx jolted awake. "What was that screaming?" Her face turned pale.

"I think it must have been a memory."

"What happened?" Ambrose came over to them. "I couldn't reach either of you."

Darius glanced over at Lyon and guilt pitted in his stomach. "We were too late."

Ambrose shook his head. "We did the best we could." He squeezed their shoulders. "It was a long shot anyway."

Lyon's spirit hovered over his body. Nyx drew back in alarm.

"It's alright. This isn't unusual," Darius whispered to her.

"Lyon now is the time for you to move on," Ambrose told him. "Be at peace now."

"No, wait. I came to tell you that something killed me. It drained my magic and —" Lyon screamed as his glowing form evaporated.

"What was that?" Nyx touched her face. "Did he move on? Is he at peace now? That didn't seem right, but I've never seen anyone's spirit leave their body before."

Ambrose shook his head. "No, something pulled his spirit away."

Darius stared at Lyon's now lifeless body in disbelief. "More like someone." Darius scrambled up. "I've seen enough spirit magic to recognise the signs. Someone stopped him from talking to us."

"Why would they do that?" Nyx frowned.

"That's what we must find out," Ambrose replied.

CHAPTER 21

The next two weeks passed in a blur of endless chores and flying around the islands as they tracked darklings. Ambrose had been so busy he hadn't had time to train Nyx much. She still hated seeing the condition of the slaves and, even worse, she couldn't do anything to help them. At least she had the illusion of freedom when she lived with Harland.

This strange place still felt so alien to her.

Nyx was already gathering supplies for her escape. Every time she and Darius went somewhere, she made a note of the escape routes and planned how she would use them. She still had to remind herself that staying here was only temporary. Getting off the island and to the lower realm would be the hardest part. How she would do that she didn't know yet. Stowing away on a ship didn't seem like an option — too many things could go wrong. Taking a dragon seemed the safest route, but she had no idea how she would steal one.

So far, Ambrose had concentrated on teaching her to control her mind whisperer abilities. As much as she wanted to control them, she still wanted to learn how to use magic itself. Darius had reluctantly started teaching her a little bit of druid magic. Their working together had at least made him trust her. She learned that druid magic came from nature itself and all druids had an affinity for different elements, whether it be fire, water, earth, air, or light. He said some druids even had an affinity for spirit magic as well, but that was much more rare. Most druids had one or two affinities, but Darius himself could tap into all the elements, though lightning was his strongest.

Ambrose called her into the sitting room one morning, and she found him sat on one of the divans. "We need to practice your powers more so you gain some semblance of control." He motioned to a scroll on his desk. "Gideon sent a message summoning you to him this evening." His expression turned grim. "I had hoped we would have more time."

Nyx's blood went cold. She had known this was coming. Darius had managed to come up with different excuses as to why she could not go there over the past few days, but she knew he couldn't keep his brother away forever. Nyx had grown used to Darius and thought they could tolerate each other now at least.

"What are you teaching me today then?" She sat down on one of the wooden divans. So far, he told her to concentrate on finding a place of peace inside her mind, but that did nothing when dozens of people surrounded her. The more she practised with her abilities, the harder they became to control. Even retreating to her grove hadn't helped.

"We are going to test your abilities."

Wonderful, more tests. How she despised them. Nyx would have thought he had tested her abilities enough by now. What more could there be?

A knock came on the door, and Alaric came in dressed in his usual forest green tunic and hose.

"I want you to test your powers on Alaric."

Nyx's mouth fell open. "What if I kill him?" Nyx didn't want to risk hurting someone else after what happened with that Redcap. She had avoided using her powers on anyone since that incident and didn't want to use them now.

"I'm here if anything goes wrong. Controlling your emotions is the key to controlling your powers."

How could anyone do that? It wasn't like she could stop herself from feeling things, no matter how much she tried.

"The people you've harmed so far have usually been a threat, yes?" Alaric asked. "We believe your power may be responding to your fear."

Alaric went and sat on the opposite divan. "What do you feel from me?"

She furrowed her brow. "Your energy is raw. Almost primal… like a wolf." He reminded her a little of Lucien, although Darius insisted he was different from Lucien.

Alaric chuckled. "The wolf is my favoured form."

Ambrose nodded. "Good, now you are going to go into his thoughts."

Nyx blanched. Had the old druid lost his mind? She didn't want to risk harming anyone again. Darius had mentioned Lucien was harder for her to read due to his shifter nature. She hesitated when Alaric held out his hand to her. "I'd rather not touch you. I touched the Redcap and he…"

Harland's laughter echoed in her ears. "Afraid they'll see you for what you are, girl?"

She flinched and glanced around, half expecting to see him, but there was no one. She had only seen him hovering around a couple of times over the past two weeks. Both times he had taunted her and insisted she would be joining him in death soon.

"I thought it would be easier. Touch opens people's thoughts more," Alaric said.

It did, but it also ran the risk of other things happening, like her influence coming out.

"I'll read you without touching you." She closed her eyes and forced away her nagging doubts. She would never learn control unless she practised. No one understood her power since there were no mind whisperers left.

Nyx found herself back, surrounded by her protective grove. Here she felt safe.

"Concentrate and let your mind go forth," Ambrose told her. "Let it guide your way."

Her power didn't guide her. It did whatever it wanted with her. Nyx waited for something to happen. Aside from a distant buzzing sound of thoughts, she heard and saw nothing.

Don't resist your power. Alaric's voice made her jump.

"Concentrate on what you want to find," Ambrose added.

The buzzing sensation intensified until Nyx found herself falling.

What's happening? Her heart lurched as the ground vanished, replaced by darkness.

Nyx found herself in a hallway with doors on each side. The doors seemed to go on forever. It reminded her of the night she and the druid had entered Lyon's mind when they had tried to save him. Did all minds look like this? Darius had insisted that happened because of her power, and it was a way for her to access people's memories on a deeper level rather than just reading their surface thoughts. Most people's heads were only a jumble of sounds and colours.

"What do you see?" Ambrose asked.

Nyx gasped, amazed she could still hear him.

"Doors," she murmured. Odd, she could never talk out loud when she got deep into someone's mind.

"Good, search through them."

Search? It could take a lifetime to look through all of these.

Nyx approached the door nearest to her. It opened on a scene of running through the woods. Exhilaration washed over her and the thrill of the hunt. *This is Alaric's memory,* she realised. Nyx pushed the door shut. She didn't want to feel that. Did Alaric know what she was doing?

She didn't like that thought either. People were always unaware of her eavesdropping, but now she couldn't be sure.

Nyx moved a little further down the hall and opened another door. This time Ambrose appeared, and the two argued over something. This must be a recent memory.

"I want you to find out what Alaric turned into when he first changed."

How old would Alaric have been when he changed? He looked about forty, so there would be decades of memories to search through. On rare occasions when she wanted to know things it usually didn't take long to find them. Most people's minds were an open book. She'd never had to search so deep in someone's mind before.

Nyx had no idea where to look so she hurried further down the hall until she came to another door and pushed it open.

Fire surrounded her on all sides, smoke stung her eyes and made her cough.

She slammed the door shut. Ambrose had said to let her power guide her.

What did you change into? She didn't like being stuck in here either. It felt like a violation in a way it never had before. She never usually read someone's thoughts on purpose. It just happened, whether she chose it or not.

The doors blurred. Nyx concentrated harder on what she wanted to find.

One door beckoned her. This time Alaric's energy felt younger. Bone and muscle cracked as he took on a new form. She winced as pain seared through her.

"A bear," she said finally. "He changed into a bear." She opened her eyes, and the world around her spun. Relief flooded through her at being out of there. The pain had felt too real.

"Good, now go back and find out who Alaric's brother is."

Nyx wanted to protest and took a moment to steady herself.

The hall loomed before her again. More doors than ever appeared. One door flipped open, and she edged closer. Alaric was in the sitting room with Ambrose again. They had on the same robes as they wore now.

"Do you think the girl truly is a mind whisperer?" Alaric asked. "They were wiped out decades ago."

Ambrose nodded. "Yes. What else could she be? Her power is unlike anything I've felt before. Think of her potential."

"Think of the danger," Alaric countered. "If the Archdruid found out, he would either kill her or try to use her for his own means."

"He won't. I'll find a way to help her. Did you find anything in the Hall of Knowledge?" Ambrose arched an eyebrow.

Nyx wondered what the hall was. It sounded interesting, and she sensed it was important. She had heard Darius and Lucien talking about the place a few times along with Ranelle, but none of them had bothered to explain what it was or where it was for that matter.

"No, everything about them has been erased by Dorian Valeran — Darius' grandfather."

Ambrose cursed. "It's a good thing the overseers took the hall from him when they did. No doubt Fergus would want its knowledge too." He sighed and ran a hand down his beard. "I want to help this girl. Perhaps she's the one the prophecy speaks of. Even if she is not —she must learn to control it."

"Agreed. I heard that some mind whisperers went mad and had to live in isolation because of their gifts."

Nyx drew back. Would she go mad if she didn't learn to control her powers? Fear bloomed in her chest. The hallway flickered in and out of existence.

She had to focus.

The flickering stopped, and she concentrated on Alaric's brother. More doors blurred past her. One beckoned, yet it didn't feel right.

Nyx hesitated and opened another door instead. A small boy was playing in a field. She opened her eyes. "Derek — his name is Derek." Her temples throbbed. "Why do mind whisperers go mad?"

The two men shared a glance.

Ambrose chuckled. "It seems you might have more control than we thought."

Nyx turned to Alaric. "You were distracting me when I searched for your brother. I felt it. You wanted me to go through the other door even though the truth wasn't there. Why would you do that?"

Alaric nodded. "I didn't think you would notice. I didn't mean to test your abilities."

Nyx frowned. "How did you do it? No one knows when I'm in their mind."

"I'm an overseer. We are taught to shield our minds since we have access to ancient knowledge. No one has walked around my thoughts as easily as you did."

"So why did mind whisperers go mad?" she repeated.

Ambrose hesitated. "Some grew overwhelmed by their gifts. It became too much for them to bear. During the realm wars, they were forced to do unspeakable things."

"Like what?"

"Like torture slaves and prisoners. Force people to…" Ambrose shook his head. "That is why you must never let others know the true extent of your powers."

"What good did this lesson do then?" She crossed her arms. "He didn't teach me control."

"It proved you can control it when you choose. Now try again."

Nyx didn't feel much like eating dinner that night. Even though she enjoyed having three meals a day, she couldn't eat anything, not with the meeting with Gideon hanging over her and dread knotting in her stomach.

"Are you going to eat?" Darius frowned at her from across the table. Most of his plate was already empty. Ambrose hadn't joined them for dinner as he had been called away, so it was just the two of them.

She pushed her food around the plate with her fork. "No." She gulped down her water.

The druids only drank wine during ceremonies or on special occasions, so she didn't even have that to give her courage. That was one thing she missed about being in the tavern, at least there she had easily been able to get wine or ale. Nor did she have access to the drug Nilanda anymore either. At least that would have dampened her powers.

"Are you worried about meeting Gideon?"

She glowered at him. "Why couldn't you waylay him again? I'm not ready to face him yet. I still can't control my powers well enough." She threw her fork down in exasperation. "What if he senses how powerful I am? He said my abilities wouldn't work against him. He could lock me up or worse." Her hands clenched into fists. Nyx hated feeling afraid. She had felt nothing but fear since she had come to this place.

Even though she had known Darius couldn't keep his brother away forever, she had hoped he would delay it a little longer.

"You said I had to keep my abilities a secret. How am I supposed to do that?"

Darius lowered his goblet. "Use your bracelet."

She gaped at him. "That's it? That's going to protect me?" The bracelet had helped to some extent, but she didn't want to rely on it. Her powers might still seep through somehow or it might lose its effectiveness. Anything could go wrong. Nyx continued, "I know what your grandfather did to mind whisperers. I also know they went mad and he killed them."

Darius' jaw clenched. "I won't let that happen to you. The bracelet represses your powers. You won't lose control around him."

"Forgive me if I don't believe a spelled bracelet is going to protect me." She crossed her arms. "What did you do to it?"

"I used my blood on it. I somehow suppress your power. It's the only thing we have to shield you."

"It makes me vulnerable too. What does Gideon want with me?" Her mind kept racing with different scenarios of what the fae prince might do with her. None of them ended well.

"He will want to test you to see if you are the one the prophecy speaks of. We heard stories about you, and that piqued his interest. Whatever you do, do not use your powers on him."

"Is he immune like you?"

"Probably, but he is protected in ways I'm not. Our father placed shields on us designed to stop any mind whisperers from compelling us." Darius took a sip from his goblet. "The shields are pretty much impenetrable."

Her shoulders slumped. Her influence wouldn't save her if Gideon did anything untoward.

"He will want you to prove your power. Do whatever you can to hide it."

That did nothing to ease her nerves.

Nyx pushed back her plate and rose. "How do I even get to Avenia? Will Sirin take me?"

Maybe she could order the dragon to take her to one of the smaller islands, and she could hide there for the night. If she found somewhere safe she could retreat into her grove so Gideon wouldn't be able to find her. Nyx wished she had a way of escaping already. Despite her provisions and planning, she didn't have a route planned yet.

"No, Gideon's personal guard will come and escort you straight to him. Don't try running away. These guards are trained to kill people, and they will drag you there no matter what."

Her heart sank — no chance of hiding then.

"Can I have some wine before I go?"

Darius chuckled. "No, you need your senses to be clear. Wine would only impair your judgement."

She scowled. "I'll be more powerless if I had some."

"Wine impairs the mind. You need to be alert." He got up to grab something from his coat. "Here." He held out a thick metal band to her. "This is for you. Wear it."

Nyx frowned. "What will this do? Turn me into a dragon?" That would be something at least. Maybe then she could kill Gideon and be free of him once and for all. Being a different race would mean she wouldn't be forced to stay here either.

He laughed. "Blessed spirits, no. Try it on."

Nyx sighed and slipped the band onto her wrist. There was nothing special about it. It was a plain grey band. If she saw it on the street, she would never give it a second look. She waited for something to happen. "What does it do?"

"Press the other side here." He pressed his fingers against her wrist.

Nyx did so and yelped when a blade came out. "Gods, druid, are you trying to kill me?"

Darius bit back a smile. "No, this is the perfect weapon. Easily concealed and in plain sight. I thought you could use something extra to protect yourself with."

Nyx tested the balance of the blade. "Not bad, but not as good as a real sword." She pressed the side again, and the blade retracted. "How does it work?"

"I copied it from an old design by the ancients. It's magic, so the blade retracts into the metal." He grabbed her wrist, so the blade came out again. "Let the blade move with you."

"I know my way around a sword, druid."

"The bracelet can be triggered by thought too. I designed it to respond to the wearer."

"You forge weapons?" She had never seen him do such a thing, but he disappeared at times, and she hadn't been able to work out where he had gone. "How?"

"Everyone should have skills. My magic allows me to withstand heat and forge metal."

Retract, she thought and jumped as the blade snapped back.

"See, I knew it would be perfect for you." He kept hold of her wrist, his fingers warm against her skin. "And it's safer than using your powers — but don't use it unless you have to. Gideon can protect himself with magic. Don't stab him unless you have to."

Nyx took her arm away as a man walked in. "I've come to bring the slave before Prince Gideon."

Nyx flinched at the word "slave." Over the past few days, Darius, Ambrose and most of the people she met had been kind to her. No one on Eldara treated her like a slave. She bit back a retort. It was best to get this over with. Besides, Darius' gift put her more at ease. She glanced back at the druid.

Good luck, he told her.

I'll need it.

Nyx followed the guard outside where he activated the transport circle. A few moments later, they reappeared inside a long hallway. Oak gleamed over the floor, and rich tapestries covered the walls.

Suits of armour were dotted down one side of the hall and looked like they were holding real weapons.

Her head spun from the sensation. She hated those transport rings.

The guard stomped down the hall without saying a word.

She guessed they must be in the Crystal Palace, but she didn't know for certain. Nyx frowned and fiddled with her spelled bracelet. Nothing warned her of danger and she had no way of knowing if repressing her power would prevent her from sensing any threats.

If Gideon harmed her, she'd make him pay.

Nyx took a deep breath as another guard knocked on a door, and she checked to make sure both of her bracelets were in place. Neither band looked very impressive so she hoped neither the guard nor Gideon would remove them from her.

"Come," Gideon called.

She flinched, and her stomach lurched. *Spirits, please help me through this. And please don't let Harland appear whilst I'm here.*

The door creaked open and she shuffled inside.

Gideon's chamber looked almost as big as the tavern. Aside from the tapestry on the wall, it didn't have a cosy atmosphere like Ambrose's house. That place felt like home — somewhere that was lived in. This room gave off a cold, harsh feeling — much like its owner.

Nyx shivered.

Gideon rose from the high back chair. "Good, you're finally here. Why has my brother been delaying your visit?" He eyed her up and down. "I have sent summons for you for almost two weeks now. What took so long?"

She shrugged. "You would have to ask him that." She met his gaze head-on. Nyx might have been terrified the first day she met him, but she wouldn't be now, or at least she wouldn't show it. She had seen how Darius put a mask on and kept his face impassive. She'd practised in front of the mirror, but had no idea if it would work.

"I'm asking you."

"We've been working on the darkling problem." True enough. Darius had told her not to lie to his brother, so she would keep as close to the truth as possible. "I've been following your brother around wherever he goes."

Gideon sneered. "Darius likes to indulge in Ambrose's delusions. I can't believe he's wasting time traipsing all over the islands, and for what? It is not possible for the veil to break and my brother is too stupid to realise it."

Nyx bit back a retort. Darius might be a lot of things, but stupid was not one of them. She still couldn't believe what a fool Gideon was for choosing to ignore the fractured veil. What would it take for him to finally see the truth and admit there was a real problem?

She knew though that if she argued, she might make things worse for herself. "What do you want with me?"

"That's for you to find out. I heard many tales from the lower realm of how a thief kept stealing things, and victims had no memory of how or when it might have happened." Gideon's usual scowl returned. "You must have known you couldn't hide your abilities forever. You would have been safer if you hadn't used them at all, especially to commit petty crime."

Did he expect her to admit to it? She would not give in so easily.

"How would people know if they forgot about it?" She raised her chin and refused to wilt under his gaze.

"Tongues loosen when they are plied with drink. I know you're the one they spoke of and you're the one who killed that tavern owner." Gideon circled her, staring at her like she was an insect. "Just as I know you're hiding your powers somehow."

Her skin prickled as his senses roamed over her once more. Power flared inside her, held back by the band on her left wrist. She wanted to use her powers on him more than anything, but she wouldn't. She would do everything she could to avoid that.

Gideon drew back and frowned.

Gods, had he sensed her power?

No, he couldn't. She had the band on.

"Guard!"

Nyx flinched, and her heart pounded in her ears. If they came for her, she'd whip the bracelet off and let her power roam free. Keeping her power a secret would no longer matter then.

A guard came in, dragging another man with him. A slave, she realised, a winged fae like those she had seen on Doringa. Long blue hair trailed down his neck, his large catlike eyes were bruised and his frame was thin from lack of nourishment.

What was Gideon up to?

"Someone has been stealing from my chamber. I've already questioned my personal guards who are loyal to me," Gideon said. "Now I want you to read his thoughts and find out if he's the one responsible."

"But I can't," Nyx protested. Blood roared through her ears as her panic rose. What could she do to avoid using her power? Would the band even be enough to hold it back?

"You will or you will both die," Gideon growled.

"And if I do?" Her voice came out stronger than she expected. "I will not help you sentence this man to death. I am a thief, not a murderer."

"Then you get to live a little longer."

Nyx scoffed at that. "You won't kill me. I'm too important. That's why you sent your brother to find me." She knew she was right. "You need me for something, don't you?"

He thought he could intimidate her — he could, but she knew he wouldn't kill her. His prophecy was too important for that.

"I only pick up bits and pieces. I became known as a good thief because I'm fast. Not because of my power or because I made anyone forget."

"Read him," Gideon snapped. "I won't keep you alive unless you prove useful to me, so don't think otherwise. You are not important. You are as worthless as dirt, and your death would mean nothing to me."

The fae servant flinched as the guard forced him to his knees.

Nyx bit her lip and headed over to him. Would her power even work? She couldn't breathe. "I — I have never read a fae before. Human thoughts are easier to pick up on."

"Try harder. If you don't, you'll die. If you refuse, I'll kill him." Gideon motioned to the guard who drew a dagger and held it against the servant's throat.

The man whimpered. "Please help me," he pleaded with Nyx. "I didn't do anything. I swear I didn't steal anything."

"You'll kill him anyway." Nyx crossed her arms. *Gods, forgive me.* She hated bargaining with someone's life like this, but she couldn't risk Gideon seeing her fear. If he did, he would know he had power over her.

"If you do as I asked you and you fail, you will receive a quick death. If not, he will suffer first."

The poor man would die no matter what she did.

She closed her eyes. Her heart pounded faster. Buzzing came from his mind, but she couldn't make out the words. "I'm not getting anything. I can't read fae."

"Then I'll have him suffer. The longer you take, the more he will have to endure. Can you really bear to watch that?" Gideon chuckled. The guard kicked the man in the back, making him crumble to the floor. "The more you refuse, the more I will have him beaten, but then again, you are a killer yourself. You probably care nothing for your fellow fae. In that case, feel free to watch him suffer and die a slow, painful death."

"Punishing him won't get me to do what I can't. My powers are unreliable, especially on a fae."

"Use your touch on him. Make sure he talks then."

Nyx shook her head. "You don't understand. I already touched him, and I can't get anything." She didn't have to pull off a convincing lie. The fae's thoughts were a jumbled mess; she couldn't make much sense of them.

Gideon sneered. "Mind whisperers can touch someone's mind and force them to do whatever they want. That's why they were wiped out."

"My power doesn't work that way. I only hear fragments of thoughts. Nothing substantial. All of those stories you think are true are nothing but exaggerations." Nyx shook her head. "I have no real power."

Gideon gave a harsh laugh. "I know you better than you think. I had people watching you for weeks. They saw how you touched people and forced them to give you whatever you wanted."

Her stomach dropped. She had told Harland how she thought someone was following her before he died. He had scoffed at that. "Why should I believe you? If you think I'm so powerful, you wouldn't have given me to your brother. That means you are not certain, are you, prince?"

"Or perhaps you need a stronger motivation. I could have one of your sisters brought here. I'm sure they'd make fine slaves."

All colour drained from her face. Could her sisters be in Andovia?

No, they couldn't be. She would know. They would call her in thought… unless they couldn't reach her. What if they were locked up unconscious somewhere? Bile rose in her throat and she forced herself to swallow it back down.

"You are bluffing." She narrowed her eyes. "You don't have my sisters. Even if you did, they mean nothing to me anymore. They didn't even do anything to help save me after I was sentenced to death." Nyx knew she somehow had to convince Gideon there was no one she cared about, no one he could use as leverage against her, especially not her sisters.

Gideon grabbed hold of her wrist and yanked it so hard her leather bracelet snapped and fell off. "Am I? Do you want to take the risk?"

Nyx gasped as Gideon then let go of her. She didn't know what to do. Should she grab hold of her bracelet again? Her heart pounded so hard she thought it would burst out of her chest. Had he sensed her power? If so, why hadn't he done anything? No, she had to stay calm. Panicking would only make things worse.

Nyx grabbed the servant. She would find out what he knew and needed her full power to do so. *Tell me if you stole from the prince.*

Nothing happened.

"Why isn't anything happening?" Gideon demanded. "If you are trying to trick me, the consequences will be dire."

"I told you I can't use my touch or whatever you called it. I do sense he is innocent. I'm good at sensing whether someone is lying." She raised her chin with more confidence than she felt.

Gideon growled at her. "Get out."

"What?" She couldn't believe it. Didn't he want to torture her some more?

"I said, get out!"

Another guard came in and made a grab for her. Nyx didn't need to be told again.

She bent, grabbed her bracelet, then ran from the room. The guard led her outside then told her to go. He slammed the door shut before she had a chance to ask how she would get back to Eldara.

Nyx found herself alone outside in a deserted courtyard. Why hadn't the guard conjured the transport circle?

Wonderful, first the prince dragged her here, then he abandoned her. She didn't know Avenia well enough to know where to go. How would she get back to Eldara, in the dark no less?

Nyx muttered a curse. Why had Gideon thrown her out? Did he even have her sisters? She didn't expect him to even know about them. If he did have them, she had to find them. But first, she had to talk to the druid.

Why hadn't her power worked? The band had come off. Had Gideon somehow known that it had been repressing her power? The druid would know the answer to that question; he knew his brother better than anyone and might know what kind of game he was playing.

Stupid, stupid. She had shown her weakness to Gideon. Nyx still didn't know why he had grabbed hold of her wrist or even why her power hadn't worked. She pulled the band out of her pocket and frowned at it. Had it repressed her powers so much it no longer worked? She would have to repair it. Gods, what if Gideon had sensed her full power after he snapped the band off her wrist when he grabbed her?

No, if he had, he wouldn't have let her go.

She sighed. *Druid?* she called. *I'm stuck now. Can you help me get back to the house?*

No response came.

Had the band made her completely powerless?

Druid?

Was he ignoring her?

Darius? She tried instead. *Come on, druid. I'm stranded.*

Her senses prickled as someone came up behind her and grabbed her before she had a chance to react.

CHAPTER 22

Darius crouched in the grass close to the open rift in Migara. Lucien strode over to him in wolf form. Night was the ideal time to track the darklings as the rift usually became more active then.

Ambrose had gone off to another council meeting, so Darius convinced Lucien to come on the hunt with him. It was strange not having Nyx around and he guessed he must have grown used to her presence. He hadn't wanted her to meet with Gideon either, but there was nothing either of them could do about it.

What are we looking for? Lucien asked. *I don't see anything.*

Darius motioned to the faint green flashes of the rift in the darkness. He hadn't conjured any orbs because he wanted them to remain hidden. *We are waiting to see what comes through.* He almost wished Nyx were there. She could sense the darklings better than anyone.

Darius kept his senses on alert and waited.

They didn't have to wait long.

A large black mass came out of the rift, blacking out the faint, green shimmers of the veil.

What is that? Lucien asked.

Darius shook his head. *No idea, but we are going to find out.*

The creature grappled up onto the embankment on the other side of the rift. Darius couldn't make out what it was.

It turned and disappeared into the distance. Darius' mouth fell open. How had it vanished? One moment it was there the next it was gone.

They had to track that thing.

Lucien leapt from the bush and darted around the rift, a blur in the dark.

Darius knew he wouldn't be able to track him on foot, so he whistled for Sirin to appear. The dragon swooped down, her skin like moonlight.

Darius scrambled onto her back and they took to the air. Darius had to keep his senses focused or he would lose track of Lucien. He sent his senses out like a net, scanning for his friend and any sign of the strange creature they had seen emerge from the rift.

Nothing.

Whatever it was, it had vanished.

Lucien, have you found it?

No, it disappeared.

How could it disappear? It looked like flesh and blood.

If it's a spirit, it could have moved between the planes easily enough.

Darius groaned. *It didn't look like a spirit. We have to find it.*

You should call your fae. She could help us, Lucien suggested.

If you mean Nyx, she's not my anything. And she can't help. She had to go and see my brother. Darius scanned the area again with his senses but found nothing.

That was a couple of hours ago. Perhaps she's back now.

Darius would be glad if she was. They could use her help.

Nyx? He reached out to her with his mind. *Nyx?*

No answer came.

Why wasn't she answering?

Something moved out of the shadows: the creature he had seen emerge from the rift.

"The girl is gone. Soon she will be dead and the way between the worlds will stay open forever," it said.

"Gone?" Darius frowned. "Gone where?" His chest tightened. Had something happened to Nyx? Maybe that was why she hadn't answered him.

The creature laughed. "You have no idea what is coming, do you, druid?"

Lucien rounded the corner. "Why don't you enlighten us?" He growled.

The creature laughed again. "The dark time shall come again. All of Erthea will burn and be torn asunder."

Darius raised his hand and cast a web of energy around it. He had to contain the creature and figure out what it was. The creature thrashed against the glowing web of energy and roared with fury. In one swift move, it broke through the web and launched itself at Darius. Darius raised his hand and fired a bolt of lightning at it. The creature screamed as its flesh smouldered, then it darted off in the opposite direction.

"Hurry, after it!" Darius called out to his friend.

Lucien blurred away, and Darius urged Sirin onward. The dragon flapped her massive wings and took to the air once again. Trees spread out like gnarled phantoms below them and Lucien vanished underneath the thick canopy of leaves.

Where had that damned creature gone? And what had it meant?

He didn't know how it could have broken through his web either. Webs were designed to contain things, only something with great power would have been able to get through.

Darius would have to get to the Hall of Knowledge and check things out, but first, he had to find the creature again. He raised his hand and cast a tracking spell. Light flared between his fingers and whirled around them before it shot out through the night sky.

Luc, have you found anything?

Again with the Luc. And, no, I haven't. That thing moves fast.

Nyx? He reached out her again with his mind but felt no sign of her. Nor did she reply.

Darius guided the dragon lower, the wind rushed past his face, and it took several moments before he found a space in the thick canopy big enough for them to get through. Sirin screeched as she drove through the gap. Giant leaves whacked against them as they descended lower into the forest. Orbs of light danced all around the dark trees that stood like silent sentinels.

Where had that creature disappeared to? He had to find it before it hurt someone or worse. Although perhaps then Gideon and the rest of the high council would take the threat of the rifts seriously.

His dragon circled around, careful not to collide with any of the overhanging canopy or endless tree branches. Darius sent his senses out again, scanning the surrounding area for signs of anything unnatural. Earth, air and water all pulsed around him in different directions. The energy here in the forest thrummed with its own steady rhythm, yet the tear in the veil prickled at the edge of his mind like an open wound. Poison was seeping out of it, and if they didn't find a way to stop it soon, he dreaded to think what would happen to the island and the rest of the realm.

Nyx? He reached out to her one more time in case she heard him. No response came.

Darius, I have lost the creature's scent. I don't know where it has gone.

His mind raced with thoughts. What did the creature want? So far things had been attacking Nyx. Were she and the rift somehow connected? If she was part of the prophecy, he supposed that could be true.

Maybe Gideon would know where she was.

Gideon? He called his brother. *Is Nyx still with you? Is she alright?* He cursed himself for the last question. He knew better than to ask such a thing. It wasn't as if Gideon would tell him if he had hurt her.

What do you want now, brother? Gideon sighed.

I need my servant back. Where is she?

How should I know? Gideon sounded impatient. *She is your servant, not mine. It's not my responsibility to keep her in line.*

She left to answer your summons. So, where is she? His hands clenched into fists as he fought to keep his anger under control. Why couldn't his brother just give him a straight answer?

She's not here. I dismissed her a while ago.

Darius gritted his teeth. *Did you send her back to Ambrose's house?* Knowing his brother, he probably would have tossed Nyx out to find her own way back to Eldara.

No, I sent her away.

You mean you threw her out without bothering to make sure she got back safely. Darius groaned. Why couldn't Gideon be considerate of others? Nyx wouldn't be able to find her way back since he hadn't shown her how to use transportation circles yet for fear she would use them to escape.

She's a servant, brother. Nothing more. If she can't find her own way around, send her to the slave islands where she belongs, Gideon snapped. *All of those stories about her seem untrue — unless she somehow hid her powers from me. One way or another, I will find out. If she proves to be useless, we might as well kill her. A powerless mind whisperer is no good to anyone.*

When did she leave? Darius knew he had to find Nyx. He had become less worried about her running away over the past couple of weeks, but he did fear she might get lost somewhere.

How should I know? I don't keep tabs on the comings and goings of servants.

Darius ended the connection and muttered an oath. Why did Gideon have to be so careless? Anything could have happened to Nyx now, but finding her would have to wait a little longer. Finding that creature took priority.

He urged the dragon lower, closer to the ground so they could see more. Sirin screeched, uneasy.

I don't sense that strange creature anywhere, she told him.

Where had that damn thing gone to? His spell had turned up nothing.

Darius gritted his teeth again and chanted another spell, this time to find an intended target. Orbs of light shot through the night sky, descending into the darkness below them.

Darius waited a few moments as Sirin circled around, taking everything in.

Nothing. His spell fizzled out and dissolved into nothingness. Why weren't any of his spells working? These spells had been used in the Forest Guard for generations, and he had druid magic on his side.

Maybe he needed to rely more on his druid magic — and the things his father had taught him. Darius hated everything about the darker side of magic, but that creature had been something born of darkness — he had sensed as much when he first saw it. Maybe dark magic was the only way to find it.

He hesitated then chanted the words to a druid tracking spell. Sparks of light crackled between his fingers as the high magic flared to life. Darius hated the feeling of exhilaration that came whenever he called upon the darker side of his powers.

The sparks curled around his fingers as he clenched them into a fist, almost reluctant to let them go. He sighed, then released the spell. *Find the creature I seek.*

The orbs shot out into the night, leaving a trail of golden light in their wake.

I sense dark magic in the air, Lucien remarked.

Darius had been so caught up in his own thoughts he had almost forgotten his friend was tracking the creature with him. *It's probably mine.*

Lucien let out a low growl. *What? You shouldn't —*

Not now, Luc. We will talk about this later. We have to find that thing so I can search for Nyx. I have a bad feeling something has happened to her.

190

A glowing beacon of light lit up the darkness below them, and he knew his spell had found purchase. He urged Sirin into a dive, and they headed straight towards it.

Luc, can you see that light? I think I found the creature.

I see it. I'm on my way.

Darius leapt from Sirin's back the moment the dragon touched the ground. "Good girl," he told her and took off in the opposite direction. Branches thrashed against him and snagged his clothes as he ran through the dense foliage towards the spell. He muttered a curse and raised his hand. With a flash of light, the branches moved aside, clearing a path for him.

He sensed Lucien coming towards him but didn't bother stopping to wait. Lucien would catch up soon enough using his speed.

When he reached the clearing, he found the creature waving his arms around, trying to get rid of the spell that lit him up like a torch.

Darius raised his hand but hesitated. He thought of all the usual methods he had learnt in the Forest Guard, but somehow he knew none of those would work, only dark magic had found the creature.

"Rhombus." He raised his hand and arcs of lightning shot from his palm, enveloping the creature in a cage of energy.

The creature screeched as the bolts of energy charged against it and knocked it to the ground.

"Tell me what you are and why you've come here." Darius raised his hand, causing more bolts of lightning to crackle between his fingers. "If you don't, I will force you to give me answers. You know I can do that."

Lucien's presence grew closer. Darius used his free hand to create a wall of energy between them. Lucien would only interfere if he saw Darius using dark magic. He didn't have time for that. He wanted answers. Now.

"You have no power, druid. You are nothing." The creature laughed and yelped as the cage of energy struck him again.

Darius, what are you doing? Lucien demanded. *Why are you blocking me? Let me through. I am coming to help you, you fool.*

Darius ended the connection and put a wall up inside his mind so he wouldn't have to hear Lucien. He had to remain focused, or he would lose his grip on this unpredictable magic. He couldn't control it all the time — not in the way his brother could. Gideon used high magic as easy as breathing. He drew more magic and clenched his hand into a fist. He muttered more words of power, words to force someone to obey, the very magic he despised his father for using. Magic that had once been used to enslave entire races.

The creature yelped. "The dark time is coming, druid. You better be ready for it." The creature screamed as its body exploded in a burst of flame.

Darius stumbled back from the force of the blast and gasped. Dark magic or not, he hadn't been the one to kill the creature. Someone else had. The question was who and what did they want with Nyx? He had to find her before it was too late.

CHAPTER 23

Nyx couldn't see anything but blackness when she opened her eyes. A piece of cloth now covered her face. How had someone managed to catch her off guard like that? Why hadn't her powers warned her about the threat? Perhaps it was because of the bracelet, but that had come off and was inside her pocket. Or at least it had been before she had been taken.

She moved and found thick rope binding her arms and ankles. The last thing she remembered was being thrown out of the Crystal Palace. *Now, where am I?*

Nyx tugged at the ropes, but they held firm. Someone's presence came to her. She didn't need her eyes to sense him. Why had they attacked her? Was it another creature that had come out of the rift?

Nyx remembered that she hadn't put the bracelet back on, so her powers should still be accessible. She moved her fingers, but the ropes refused to budge—stupid magic.

"Hello?" Her voice sounded weak. It surprised her how her captor had not put anything over her mouth to stop her from calling out for help.

Someone was nearby, that much she knew. If they wanted to kill her, they would have done so already.

"Where am I? What's going on?"

Still no one answered.

Nyx's power burned just below the surface. She had half a mind to relinquish her hold on it and use her influence, but Ambrose kept telling her not to do that. He said she had to calm her mind and learn to hold her power in or else she would lose any grip she had on it.

Nyx had scoffed at the other druid during some of their earlier lessons together. She had been practising the different techniques he had shown her. It still surprised her how much he knew about mind whisperers. She took a deep breath to calm herself. Her head pounded harder.

To the underworld with calm. She wanted out of there. Now!

Her power flared but didn't explode outwards as she had expected.

Why hadn't it worked? Has she been drugged? Or her powers bound?

She couldn't be sure.

The other presence grew stronger as someone stalked towards her. They reached out and yanked the covering off her eyes.

Light blinded her for a moment as her vision adjusted.

A face came into view, the face of the winged servant Gideon had forced her to use her power on earlier. She gasped. "You." She glowered at him. "What are you doing? I thought they were going to kill you." Nyx glanced around, half expecting to find guards there, but found none. "Did the prince put you up to this?"

"The prince believes I'm dead, and it will remain that way."

"I don't understand. Why did you kidnap me?"

He laughed. "You don't know, do you?"

"Know what?" Nyx demanded. "If you think I'm part of some stupid prophecy, you —"

He cackled. "Can't you feel it? It's all around us."

Nyx took in her surroundings. Glowing crystalline walls surrounded them with crystal torches lighting the tunnel.

Nyx realised they must be somewhere underground. She tugged at her bindings and energy prickled against her skin.

"Don't bother trying to escape. I know how to bind, mind whisperer," he told her. "You are the key to getting what I want."

At the end of the tunnel, green plumes of smoke rose from cracks in the earth.

A rift.

"You're the one who fractured the veil." She scanned the fae with her senses. Her magic couldn't have been fully bound as she could still sense things.

The name Mervyn came to her.

"Mervyn, is that your name?"

His dark eyes narrowed. "Clever girl." He raised his hand, and the cracks of the rift grew larger.

"I don't know what you believe about the prophecy, but I'm no one. I can't bring about a dark age," she insisted. "You saw what happened at the palace. I'm not the one the prophecy speaks of."

Nyx knew she had to find a way out of there. She didn't want to find out what he had planned for her.

Mervyn snorted. "I couldn't fracture the veil even if I wanted to. I, like the other Andovians, have been forced into servitude. Our race is being destroyed by the Archdruid and that priestess who calls herself queen. Now is the time of the calling. The break in the veil is the first step, that's why the dark things and creatures banished from this world are walking free once more."

"What does that have to do with me?" Nyx demanded.

"You are the key. The darklings are gathering power."

She had to keep Mervyn talking and keep him distracted, as well as figure out a way to escape. If she could sense things, maybe she could call for help with her mind.

Druid? she called. *Can you hear me? Darius? Anyone? I need help.*

She waited, but no answer came.

Mervyn yanked her up. He pulled her towards the ledge. Worse still, he had bound her arms and wings together so she couldn't fly.

"No, don't." Nyx dug the heels of her boots into the ground. "You could at least tell me what this is all about. I deserve an explanation – I tried to save you back at the palace."

"You're part of the prophecy — that's obvious. You're the one who set her free."

"Set her free? The person who broke the veil?"

Mervyn yanked her forward.

Gods no. Some of the ground fell away.

Get away! She let go of her power and willed him to let go of her. Power reverberated through her like thunder without sound.

Mervyn didn't let go but did flinch. "Your powers won't work on me." He backhanded her so hard stars flashed in front of her vision.

Mervyn yanked her towards the rift once more.

Nyx struggled and thought, *No!* Then, a burst of energy slammed Mervyn into the far wall.

Nyx wriggled her fingers and the ropes finally loosened. She yanked them off.

Mervyn gaped at her. "Impossible, I bound you with runes to stop any mind whisperer. That's why your touch didn't work on me."

She shrugged. "Guess I'm special then. Now you're going to tell me what I want to know." She raised her hand, light sparking between her fingers. "Or maybe I'll use my powers and burn my way through your immunity."

Mervyn hissed and drew back. "Why should I tell you anything?"

"Because I'm sick of people coming after me. I want answers. Now." She grabbed his arm and let her power flow free. Energy reverberated through the air like thunder without sound.

Mervyn stumbled backwards and would have fallen into the rift if Nyx hadn't kept hold of him.

"I told you your power won't work on me." Mervyn gripped hold of her arm and used his other arm to reach for her. Nyx blocked his blow and punched him in the face. She had dealt with enough drunkards at the tavern to know how to defend herself.

Mervyn crumbled to the ground.

"Nyx?"

Ranelle ran towards her. "What happened?"

"Guess I hit him harder than I thought." Nyx frowned. "What are you doing here?" She wondered if Ranelle was somehow connected to Mervyn, but she didn't sense any deception from her, only concern.

"I heard you call out for help. Darius told me to look for you."

"We need to take him somewhere. He knows things about the darklings." She motioned to Mervyn.

Ranelle gasped. "He works in resistance with me."

"Yeah, well, he tried to kill me. Were you part of this?" She scanned Ranelle with her senses deeper.

Ranelle shook her head, and her thoughts and emotions didn't waver. "Of course not. I had no idea about Mervyn. I swear to you."

Nyx rubbed her aching knuckles. "We should call the druid."

"He's out hunting for darklings. We will have to deal with him ourselves. I know somewhere we can put him," Ranelle said. "It's too dangerous to take him back to Ambrose or Alaric's house." Ranelle conjured some ropes. "Help me tie him up."

Nyx waved her hand, and the ropes wound themselves around Mervyn. "Where are we going to put him then?"

Ranelle's eyes widened. "You are getting good at moving things with your mind. I know somewhere we can take him." She bit her lip. "It will hold him until we can figure out what to do with him."

"Where?" Nyx glanced around, uneasy. She hated the thought of being underground where she could be buried alive.

"This tunnel was part of the resistance's underground network. We grow our own tunnels through crystals so we can move around easily underneath the different islands. It's the only way to stay one step ahead of the guards." Ranelle yanked Mervyn to his feet. "Good thing you called for help or I might not have found you."

Together they dragged Mervyn up the tunnel and took him to a small separate cavern. Ranelle sealed its entrance with runes.

"Looks like you hit him pretty hard. We'll have to wait for Ambrose and the others to get here before we can question him." Ranelle ran a hand through her long hair. "Whilst you're down here, would you like to meet some other members of the resistance?"

Nyx scoffed. "I shouldn't be around anyone." She wanted nothing more than to find the druid and see what they could glean from Mervyn. Her mind raced with unanswered questions, questions only Mervyn could answer.

So far Darius hadn't responded to any of their calls. Ranelle insisted that was not unusual since Darius sometimes blocked out mental calls when he was busy.

"Many in the resistance are being killed," Ranelle replied. "Nowhere is safe on these islands, not with the Dragon Guard killing anyone suspected of working with us. War is coming, and everyone in Andovia will be affected."

"Everyone here is affected by the Archdruid's tyrannical rule," Ranelle told Nyx. "As a former slave, you should know better than anyone how much people long for freedom. That's why I thought you might want to help."

Nyx shook her head. "I don't see what good I can do. I'm a danger to everyone around me. You of all people should know that."

"Let me show you something." Ranelle motioned for her to follow.

Nyx hesitated. "I need to get back to the druid." She would also be glad to get back to the warmth and safety of Ambrose's house.

Ranelle shook her head. "We'll catch up with him later." She motioned for Nyx to follow once more.

Nyx and Ranelle travelled deeper into the caves. It amazed her how much had been carved out of solid rock. The rocks here shimmered with a rainbow of colours, sending pools of iridescent light dancing around the caverns.

"This place is beautiful. How large are these caves?" Nyx asked.

"They run for several miles under the island. Most people don't even know of their existence." Ranelle motioned to the glistening walls. "The stone here can channel magic, and we use it to create barriers and cast protective wards." She went over and picked up a large lump of glowing crystal. "We can also use these to create new tunnels. We are forever having to move them to stay one step ahead of the Guard."

"I still don't understand why you think I can help." Nyx shook her head. "Or why anyone wants to use me for my powers. I can't even control them, let alone use them to help." Tonight had been a perfect example of that, she hadn't been able to use her influence on Mervyn even though she had wanted to.

Sprites danced overhead, their laughter like the sound of tiny bells.

"I know what it's like not to fit in in your homeland. My people, the wyverns, are cursed to remain in human form. They despise the fact I am half-fae – or at least my father does. I came to Andovia because I wanted to belong somewhere. Despite the fear of the Archdruid and the awful things he and the high court do, there is still good here. I found that by working with the resistance. It's one of the few chances we have of doing good in this chaotic world." Ranelle set the crystal back on the ground, and it exploded with a rainbow of light, expanding over the wall like a spider's web.

Nyx gasped as the light formed into a glowing portal of shimmering light and a tunnel grew within it. She wanted to stay there and watch the entire process, but Ranelle motioned for her to follow.

"Let me show you some of the people we help down here."

Nyx reluctantly followed her friend. She still wanted to get back to Ambrose's house soon. She needed to talk to the druid and tell him what happened with Gideon and find out if he knew anything about her sisters. She didn't want to believe what Gideon said, but she couldn't ignore the possibility that he might have them.

The tunnels opened up and expanded into different smaller caverns where people seemed to be living. All kinds of fae moved around. Some looked on edge and others took curious glances at Nyx and Ranelle as they approached.

Most of them were fae with distinctive features that made them resemble fae more than human. It was so unlike the fae she had seen on Eldara.

Some of their thoughts buzzed at the edge of Nyx's, and she sensed their fear. These were the fae that were sent to the slave islands or forced into servitude. Nyx was surprised by how many people there were down here. People hadn't liked the Archdruid's rule back in her own realm, but no one there had been concerned enough to do anything about it. They preferred to keep to themselves and dole out their own justice.

"This is Lorek." Ranelle stopped when they came to a huddled figure in the corner of the main cavern. People sent sympathetic glances his way, but no one seemed to want to go near him. "He used to work at the palace as one of the Archdruid's personal slaves. The Archdruid liked to torment him."

Nyx expected to be overwhelmed by the man's thoughts, yet his mind remained silent. She frowned. "What's wrong with him?" People usually had something going through their minds, whether it be thoughts, images, or different feelings. Some people gave off stronger readings than others, yet she felt nothing from this man, only a strange emptiness. She wondered if he might be immune to her power like the druid was, or perhaps he had a mental shield like Gideon. She doubted such a thing was possible, not for a servant at least. The Archdruid wouldn't have cared enough to put mental blocks on his slaves.

Ranelle placed a sympathetic hand on Lorek's shoulder and gave it a squeeze. "His mind is broken. The Archdruid likes to scan the minds of his servants and slaves to keep them in line. We tried to help him, but there's not much more we can do. His body is here, but it's like his spirit is gone."

"How could someone do that? The Archdruid isn't a mind whisperer, is he?"

"No. The Archdruid and other members of the high court have power and technology that can breach someone's mind. I suppose it is one of the reasons why they feared mind whisperers. They were always stronger than any of the magic and technology they could wield." Ranelle turned to Nyx. "Maybe you can help him."

Nyx gaped at her. "Me? How?"

"I've read about mind whisperers and the things they could do. The Archdruid might have tried to wipe out all the information, but some of it remains. Some of them could heal people's minds. Maybe you could go in and see if he is still there."

So that was why Ranelle had wanted her to come here. She thought Nyx could help save people. Nyx didn't know whether to be intrigued or terrified by that. She chose the latter. How could anyone want her to use her powers on a broken man? Her curse could rip him apart — she had seen that much during the time she had lost control and almost hurt Ranelle and Lucien.

She took a step back and shook her head. "I'm sorry I can't. I don't want to hurt anyone else." Nyx half expected to hear Harland goading her again, accusing her of being a killer. She had enough blood on her hands already and didn't want any more.

"If you lose control, perhaps I can pull you out. It's worth a try, isn't it?" Ranelle persisted. "How else will you learn to control your gift unless you use it and understand how it works?"

Do I have a choice? Nyx wondered. It sickened her to see the state of this man, but she had seen it before in the slave markets when slaves who had been broken had lost all the light and life in their eyes. They too were empty vessels devoid of souls.

But then again, Ranelle did have a point. Nyx bit her lip. "Okay, I'll try." She reached into her pocket and put the leather bracelet back on. There was no way she would attempt this without her power being reined in. For all she knew it might not even work.

She placed her hand on Lorek's shoulder and closed her eyes. Her power simmered beneath the surface, aching to get out and burst free from the confines of her body. The leather bracelet burned her wrist, forcing her power back inside as though it were a caged animal fighting to get loose.

Nyx took a deep breath and let her power loose. Energy vibrated through her entire body as her senses latched onto the man huddled beneath the dark cloak.

There were no doors here, no sounds of thought or feeling. Instead, she appeared to be standing in a void of darkness. Nyx flinched. She had never encountered this in anyone's mind before.

What had the Archdruid done to this man? What kind of torture caused something like this? She had seen abuse often enough throughout her life, including from Harland when he had beaten her sisters, but this was far beyond that.

She wandered deeper into the darkness and everything inside her screamed to pull back and get out of there.

Nyx opened her eyes, her power reeling from the emptiness she had found. "There's nothing there. I saw only blackness inside his mind, which was odd." Even the thoughts of the broken slaves she had met before had echoes inside their minds or at least some remnant of their former selves. "There's nothing I can do for him. I don't know how to bring back someone's spirit."

Ranelle's expression turned grim, but she nodded. "I feared as much. Come on, the tunnel I set up earlier will lead us to the edge of the island. From there we can fly back to Ambrose's house. I will make sure you get home safe." She turned and motioned for Nyx to follow her again. "At least that proves you can use your power."

That didn't bring her much comfort. Nyx shivered and wrapped her arms around herself. "I don't understand how someone could do that to another person. If his soul is in there, I couldn't feel it."

"I know, but it's hard to change the way things have been done for centuries."

"Why do you do it then?" Nyx knew it was impossible to go against the Archdruid. Even if they had an army, it wouldn't be any match for his power or that of the fae of the high court.

Ranelle frowned. "Because it's the right thing to do. Who else will fight for these people if not us? They don't have anyone else and I believe everything we do, no matter how small, does help. They may not seem like much, but I have to believe that." She paused. "How did your meeting go with Gideon tonight?"

Nyx grimaced. "Not as I expected. Do you think it's possible Gideon has my sisters?" She might not have known Ranelle for long, but she did trust her now. "I know Mervyn said Gideon would do anything to get people to do what he wanted, but... if they are here in Andovia somewhere, I have to find them."

Ranelle shook her head. "Gideon does lie about a lot of things. He'll say and do anything to bend people to his will. So no, I don't think your sisters are here. We always monitor the slaves coming in and out of the islands, and there has been no sign of them."

But that didn't mean her sisters weren't nearby. It wasn't like she could go back to Joriam to check on them as that was too far away. The druid would know what to do. The sooner she spoke to him the better.

CHAPTER 24

Darius avoided Lucien's scrutinising gaze as they headed back towards the rift together. He had lost control of his sorcery again and worse still his friend had been there to witness it. He had expected Lucien to scold him for using dark magic, but to his surprise, it hadn't happened yet. What was he waiting for? He always lectured Darius whenever he tapped into the darker side of his gift. Yes, it was dangerous, but it had been necessary at the time. At least that was what he kept telling himself.

The high magic he had used earlier left his senses reeling. His power ached to get out. He still had no idea what the creature had been or what it wanted. He suspected it had been looking for new victims.

Twigs and branches snapped as they trudged back towards where they had found the rift. As much as Darius wanted to find Nyx, he knew they had to check the rift one more time in case anything else had come out. He only wished Ambrose could be with them instead of at another council meeting. The older druid might have a better idea of how to deal with the spirits and whatever else came through.

"We should go to the Hall of Knowledge later," Darius finally broke the awkward silence between them. "Maybe we can find something there about what's coming through the rift."

Lucien glowered at him. "Why did you use high magic earlier? You know damn well you shouldn't touch that stuff. You're almost as bad as Nyx when she loses control of her power."

Darius frowned. "I'm fully trained on how to use my abilities."

His jaw tightened. Nyx could barely control herself, let alone her powers. "Besides, it worked, didn't it?"

Lucien let out a low growl. "Maybe, but you take a risk every time you use high magic like that. It's dangerous, and you know it."

"My brother has no trouble controlling it, does he?" Darius muttered under his breath.

"Do you want to be like him?"

Darius looked away, and his hands clenched into fists. No, he despised everything about his brother and how Gideon used his powers. That was why Darius had always vowed to be different from him. "No, but I will do everything I can to find out who is opening these rifts and letting things through. And why." He ran a hand through his long hair and trudged on ahead.

He would be glad to get home again. Maybe Nyx would be there. One good thing about her was she didn't question him over his use of power.

The rift came back into view. More columns of toxic green mist rose into the night sky. Darius sent his senses out again and scanned the area with his mind. He winced at the poison coming out of the rift. The trees, grass and everything else around it had already withered away.

Dark shadows swirled in and out of the plumes of smoke. Wonderful, more darklings.

Darius put a hand out to stop Lucien before he could go any closer.

"Now what?" Lucien lowered his voice, fearful of attracting any unwanted attention.

Darius switched to talking in thought so they wouldn't be overheard. *If we could create a web of energy and keep it contained, then maybe we could force them back through the rift.* But he had tried using webs on the spirits before and they had had no effect.

I have some crystals with me if that would help.

What kind of crystals?

Lucien pulled out a lump of clear crystal. It was a natural piece of stone that occurred over on Eldara and could be used for a lot of different things — especially channelling energy. The druids liked the stone, and so did the fae as they often used it in their spells, rituals and even in defensive wards since it was good for storing energy.

Good idea. Darius nodded. *How many do you have?*

Lucien rummaged through his pack and produced four pieces of crystal. Not as many as Darius would have liked, but it would have to do.

I will take two and put them on this side of the rift. You need to put the other two on the other side. Do you think you can get around there without being detected? Darius took hold of the crystals and clutched them in his hands.

Lucien smirked. *Of course I can. I move a lot faster than they do.* He ran off in a blur of movement.

Darius chanted the words to a cloaking spell and light flashed around his body. He hoped it would be enough to conceal him, but he didn't know if it had worked or not. Cloak in place, he edged nearer to the rift, his heart pounding in his ears. Just being near the dark spirits made him uneasy.

He dropped into a crouch and placed one of the crystals near the edge of the rift. The toxic smoke burned his lungs, and he covered his mouth to repress a cough. Darius reluctantly drew magic so he could breathe easier, but doubted it would last long. Crawling, he made his way along the edge of the embankment to where he would need to place the other crystal. Lucien wasn't anywhere in sight and moved too fast for him to see anyway.

Stones dug into his arms and torso as he continued crawling along the verge. The smoke stung his eyes and burned his lungs more. He wished he had thought about conjuring a shield earlier, although that would have used a lot more power than he would have wanted and might have drawn the darkling's attention.

My first crystal is in place, Lucien told him. *Are yours?*

Almost. I just need to place the second one. Just a few more feet and he would reach the ideal spot. He sensed the other crystals nearby and decided this would be a good point for the crystals combined energy to flow together and form a web that would cage the spirits in.

The darklings continued to circle over the rift like cloaks flapping in a breeze. Darius wondered what they were circling for. Were they waiting for something? Someone? Most of the darklings they had seen so far had been searching for something or attacked someone, just like one had the night when he had gone to Joriam to find Nyx.

One of the darklings drew near, and Darius felt himself fall.

He winced as the air whooshed from his lungs, but his shield stopped him from falling any further into the rift.

A screech rang out, and the darklings swarmed towards him.

Holy spirits! Darius raised his hands. Lightning bolts arced over his head, forming another growing shield of energy. One by one, spirits battled against his shield like flying rocks.

Wonderful, now he was stuck in the rift with one shield keeping him afloat and another keeping the darklings at bay.

Luc, get the other crystal in place. More lightning shot from his palms.

I'm trying, Lucien replied. *These damn spirits keep coming for me.* Darius had no doubt Lucien could stay one step ahead of them using his speed. *Do you want me to help you get out of the rift?*

No. Darius knew he couldn't keep this up forever. Sooner or later one of his shields would fail and he'd end up either being attacked or at the bottom of the rift. He didn't know which would be worse. *Hurry up!*

I'm trying. The bloody things keep blocking my way.

Move faster.

Darius knew he had to get out of there. He didn't want to risk landing in the rift or being at the mercy of the darklings. He had to think fast. Spells raced through his mind. Druidry wouldn't work. He would have to use his high magic again.

Darius gritted his teeth and reached for magic. High magic didn't always require words, only intention, which was what made it so dangerous.

He raised his arms, lightning exploded in all directions. The darklings scattered like flies. Darius called on the air and used the currents to propel the shield underneath him up and out of the rift. Once he reached the edge of the embankment, he jumped off the shield.

Darius landed on his feet and raised his hand. His magic burst to life, glad to be free from the confines he had kept it locked away in. Exhilaration rushed over him. Lightning shot through the air and each darkling screeched as the bolts struck them.

Darius marvelled at his power as it made contact with solid flesh. Darklings could become corporeal when they chose. Their screeches rang through his ears, but part of him enjoyed it.

"Darius?" Lucien's voice sounded far away. "Stop this."

Darius ignored him and let his power fly free. In a few moments, he would rip these creatures apart. He gathered more magic, forcing it out and willing it to kill the spirits.

In the back of his mind, all the endless hours of enduring his mother's teachings came back to him. Mercury knew how to control spirits and could bend them to her will, but his father used high magic.

The darklings continued their unholy wailing, but none of them had been vanquished yet. Something resisted his power and pushed against his magic. Someone else must have the power to control these things, but who?

The other darklings dispersed, vanishing back into the depths of the rift. Only one remained. Its features were skeletal. Its eyes flashed with eerie orange light.

"Who are you?" Darius demanded. "What do you want?"

"The darkness is coming," the creature hissed.

If it wouldn't talk, he would make it. Darius didn't hesitate and sent out a mental command. Lightning shot from his hand as he let his magic loose. The bolt shot straight through the darkling.

"Darius?" Lucien called out as he rushed back towards him.

"Druid?" Nyx asked. "What are you doing?"

"You need to stop this." Ranelle came up behind them. "This is high magic. You know better than to use that again."

How else would he get answers? He was sick of watching people die.

"Druid?" Nyx put her hand on his shoulder. "Stop."

Darius' hands fell to his sides and his power dissipated. They were right. This was the wrong way of doing things. The darkling shot down and disappeared into the rift.

Darius wiped the sweat off his forehead. What had he almost done?

Darius didn't say anything as he and the others transported to the underground tunnels. Nyx and Ranelle had told him about what happened after a resistance member grabbed Nyx outside the palace. Lucien had gone to grab Mervyn and take him into a different chamber so they could interrogate him, and Darius agreed leaving him down in the tunnels was too risky. He didn't like the idea of locking Mervyn up down here, but they had nowhere else they could take him without the risk of being seen.

Darius had been surprised to hear someone from the resistance had dared to try and kill Nyx. Why were people so interested in her?

She might be powerful, but he hadn't seen anything from her so far to indicate she might be the one the prophecy spoke of. Still, he was glad they had a potential lead at last. If they could figure out who was opening the rifts, maybe they could find a way to seal the veil once and for all.

Darius called for Ambrose to come and help, but his mentor said he was out in the lower realm searching for rifts and could not return for a few hours. That had disappointed him, but Darius guessed they would have to manage by themselves for a while.

Lucien dragged Mervyn into the chamber and Darius set wards in place to prevent him from escaping.

He didn't know Mervyn well and had only seen the other fae a few times, lurking around the palace.

"Will your touch work on him?" Darius asked Nyx.

"My what? Oh, you mean my influence." She shook her head. "No, I already tried to use it on him twice. It had no effect. He is somehow immune to it." She frowned. "How else are we going to get answers out of him?"

That was a good question and one Darius didn't know if he could answer yet. There were many ways of getting someone to tell the truth if you knew how to find their weakness and exploit it. He had learnt that much from watching his parents over the years. But they didn't have time to waste, nor did he want to torture Mervyn either.

They needed answers now.

After Lucien dropped Mervyn off inside the cave, he and Ranelle went to check on the rest of the resistance members who were living in the tunnel system and to check out Mervyn's quarters to see if they could glean any information.

"You," Mervyn spat the word out with disgust when he caught sight of Darius. "Not even you can make me talk. I serve a greater power than anything you mere children could possibly imagine."

Can you listen in on his thoughts? Darius asked Nyx. *You said Gideon forced you to use your powers on him earlier. Go into his mind and see what you can find.*

Nyx hesitated. *His mind is so jumbled. I found it hard to get anything from him. He somehow manages to confuse me with conflicting information.*

Try anyway. He must know something about the person who fractured the veil. Why else would he want to kill you?

Nyx went over and placed her hand on Mervyn's head. She closed

208

her eyes and her brow creased in concentration. After a few moments, she drew back. *His thoughts are still so confusing. I can't find anything.*

Darius sighed, and spells raced through his mind. With a few words he could get Mervyn to speak the truth, but that would mean using high magic again. He had lost control once that night already and he didn't want to risk doing so again.

"See, your powers are useless against me." Mervyn sneered. "The darkness is coming, and there's nothing either of you can do to stop it."

"Who broke the veil?" Darius crossed his arms and leaned against the wall. "I am a Valeran. You know I can make you talk if I choose to and I won't need her powers to do it." He inclined his head towards Nyx.

Are you going to use high magic again? Nyx narrowed her eyes at him.

Not unless I have to.

I could pull you back if you need me to. It seems I have the same effect on you that you have on me when I lose control of my powers.

Mervyn scoffed at the threat. "I've watched you, boy. You are a coward compared to your brother, and your powers are weak, pathetic. You won't do anything to me. You don't have it in you." He gave a harsh laugh. "The only one with power here is the mind whisperer and she is almost as useless as you are."

Nyx put her hands on her hips. "Then why did you try to kill me? Clearly, I must be important for something?"

Mervyn fell silent and looked away.

Nyx moved closer to Darius. *What are we going to do with him, druid?*

Darius sighed. *I'll have to use a spell on him. We don't have time to get the information out of him any other way. When I spoke to Ambrose on the way here he said the rifts are becoming more widespread.*

She had been right about one thing. She could probably pull him back if he lost control again. Still, the spells that forced people to bend to his will were the ones he hated the most. The mere thought of them sickened him.

I'll use one of my father's spells, he added.

Nyx gaped at him. *What? No. That goes beyond high magic and into the realm of dark magic.*

What other choice do we have? Your powers don't work on him.

What if you cast some sort of spell on him and I try to go into his mind at the same time. Maybe in that moment of weakness, I might find a way in.

How do you know your power will work? We still know very little about how to control your abilities.

Nyx shrugged. *I don't know. Just have a little faith in me, druid.*

Darius knew it was worth a try and began chanting a spell.

Energy charged through the air as the spell hit its intended target. Mervyn squirmed in the corner of the chamber and whimpered as if in pain.

Nyx walked over and touched his head once more. *Curse it. It's not working.*

Darius said the next part of the spell and walked over to her. He put a hand on her shoulder. Something jolted between them as he uttered the final verse of the spell.

The glowing crystalline walls of the chamber around them faded until he found himself somewhere else. Crystal torches glittered on the walls, and he knew they must be in one of the servant passageways at the Crystal Palace.

"We are inside Mervyn's mind," Nyx gasped from where she stood beside him. "How? He was immune to my powers."

Darius shrugged. "The effects of the spell must have worked and allowed you in. Allowed us in."

"Where are we?"

"At the palace. We need to see this through and find where it leads us. Concentrate on what you want to see. Force him to show us what he knows." Darius would do the same since he had cast the spell.

They stood there waiting.

"Do you feel like Mervyn is deceiving you?" he asked.

Nyx shook her head. "No. His thoughts would be more jumbled if he were. Your spell must be working."

"Mervyn, show us what you know about the person who fractured the veil," Darius commanded. He knew he had to stay in control or the darker side of his magic would take hold of him.

Mervyn travelled down to the end of the hall. Darius didn't recognise this part of the palace although he had travelled through its many corridors for most of his life, even the ones the servants used. He pulled on one of the crystal torches that illuminated the space, and a wall slid open. Mervyn peered around the corner. Glowing green light glittered around the open chamber as a black-cloaked figure stood with their back to him. Cracks appeared on the floor and the familiar green plumes of smoke they had seen emanating from the rift rose into the air.

As if sensing Mervyn's presence, the figure whirled around, but their face remained hidden by a veil of blackness.

"You dare intrude! If you speak of this to anyone, you will die!" a voice hissed.

Darius gasped as he and Nyx were forced out of Mervyn's mind.

Blood trickled down the fae's face as his eyes turned glassy in death.

"No!" Darius cried, but he knew it was too late.

Whoever Mervyn had seen had ensured their identity would remain a secret once more.

Darius and Nyx headed to the palace after reconvening with Lucien and Ranelle. Lucien told them they had found nothing within Mervyn's chamber, so the four of them went to search the palace instead. After a couple of hours of searching through all of the servants' hallways they found nothing. None of the passages they opened looked anything like the one they had seen in Mervyn's mind.

Afterwards, they retreated to the Hall of Knowledge so they could go over the events of the night.

The warmth of the hall enveloped them as they headed inside. Darius usually found this place welcoming, but it did little to ease his warring emotions. He couldn't believe they had come so close to finding answers only to fail yet again.

Ranelle went and brought a tray of tea in for them.

He marched off through the foyer. A beam of energy shot down and scanned him for a moment, then it winked out.

The hall had security which made sure no one aside from the overseers and a chosen few were admitted entrance. Legend stated the hall had been destroyed, but the overseers had used their combined power and help from the druids to move it to a safe location. Here the whole hall laid hidden on a separate plane of existence away from anyone who might misuse its knowledge, including the Archdruid. Hiding the portal's entrance in the great library had been a genius choice as no one would ever think to look for it there.

Darius breathed a sigh of relief. "Keeper?"

In a flash of light, the keeper appeared. It was a fae looking creature with pointed ears and wispy hair. The keeper looked neither male nor female in its features.

Nyx gasped when she caught sight of it. "What is that thing?"

The keeper's long hair fell down their shoulders and it had pointed ears and catlike eyes. Its lower body was made of smoke, only the torso looked humanoid.

"Nyx, this is the keeper of the hall. They can help people find what they are looking for."

Nyx closed her mouth. "Oh. Right." She averted her gaze.

Shelves stretched as far as the eye could see. It put the great library to shame. With its sweeping wooden columns and gleaming oak floors, this place felt almost sacred. Darius loved it here since it felt like pure freedom. "Can I get you something, my lord?" the keeper asked him.

"Fetch me everything you can find on evil spirits and about the veil between the worlds."

Lucien and Ranelle trailed behind them. "You've already looked for that information," Lucien remarked.

"We need to go over everything again," Darius said before he walked over to Nyx

Darius listened while she told him what happened with Gideon.

"Do you think he has my sisters?" Nyx asked. "Or that he senses my power?"

Darius hesitated. "If you had exposed your power, I doubt he would have let you leave. As for your sisters… No, I haven't heard of any new slaves being brought here."

"But he could have them?"

"If he does, I would have heard. Your sisters are safe in Joriam."

Nyx breathed a sigh of relief then yelped as the keeper flashed into existence. "Good gods, do you have to do that?"

The keeper didn't look bothered by Nyx's outburst. "Here's all the information you asked for, my lord." The keeper placed a tablet on a wooden table. "Do you require anything else?"

"No, thank you." Darius took hold of the tablet.

The keeper faded into smoke.

"Wait a minute." Nyx bit her lip. "Can you find something for me too?" She glanced at Darius as if asking for permission.

Ask whatever you want. He waved his hand in dismissal and picked up the tablet.

"Yes, my lady?" The keeper materialised again.

"Lady? Me?" Nyx laughed then hesitated. "Can... Can you find me information about mind whisperers? Their history, names and stuff."

The keeper bowed their head and disappeared.

"We already looked for that information," Darius remarked. "Someone erased it all. Likely my grandfather."

Nyx slumped back into her seat. "I need to know more. I couldn't have just appeared from nowhere. One of my parents had to be a mind whisperer, didn't they?"

Darius nodded. "I guess." He shrugged. He didn't know enough about mind whisperers to know about her lineage.

"What do you think you will find here?"

"Someone broke through my power tonight. Now I need to figure out who and why they did it."

CHAPTER 25

Nyx stalked into the Hall of Knowledge. It still felt strange being transported somewhere by the sphere back in the great library. Even after several weeks of living in Andovia, she was not used to the sensation, but she liked the solitude she found here away from all of the voices outside.

Ambrose had agreed to start training her here since she could focus better than in the outside world. Nyx would have been half glad to stay here all the time if she could have. Not being subjected to anyone else's thoughts but her own was a dream come true.

"You are late," Ambrose observed.

"Sorry, I was busy. The druid and I have been flying around and checking for more rifts." She yawned. "What are we practising today?"

Between training with Ambrose during the day and now Gideon at night, she couldn't remember half of what they suggested.

"You look tired. How have you been progressing?"

"Progressing?" Nyx rubbed her temples. "Define progress?" She fiddled with the leather bracelet on her wrist.

Ambrose frowned. "You're wearing that a lot."

Nyx shrugged. "It keeps my power under control. Plus, I never know when Gideon might summon me."

Gideon had insisted on her coming to see him every evening over the past few weeks. Every time he got her to test her power on different people — for what reason she had no idea. He brought someone new in every night and forced her to read their mind or use her influence on them.

"You can't rely on that all the time." Ambrose motioned to the bracelet. "If you do, you'll never achieve true control."

Nyx sighed. She had taken to wearing the band more often, both because it made her feel closer to her sister and because it gave her peace. She reluctantly slipped it off and set it on the table. "So, what are we doing today?" She drummed her fingers on the arm of her chair. Nyx wanted to get this over with so she could get back to helping the druid with hunting for rifts and aid the others with research. Three more people had died since the night Darius had lost control and they were still no closer to finding out who was creating the rifts or why.

Nyx was glad the attacks against her seemed to have died down. She had no idea why, but she wouldn't question it. The more she could focus on helping the others, the better.

So far, Ambrose had her practising on him or, on occasion, Alaric when he was available. Ambrose liked her to wander around his mind to find answers. It had been the same routine for weeks now, and Nyx found it tiresome.

"We're going to try something a little different today." Ambrose rose and tapped his staff on the floor.

A woman appeared in a flash of light. Long silvery hair flowed down her shoulders, her eyes were azure and her skin was almost opaque. She looked so fresh, like a spring morning.

Nyx found that odd. No one ever looked this perfect. Something was strange about her.

"You want me to read her mind," Nyx guessed.

Ambrose's thoughts were silent behind his shield. The woman's thoughts were silent too, as well as her energy, which Nyx found even stranger. Everyone had energy around them, especially everyone she met on Andovia. Even her human tribe had different energies – she had learnt to recognise that much in her endless training sessions. Nyx opened her mouth to ask how this woman could have none, but Ambrose cut her off. "No, I want you to tell me who and what she is."

Nyx's mouth fell open. "What? Why?" He'd never asked her to do such things before.

"Because you need to learn to control."

The woman blinked but said nothing, that unnerved Nyx even

more.

"Are you okay with me doing this?" Nyx asked her.

Nothing.

That struck her as strange. Everyone Gideon brought before her was terrified of her being a mind whisperer. They trembled, screamed, or tried to run.

This woman didn't look at all bothered.

Gods, this woman was strange.

Nyx hesitated. "Are you okay with this?" she repeated. Nyx didn't know why, but she felt like she needed to ask permission. Odd, since she always used her powers on people whether they wanted her to or not. Still, the woman remained silent.

Say something, Nyx wanted to shout at her.

Unless Ambrose had told her to keep her mouth shut. Perhaps this was all part of the test.

Nyx glanced over to Ambrose and let her power roam over him. Bam. His shield had somehow become much stronger, either he had something with Darius' blood on it or he had a new mental block that shielded him against her.

Sneaky old goat. Nyx sat back and let her power flow free again. That was another reason why she liked the bracelet because she didn't have to hold her power in. Her power latched onto the strange woman. Nyx braced herself for the inevitable onslaught of thoughts.

Only silence greeted her.

Nyx furrowed her brow and probed deeper. The woman didn't have any shields or blocks — none that she could sense.

"Do you mind if I touch you?"

Again, the woman stayed silent.

"Say something," Nyx banged her fist on the arm of her chair.

The woman didn't so much as flinch or react at all. Nyx took hold of the woman's arm. To her surprise, her fingers connected with solid flesh. She had wondered if the woman might be a spirit.

Nyx sent her senses deeper. *Who are you, what are you?* Nyx closed her eyes.

She expected to find herself in a hallway of doors or assaulted by the constant buzz of thoughts.

Instead, only faint whispering greeted her.

That couldn't be natural. Everyone had thoughts, memories and feelings – things that made up who they were.

She couldn't make out who this woman was or feel any resistance from a shield.

Nyx reached out with her senses to catch onto the whispering. There had to be thoughts, even if this woman seemed to have nothing but air in her head. The whispering grew louder, but she couldn't make out the words at first.

Come on, show me who and what you are.

There had to be something here. She had taken her bracelet off, and her power flowed free. Was it exhaustion? Ambrose always said her emotions would affect her powers too, like when she got angry or afraid.

Nyx pushed against the woman's mind into blinding light. Roaring filled her ears.

She covered her eyes and found herself somewhere else. A man with huge gossamer wings stood, using a stylus to draw glowing symbols in the air.

She had seen the druid use runes, but these didn't look like them.

Nyx moved closer, surprised by the sight of the fae. He didn't look anything like the Silvans. His ears were pointed, his eyes edged with colour.

He drew more runes and light flared so brightly, dazzling her as he chanted strange words.

Then a figure stood before her — the woman she had been reading.

Nyx slumped back onto the floor, the world around her spun and her stomach recoiled.

"Are you alright?" Ambrose made a move to guide her.

"She's — she's not real." Nyx swallowed the bile in her throat. "You tricked me!"

"How do you know that?" Ambrose leaned on his staff.

"Because I saw the man who created her. She can't talk — she has no real mind of her own. What is she?" Nyx frowned and flinched at the too perfect creation as it blinked at her. She looked real, yet somehow not.

Ambrose's eyes widened. "Wait, you didn't see me activate the spell used to create her?"

Nyx shook her head. "No. Why did you trick me?"

"It was a test. Nyx, tell me what you saw. Everything." Ambrose sounded excited.

She shrugged. "A male winged fae."

"Did you see what he did or said?"

She furrowed her brow. "Oh, I get it. You wanted to make sure I could tell the difference between a real person and this thing." She motioned to the woman.

"Nyx, tell me what you saw and heard." Ambrose rose and sounded more urgent.

Nyx bit her lip. "I told you, a male winged fae. He drew some symbols — runes — but different from your druid ones."

"Can you replicate them?"

She shrugged again. "Maybe. He said something like, 'Created in thought form, in magic and blood born.'" She tapped her chin. "Those are the words. That sounded strange at first, but now I understand them."

Ambrose gaped at her. "Blessed spirits, you saw her being created." He clapped his hands. "Incredible. Yes, she is a thought form – only more advanced. They were used as servants by the ancestors. This means your power has grown."

Oh, joy.

"How so?" Nyx leaned back in her chair then motioned to the thought form. "Can you get rid of her now? She unnerves me."

Ambrose tapped his staff on the floor and the woman vanished in a flash of light.

Nyx breathed a sigh of relief.

"This is incredible." Ambrose rose and began pacing. "The spell for a faerie – that's an old term for thought forms — has been lost for centuries. Most of them have been destroyed. She is the only one left of them we possess."

Nyx frowned. "How could I have seen that? I'm not a seer." That thought made her chest tighten. Gods, she missed Domnu.

"Whenever anyone casts a spell, they leave a mark — a trace of energy, perhaps a trace of their thoughts, which is what you sensed. Incredible." Ambrose stopped pacing.

"How does this help me control my power?" She crossed her arms.

"You're getting better every day. You just need to learn not to rely on that band so much."

The outer door burst open as Darius rushed in. "The rift on Migara just expanded, and a mass of land fell into it. We've got bigger problems now."

CHAPTER 26

"What do you mean the rift expanded?" Nyx asked as she, Darius and Ambrose hurried out of the great library.

Darius pushed his long hair of his face and called for Sirin. The dragon swept down like a silent phantom. "Exactly that. The rift expanded, and everything fell into its depths." Darius scrambled up onto the dragon's back. He pulled Nyx up behind him.

"I'll meet you there." Ambrose drew a circle around himself and tapped his staff on the ground. He then vanished in a flash of light.

Nyx gripped onto him as Sirin took flight.

Darius raised his hand and caught hold of an air current and channelled his magic. Flying all the way from Migara took time since it was on the other side of the realm. They didn't have time to waste.

Wind whooshed past him as he used the current to catapult them forward.

Nyx screamed and Sirin screeched. "What are you doing?"

Migara finally came into view. The great expanse of the wilds stretched out before them.

"Using the air to make us travel faster." Darius patted the dragon's head. "Sorry, girl."

Nyx gave him a shove. "Hey, I deserve an apology too. I almost fell off." The dragon screeched. "See, even she agrees with me."

"Fine, I'm sorry to both of you," Darius grumbled. "But we need to get there fast." He urged Sirin to the ground.

The glowing green light and toxic fumes were visible even from up here.

Once they reached the ground, Nyx ran off in the direction of the rift. The wilds lived up to its name. Thick foliage covered the rocky terrain and trees stood in every direction. Everything here was wild from the trees, plants and the land itself. Unlike the majesty of Eldara, this realm was untamed and alien.

Leaves caught his tunic and branches groaned. Nyx yelped and dodged one as it made a grab for her. The trees on Migara had always moved and been unpredictable, but with the open rift, their energy had become much darker.

Darius pushed the branch away. "Maybe you should fly."

"Good idea." Nyx spread her wings and took to the air. More branches made a grab for him.

Nyx leaned down and grabbed hold of his arm.

Darius bit back a cry of alarm as she lifted him off the ground. Then her wings buckled. Darius hit the ground again with a thud. "You can't carry me. Go. I'll catch up."

Nyx hesitated then flew off above the tree line.

Darius raised his hand and sent out an invisible burst of energy. The branches at once retreated, clearing his path. He bounded ahead until the green shimmers and dark shadows came into view. Darius coughed as the fumes hit him and headed over to where Nyx, Ambrose, Alaric and Lucien were standing.

"This is not good." Ambrose leaned on his staff. All of them stumbled backwards as more earth fell away.

"Wait." Darius caught hold of Ambrose's arm., both to hold himself upright and to stop the other druid from falling in. On the other side of the rift trees groaned as the side of the embankment gave way. People screamed, and several ran away or took to the air.

Nyx clutched her head. "Oh no, I left my bracelet behind." She sank to her knees.

"I'll conjure a shield." Ambrose raised his staff.

Darius made a move to go and help her. Holy spirits, she hadn't been overwhelmed like this for a while. Had she been relying on the bracelet the whole time?

"Not you." Nyx winced and used her free hand to motion to the rift. "It's from there."

Alaric glanced at Ambrose. "How can she be hearing thoughts? Has anyone fallen in?"

If they had, Darius doubted they would still be alive.

"No one has fallen in that we know of," Lucien added.

"Unless they fell in before we got here." Darius went over to Nyx and put a hand on her shoulder. She relaxed and breathed a sigh of relief.

"We need to report this." Several people from the Forest Guard were already there trying to help. Darius knew most of the people that lived in the wilds wouldn't stick around and would retreat into hiding.

"The Archdruid must know," Alaric added.

"He's not here," Darius reminded them.

"Then the queen and your brother must know. Migara is in danger of being swallowed by the rift," Ambrose said. "This cannot continue. All of the islands are in danger."

"I agree, but they both ignored the problem." Darius kept a hand on Nyx as she scrambled up.

"This can't be ignored. Summon your brother here."

Darius hesitated. He alone had the power to summon Gideon, but despite the danger part of him did not want to do it. "What about Nyx? He will sense her power."

Ambrose pulled an amulet out from under his robes. "Here." He slipped it off and held it out to her. "It's spelled with Darius' blood. Put it on."

Nyx frowned at him. "I knew you were blocking me out." She put the amulet on and hid it beneath her tunic.

Darius hesitated then raised his hand, reaching for the familiar feel of his brother's presence.

Light flashed as Gideon himself appeared. His dark eyes narrowed. "Brother, what do you think you're doing?" His voice held a hard edge.

"Look." Darius motioned to the open rift. More earth fell away, crumbling into the fumes and turned to ash as it went. Gideon frowned, but Darius caught a flash of surprise in his gaze. With a groan, more land fell away. Fae and dryads screamed as they turned into ash in the rift. "Still think this isn't a problem, brother?"

Gideon's jaw tightened, and he edged closer. He raised his hand. "The veil... It's fractured."

"We have been telling you that for weeks." Nyx raised her chin.

Careful. Now is not a good time to push him, Darius warned her.

"You're the closest thing we have to an Archdruid, prince. What are you going to do about it?" Nyx arched an eyebrow.

Gideon glowered at her. "I —"

"The rift must be closed," Ambrose spoke up. "Everything we've tried so far has failed."

A darkling shot up and out of the rift. It hovered for a moment, its skeletal body shimmering in the sunlight. Gideon raised his hand and hit it with a ball of energy. The darkling screeched and dived back into the rift. "Gods below," Gideon growled.

"So, how are you going to fix this?" Nyx put her hands on her hips.

Gideon turned his scowl onto his brother. "Can you keep your slave in line?"

"She's not a slave," Darius said without thinking. "And she's right."

"Fine, then I'll close the rift." Gideon raised his hands and light flared between his palms. The ground beneath them groaned and trembled. More land fell away, forcing them to step back. Darius grabbed his brother's arm and pulled him back. Gideon yanked his arm away. "I don't need you to save me."

Darius shrugged. "You're welcome."

"Your power alone isn't enough, my prince." Ambrose clutched his staff tighter. "The veil is fractured. We need to find another way."

"We need the power of the Archdruid," Alaric spoke up. "He's the only one who has a connection to Erthea itself."

Gideon turned his glare onto the overseer.

"He has a point," Darius agreed. "Father has the power. Nothing we've done so far has worked."

True, Fergus did have a connection, but Darius dreaded to think what might happen if Fergus used his power. With his dark magic, what kind of damage would he do?

"We need to talk to Father." Gideon gritted his teeth. "He won't like it."

"Summon him or call him. We can't ignore this problem anymore." Darius pushed his hair off his face. "Neither can he, or all of Andovia could be swallowed up in a matter of days."

Gideon blew out a breath. "Fine." He motioned with his hands and light flared between his palms. It swirled around until a life-like image of Fergus appeared.

Fergus Valeran's expression hardened at the sight of them. "What is the meaning of this?" Fergus hated being summoned by anyone.

"Father, we have a problem." Gideon motioned to the growing rift behind them.

"Migara is being swallowed up by the rift and the tear in the veil has grown worse," Ambrose told the Archdruid.

Fergus' gaze flickered to the rift. "What do you expect me to do about it?"

"Father, your power could heal the rift," Darius spoke up. He didn't want to endure his father's ire, but he would do whatever it took to fix the rift. "Dark creatures are coming through."

"He's right," Gideon admitted. "If we don't do something, all of Andovia will be destroyed."

Fergus rolled his eyes. "Nonsense."

"Father, look around you." Darius motioned as another mass of the land gave way behind them. "You're the Archdruid and the only one who can fix this. You don't want to lose your entire realm, do you?"

Fergus gritted his teeth. "Let Migara fall. It's a useless wasteland."

Darius bit back a sharp retort. Hundreds of people still lived on Migara and would die if the rift consumed the island.

"But, Father, what about when it spreads further?" Gideon protested. "The crown jewel in your empire will be destroyed."

Fergus laughed. "All lands belong to me, boy. Losing a couple would be no loss."

Nyx pushed her way forward. "What about all the innocent lives that will be lost? Your sons are here." She motioned to Darius and Gideon.

Fergus laughed again. "Evacuate, then. I have more important matters to contend with. Do not summon me again if you know what's good for you, boy." Fergus backhanded Gideon so hard the prince fell to the ground. Then, the image of Fergus winked out.

Darius knew then they were on their own. He muttered an oath and turned to his mentor. "Now what?"

"I can't say I'm surprised." Ambrose shook his head. "The Archdruid will do nothing to help us unless it serves his own purpose."

"How dare you —" Gideon thundered.

Darius put an arm on his brother's shoulder. "He's right, and you know it. We need to figure out our next move."

"Leave us," Gideon snapped at the others. "All of you. I want to talk to my brother alone." As Ambrose hesitated, he spat. "You too, you old fool."

Ambrose, Alaric and Lucien all wandered off.

"I said alone." Gideon scowled at Nyx.

She raised her chin. "I'm his servant, remember? I go where he goes." She inclined her head to Darius. "I also stay where he stays."

"You —"

"Gideon, enough. Leave her out of this." Darius stepped between them. "We both knew Father wouldn't help. For all we know, he could have caused this."

Gideon turned his scowl on his brother. "He wouldn't —"

Nyx scoffed. "Oh, he would, and you know it."

"You need to keep this girl in line, brother."

"I have about as much luck controlling her as I would the wind." Darius chuckled. "There has to be a way to fix this."

"What do you suggest?" Gideon snapped. "We can't —"

A scream made both brothers turn to see Nyx had fallen in the rift.

"Nyx?" Darius bounded over to the edge, but she had already disappeared.

Now he didn't know how, but he would get her back.

CHAPTER 27

Nyx screamed as she fell into the toxic fumes of the rift. She flapped her wings to slow her descent, but it didn't help. She reached out and grabbed hold of a rock ledge, gasping as she finally stopped. Gods, how could she have fallen? She hadn't been anywhere near the edge when the ground gave way.

Nyx gripped the ledge tighter and heaved herself up. All at once, the rock gave way and she found herself falling again.

"Druid?" she yelled.

But it was no good. She couldn't sense either of the Valeran brothers anymore.

The blackness swallowed her; she fell through emptiness. Would she keep on falling forever? Rocks and any sign of landmass had faded. There was nothing left to grab onto in her descent. Her stomach recoiled at the sensation. She flapped her wings. Still they did nothing to stop her fall.

Make this stop! Nyx screamed as the wind rushed past her, and she hit the ground with a thud. Mist surrounded her.

A figure appeared, and Harland's grinning form came towards her. "Nyxie, you have finally come to join me in death."

Nyx's wings drooped. "I'm not joining you in anything, Harland. You're dead. You can't hurt me anymore."

He laughed. "Oh, you know I can and will."

Her heart pounded in her ears, reminding her that she wasn't dead yet.

Nyx scrambled up. "I'm done being haunted by you."

Gods, why couldn't Ambrose or the druid have told her more about spirits and how to defeat them? Why hadn't she confided in them about Harland?

Harland chuckled. "You always were the defiant one. You will be mine." He grabbed hold of her throat. "You just need to give in and let go."

Get away from me! Green light flared between her hands and she sent him stumbling backwards. Somehow this felt familiar.

"I — I hit you with light that night at the tavern," she realised.

"Yes, when you killed me."

Nyx shook her head. "No, you — you were different. The darkling — I remember now. The darkling possessed you. I used my power to protect myself and Kyri." She breathed a sigh of relief. "The darkling killed you, not me."

Harland stumbled. "Lies. If it weren't for you that thing would never have taken me. You are responsible — it was there for you."

"How do you know that?"

Harland gave a harsh laugh. "I know more about you than you even know about yourself. If I hadn't kept you hidden away in Joriam these past few years, you would be dead already. I protected you."

"What else do you know about me?" she asked. Her power roared to life. Her hand ached to reach out and use her influence on him.

Harland grinned. "Why don't you join me? Then you can learn what you need to know." He reached out for her again. "It doesn't have to hurt."

Nyx took a step back. "And then what?" She narrowed her eyes.

"The veil is breaking – you know that. Someone has to control the other side. Why not us? With your powers, we would be unstoppable."

"That's why you want me." Nyx shook her head. "You've always wanted power – that's why you kept me and my sisters. No one is ever going to control me again." More light flared between her fingers. Nyx might be able to fend him off, but for how long?

This place was unnatural. She didn't want to stay here and knew she needed to find a way out, or at least get away from Harland.

He lunged at her again.

Nyx struck him with her light, and Harland screamed. She glanced at her hands. Whatever the strange light was must hurt spirits. If only it could destroy him.

Harland screamed as static rippled over him and his face contorted with pain.

Nyx decided it was time to run. She turned and fled, mist enveloped her like a heavy blanket of grey, cold and impenetrable.

Nothing but greyness stretched out before her.

She would call this place The Grey.

Nyx glanced behind her to make sure Harland hadn't followed. Her heart pounded in her ears. There had to be a way out of here. She pushed through; the mist so thick it felt like something tangible. Nyx didn't want to think about what it might be. She needed to get out of there.

Gods, help me to find a way out. Nyx had never been much of a believer in the gods her tribe worshipped, but she needed some divine intervention now. Or perhaps she should call on spirits as the druids did. Those were real enough from what she'd seen. *Okay, spirits, please help me find a way out of here.*

Light shimmered around her, and she stumbled out of the mist and into inky blackness. Nyx raised her hand to illuminate her path and chase away the shadows.

Something moved in the darkness.

"Put that light out," a scratchy voice hissed. "Get out of here." The creature's face looked like it had been carved from bone. Its eyes were black, lidless holes and sharp pointy teeth peeked out from its mouth. Its body was covered with a black cloak with what looked like mist draped around it.

Uriel. The name came to her, but the strange creature's thoughts remained silent.

The Uriel hissed and backed away. "Soul seer — how did you get into my domain?"

"I'm trying to find my way back to…" Nyx trailed off. "What did you call me?" She didn't want to let the Uriel know of her ignorance. Instinct warned her to be on her guard.

"Soul seer," the creature rasped. "I will not yield to your touch."

"I'm not here to hurt you. Gods, not all mind whisperers are bad." She crossed her arms. "Where am I?"

The Uriel lowered its gnarled hand. "You don't know?"

"Would I be asking if I did?" She put her hands on her hips. Nyx didn't get the sense of where The Grey was, but it didn't feel like Erthea. The Uriel fell silent and turned away from her. "Hey, I will use my touch on you if you don't give me answers."

The creature shuddered. "You don't know whether your power will work on me."

"Ha, I know you are fae of some kind. My power works on anything living." She sounded more confident than she felt. Nyx raised her hand and power simmered beneath her fingers, aching to get out.

Despite knowing the thing's name, Nyx didn't know what a Uriel was or what they could do. She didn't want to touch the creature unless she had to. The thought made her stomach churn.

"The veil is splintered. This is a gap between Erthea and the world beyond."

"That...doesn't sound helpful at all." Nyx sighed.

The Uriel laughed, the sound like nails scraping against rock. Nyx flinched. "You can move between places at will, girl. The veil is open, and many things can freely walk now."

"What do you know about that?" Nyx frowned.

Another screech. "More than you, no doubt."

"Okay, why not enlighten me?" She flexed her fingers. One touch would be all it took, and the Uriel knew it.

"I do not know who broke the veil. It's not my concern."

"Do you know why they broke it?"

"That's not my concern."

"So, you don't care if the world plunges into chaos? You must be an under fae then with no real power."

The Uriel screeched so loud Nyx had to cover her ears. "Do not call me under fae. I am as old as Erthea itself. You are only a child, soul seer. Run along and play." The creature lunged for her.

Nyx raised her hand. "I don't have to touch you to release my power." She loosened her hold on her magic. It roared to life like an overflowing river. With one strike, it could destroy everything in its wake.

The Uriel froze. "I do not know anything."

How could she know this thing's name but nothing about it? It made no sense how she could remember these things.

"You seek answers," the creature observed.

"I want to know why the veil is breaking and how to fix it."

"Not about the veil. About yourself. Where you come from and who you are."

Nyx's mouth fell open. "How – how do you know that?"

"I hear the spirits. They talk of you often."

"What do they say?" Nyx didn't know if she wanted to know or not. What if she didn't like the answer?

"You are fae born and of Andovia. You don't remember your past."

Nyx narrowed her eyes. "How do you know about that?"

"Like I said, the spirits talk. You can hear for yourself if you listen closely enough."

"I don't want to listen." Just thinking of Harland made her feel like she might conjure his presence. Seeing him again would scare her more than being stuck with this creature.

"Or are you afraid of seeing a certain spirit?"

"You know about that?" She furrowed her brow.

"I hear things. That Harland likes to brag about how he possessed a mind whisperer for seven years. I'm surprised he didn't use you for more than petty crime."

Nyx slumped onto a large rock. "Are you going to tell me how I can get out of here or not?" She rested her chin on her fist.

"You can leave any time, girl."

"What if I end up in the grey mist where I just came from?"

"That's up to you. Will yourself to where you want to go."

Nyx rose again then hesitated. *Uriel. Old fae, old as Erthea. They can see into the future and are known for their wisdom.*

"What do you know about me?" she asked it.

Another screech. "You are more important than anything."

"I know things," Nyx admitted. "Knowledge comes to me, but I don't know why." For a moment, she wondered why she had admitted that to a stranger of all people, but her instincts weren't warning her of any danger like they usually did.

The Uriel gnawed on a piece of bone. "That's because you don't remember who you were."

Nyx looked away to avoid showing the creature her disgust. "Who is that?" She had always wondered about her life before she ended up with Harland. Everything before then remained a mystery, even how she ended up in the forest under the Ashwood tree.

"That I do not know. Perhaps you should dispose of his spirit if he bothers you so much."

"How?"

"You have power, use it. Show him he has no hold over you."

Nyx hesitated. "Thanks." She got up and turned to leave.

"Darkness is coming. Stay close to that young Valeran druid. Your destinies are intertwined."

Nyx frowned then turned and stepped back through the darkness. Time to face her fears once and for all.

Nyx blinked as she passed through the mist again, then stopped. The Uriel had told her she could go anywhere. This was what she had been longing to do for weeks. Freedom. The chance to finally escape from Andovia. Yet her escape had become less and less important; she had been too busy helping the druid and the others to think about it much. She did need to find her sisters though and make sure they were safe.

Nyx raised her hand and pushed her way through the heavy mist. She gasped when she realised she now stood outside Farrell village — her former home.

How had she got here?

The Uriel must have been right. Nyx folded her wings back.

"I am light, hide me from sight."

Light flashed around her as she took to the air and flew towards the tavern. It looked smaller than she remembered. Strange, this place had once been the centre of her life. So much had changed since the night Harland died, and she had been sentenced to death.

Nyx landed outside and peered through the dirty window.

Inside only the faint buzz of Mama Habrid's thoughts came to her. Where were Domnu and Kyri? She didn't feel their presences anywhere nearby.

Nyx pushed the door open and dropped the glamour spell. There was no one around to see her here.

A thick layer of dust covered the bar and the room stank of cheap ale.

Nyx hurried into the kitchen where she found Mama Habrid sweeping the floor. She had never liked the crotchety old woman who had been so quick to blame her for Harland's death.

"Where are my sisters?" Nyx demanded.

Habrid looked up and screamed at the sight of her. "You — you are dead! Demon! Unholy spirit!" She swung the broom at Nyx.

Nyx ducked and avoided the blow. She waved her hand and

incinerated the broom with her light. Habrid screamed. "Where my sisters?" Nyx grabbed the old woman by the throat and let her power burst free. It shook the air around them like thunder without sound and cut off Habrid's cries. "Tell me."

Habrid blinked, dazed. "I — I sold them. Couldn't afford to keep them no more."

Nyx's heart lurched. "What?" She gasped. "Who did you sell them to? Where are they?"

"Don't know. Didn't care to ask."

Nyx gritted her teeth. "Forget I was here. I am dead to you." She hurried back outside. As much as she wanted to find her sisters, she knew she had to get back to Andovia.

This place had never been her real home. She was dead to it and would never return.

She did scan the old woman's mind before she left, though. She only hoped the druid and his resistance contacts could help her find her sisters.

Nyx found her way back to the spot she had arrived in and walked back into the heavy mist. The heavy mist surrounded her once more as she passed back into The Grey. She shivered. She had to get back to Migara now and focused her thoughts on the druid. Instead, she remained surrounded by mist. Why hadn't it worked? She had gone to throughout without any problems.

"Going somewhere, Nyxie?" Harland's voice sent a chill down her spine.

Not again.

She knew she had to deal with him once and for all or he would never stop haunting her. Nyx took a deep breath and turned to face the spirit.

"You can't run any more, girl. You belong to me."

"I belong to no one but myself. Tell me what you know about my past." She raised her hand and unleashed her power again. Thunder boomed around her, but Harland only chuckled.

"That's not how this works. I may not have had much power over you on Erthea, but I have power here." His fingers wrapped around her throat. "You're mine, and I will have you."

The light appeared again in her hands. "Wrong. I have the power, not you." She gripped him, his spirit becoming corporeal as her power flowed free.

Thunder boomed around them. Nyx gasped as energy surged through her. Pain exploded inside her head. She stumbled back.

Harland laughed and made a grab for her again. "You never could handle your curse."

"It's not a curse. You only made me think that so I wouldn't realise how powerless you were." Nyx raised her hand again. "I banish you. You have no power over me."

Harland screamed as his spirit evaporated.

Nyx breathed a sigh of relief. Finally, he was gone.

"Help," a voice whispered in her ear.

She jumped and raised a glowing hand. Now what? How could she get free of this place?

"Help me," the voice grew louder, and the figure of a blonde woman appeared.

"Who are you?" Nyx's senses reeled from the power she had used. "You look familiar. You were one of the victims of the darklings. What are you doing here?" Nyx frowned. She had no idea why the spirit thought she could help.

"Stop it."

Nyx frowned. "What?"

A shadow moved in the darkness, and something with glowing eyes came towards her.

"Stop it before it kills anyone else," the spirit said.

CHAPTER 28

Darius stared down the rift where Nyx had fallen in, unable to believe she had vanished.

"How could you let her fall in?" Gideon demanded. "Why didn't you use magic to save her?"

"I didn't get the chance to." Darius glared at his brother. "Let's not argue about whose fault this is and focus on how to fix it. Plus, since when do you care about her safety?"

"I know she has power which you've somehow been hiding from me, brother. If she is part of the prophecy, then we can't just let her die."

Darius opened his mouth to protest and closed it again. "She is not part of the prophecy."

"Then why have you been trying so hard to shield her powers?" Gideon narrowed his eyes.

"Gideon, not now. Nyx will die if we don't get her out of the rift."

Gideon scoffed. "She's probably already dead."

Darius flinched. He might not have liked Nyx at first, but she had become his friend in the short time he had known her. He didn't want to lose her.

"Don't say that. She's strong – she can survive anything." Then, turning away from his brother, he thought, *Nyx?* He reached out her with his mind, but her presence had vanished.

Next, he tried a summoning spell, but that didn't work either. "How else can we get her out?" Darius paced back and forth.

"Why not just leave her? If she is not part of the prophecy, as you claim, this is not important." Gideon had been trying spells too, but they hadn't had any effect on the rift. "We need to focus on closing this before it reaches Avenia."

"We need to find Nyx too."

"Why? She's a criminal. Or have you formed a romantic attachment to her?"

That sounded so ridiculous Darius laughed. "Romantic? Spirits, no. I just don't want her to die."

"Is she more important than closing the rift?"

Darius considered this, then shook his head. No, just because she was a good friend didn't mean he would sacrifice hundreds of lives to save hers.

"Maybe there's a way we can close the rift. I'm sure Father has something in his vault," he added. "Maybe we can somehow channel his power." He glanced down at the rift. If they closed it, Nyx would be gone forever, unless she somehow found a way out. Maybe they could find some way to save her in the vault before they closed the rift.

Gideon's eyes narrowed. "How do you know about the vault? Father —"

"Father isn't that good at keeping secrets and I've spent a lot of time travelling with him over the years."

Gideon glowered at him. Darius knew his brother had always resented him for that. He never understood why, though. Fergus was incapable of love and had never been a father to either of them.

"Let's go." Gideon grabbed his arm and transported them out in a flash of light.

They reappeared in an empty hallway back at the Crystal Palace. Darius shook off the feeling of dizziness. He had always wished he could transport himself from one place to another, but he'd never been blessed with that ability.

Gideon let go of him. This hall seemed to end with an empty wall. No door or passageway lay beyond, or so it appeared.

Even Isabella didn't know about this place, or if she did Fergus would have made sure to seal it from her. The only person he shared it with was Mercury. Darius had only been able to sneak in a few times. One time his father had caught him and had beaten him so hard he hadn't been able to move for days.

Gideon pulled down one of the crystal torches attached to the wall, and Darius pulled the other.

A door appeared etched with glowing symbols. Different runes flared to life, and only the right combination would allow anyone through. Fergus changed the combination on a regular basis.

"I haven't been able to get in here in months," Gideon remarked. "Father will kill us if he —"

Darius tapped different runes which glowed red for a moment before turning blue. The door creaked open. Darius headed in as a beam of energy shot down from the ceiling and advanced towards them. He pulled a crystal out from under his tunic and held it up, so the beam struck it, then winked out.

"How did you do that?" Gideon demanded. "I've never been able to get in here without being caught. Father beat me within an inch of my life the last time I tried."

"I have my ways." Darius wasn't about to share one of his secrets with his brother.

"Then why should I help you close the rift?"

Darius sighed. "Because you don't want to lose the realm you're destined to rule, do you?"

Gideon muttered an oath. "Fine, but I will find out how you did that."

They headed down the passageway which opened into a much larger room. Darius often wondered how something so vast could remain hidden within the palace itself. Perhaps it worked like the magic that kept the Hall of Knowledge secret.

Inside the vault, the ceiling shimmered with crystal chandeliers, glittering like diamonds. Bookcases stood against almost every wall with shelves full of books, scrolls, crystals and other artefacts. It could take years to search through everything in here. Most of this had been passed down over thousands of years through different Archdruids.

Darius hated the feeling of darkness that hung heavy on the air despite the room's light and grandeur.

"I don't even know where to begin." Gideon shook his head.

"I know a way to find what we need." Darius went over to a shelf and picked up a dark leather-bound book. It looked unremarkable and inside the pages were blank. "Show me how to seal a rift in the veil of existence." Darius closed the book again.

"What are you doing?" Gideon asked.

"This book acts like a keystone. It's spelled so it can show you what you're looking for." Darius flipped open the book, and the words appeared on the page. "Our father doesn't have the patience to look for anything."

"He's always disorganised." Gideon looked amazed. "How do you know this, brother?"

Darius shrugged. "I've spent a lot of time here." His mother had brought him here for lessons too. Fergus only allowed Mercury in here, so it hadn't been hard to use his parents' magic to trick the sensor.

Together the brothers sat and read through the book. It talked of the veil and how it separated the world of the living and the dead as well as different planes of existence.

Gideon tossed the book aside in disgust. "There's nothing in here on how to seal the rift."

"You didn't think it would be that easy, did you?" Darius asked. Then, with his mind, he thought, *Nyx, can you hear me?*

No response came. He had started to miss the feel of her presence – something he would never have thought possible. Nyx had to be somewhere. She wasn't dead – or at least he didn't think so.

"Father should have something in here." Gideon crossed his arms.

"I doubt the veil has ever been damaged before." Darius picked the book up. "Maybe we need to look for something else."

"Like what?" Gideon rose from his seat.

"Maybe your mother could help."

Gideon laughed. "My mother couldn't stop something like this. She has power, but not the skill or desire to use it. Your mother, on the other hand — it sounds like something she could do."

Darius scoured the book again. Maybe Gideon had a point about his mother. This would be something she might do. His stomach twisted into knots. What if she was a suspect? He and Ambrose had spent hours going over who might have damaged the rift and what their reasons for doing so might be His father seemed like the logical choice, but despite his mother's lust for power, he had never thought she would resort to endangering Erthea itself.

"Keep looking through this. Maybe you can spot something. Look for anything that mentions the Archdruid's connection to Erthea." Darius handed his brother the book and headed to another section of the vault. He moved past the different rows of shelves until he came to an area where he knew Mercury kept her books. The door to the vault could be accessed from anywhere even if the Archdruid was thousands of leagues away.

Darius hesitated. His mother kept her things hidden in here – hidden even from Fergus. She would flay him alive if he revealed her secrets to Gideon. He moved along the shelves until he found a black book. He pulled it down. Magic burned his fingers from the magic Mercury had placed there to protect and shield it. Darius doubted even his father ever got to view the pages of this book.

"Malchem," he muttered the words he knew his mother used to unlock it. The book finally snapped open. Words flashed in and out of existence. Mercury wrote all of her knowledge of spirits and sorcery in here. She had done so since she was a child.

Show me how to break the veil. He couldn't risk saying the words out loud for fear Gideon might hear him. Words appeared across the page. *Only blood magic is strong enough to break through the veil.*

Darius' blood went cold. Spirits, had Mercury done it? Had she torn the veil?

How can it be sealed? He prayed it wouldn't involve more blood magic. If it did, he couldn't say he was surprised. His mother liked the black arts even more than Fergus and did everything she could to increase her power. Being second wife to the Archdruid would never have been enough for her.

Nothing appeared this time. Mercury must have known how to reverse the damage, unless she wanted all of Andovia to fall into the rift.

He read further. It talked about the tear in the veil and what might happen. There was nothing to indicate why she had done it. Mercury was meticulous in what she did. She planned everything out in minute detail in case anything went wrong.

Why hadn't she written more about what her intentions were or what she wanted to achieve? Unless she hadn't been the one who had done it.

Darius wouldn't jump to conclusions. Unless she hadn't been the one who had done it.

He wouldn't put that past her.

Druid! Nyx's scream tore through his mind.

Darius jumped, and the book fell from his hands. *Nyx? Where are you?*

I need help. Something is after me!

CHAPTER 29

Darius stared down the rift where Nyx had fallen in, unable to believe she Nyx screamed as she landed on the polished oak floor and had no idea where she had ended up. She had been focused on getting back to Migara, but then she had thought of the druid and passed out of The Grey again. At least she had ended up with the druid this time, although she wished Gideon were not there.

"Nyx, are you alright?" Darius bent beside her.

"Monster..." she breathed.

Darius frowned. "Where?"

Her senses reeled from the creature's dark energy. Suddenly, the creature she had encountered in The Grey appeared. "There." Nyx motioned towards it.

She had thought it was terrifying in the mist, but now in the light it looked even more so. It was all rippling muscle and jagged fangs.

It lunged straight for her. Nyx flapped her wings and shot up onto one of the ceiling beams. Her heartbeat thudded in her ears.

Darius struck the creature with lightning and Gideon with a fireball. The creature shrieked but bounded towards them. It knocked Gideon aside and sent him flying. He crashed to the floor and laid there, unconscious.

"What is this thing?" Darius called up to her.

"How should I know?" Nyx grabbed the sword from the wall and swept down. The blade sliced into the creature's neck but went no further. Holy spirits, why wouldn't the sword slice the head off?

"I found it in The Grey," she told the druid.

"The what?" He frowned up at her.

"A place between life and death. A spirit told me this thing is what's been killing people."

Darius raised both his hands and hit the creature with lightning bolts.

Nyx swept down and kicked the creature in the head, then she leaned down and grasped its shoulder. This time she let her full power flow free. Her eyes turn black, and energy roared through the air like thunder with no sound.

Nyx winced as energy sparked between her fingers. She dropped to the floor; her energy spent.

The creature stumbled backwards, and its dark eyes flashed. "The darkness is coming," it rasped. "You cannot stop it."

Gideon scrambled up and raised his hand. Energy reverberated through the air as he used his magic and cast a wave of energy around the dark creature. He said the words of a spell and Nyx flinched from the dark energy. "Tell us who summoned you."

Darius went over and helped Nyx to her feet. "Are you alright?"

She nodded. "What is that thing?" She motioned towards the creature. Nyx knew it was not a darkling.

The creature struggled against Gideon's magic and burst free from the web. It lunged straight towards the prince again until a blast of light sent it crashing into the far wall.

Ambrose stood in the doorway; his staff radiated with energy. "That is a Lalpest, a creature banished from this world centuries ago. Only the darkest of magic could have bought it back through the veil."

The Lalpest struggled as Ambrose's magic seemed to be the only thing that had any real effect on the creature so far. He snarled at them. "It's too late to undo the damage caused. The veil will fall, and all of the creatures banished to the underworld will walk Erthea once more."

"Tell us who broke through the veil." Ambrose tapped his staff on the floor and more energy pulsed from the glowing orb. "What is it they are looking for? They have been stealing power for a reason, why?"

"She searches for the one banished long ago. The one who will set all of the fae free."

"You mean one of the chosen that the prophecy speaks of?" Nyx put a hand to her chest. She still didn't believe she was part of a prophecy.

The Lalpest laughed, a harsh guttural sound. "No, the true queen of the fae. That witch who sits on the throne knows she will never have real power. That is why she's trying to find the one who does."

All colour drained from Ambrose's face. "Impossible. The fae queen was banished more than a generation ago when the Archdruid took power. She is gone from this world and will never return."

Gideon froze. "Wait, are you saying my mother did this? That's ridiculous. Why would she need to? She is already the queen of the fae." His hands clenched into fists. "You are lying!" He stepped forward to strike the creature, but Darius put a hand out to stop him.

"No, she is a priestess, nothing more. She has no divine power as the true Andovian queen did."

"The Andovian queen is dead. No one can bring her back. Ever," Ambrose snapped and raised his staff once more. He chanted strange, intricate words of power that sounded beautiful yet terrifying at the same time. Light blew from his staff, so bright Nyx had to raise her hand to shield her eyes.

The Lalpest screamed then exploded in a blaze of fire.

Ambrose stood there, breathing hard.

"These are lies," Gideon snapped. "My mother wouldn't do such a thing. She doesn't have the power. This must be your doing." He advanced towards Ambrose.

This time Nyx stepped in his way. "He's telling the truth. That much I can tell."

Gideon glowered at her and Darius put a hand on his brother's shoulder. "Think about it," he said. "Your mother doesn't have the respect of the fae. Her power and influence are waning, and you know it. How much longer do you think it will be before our father casts her aside? She serves no real purpose to the Archdruid anymore, and the high fae are growing restless."

Gideon shoved Darius aside. "You are all wrong and I will prove it." He stormed out of the room.

"Go after him," Ambrose told them. "Before he does something stupid. If the queen is confronted with what she has done, she might turn against him."

Nyx and Darius raced out of the vault and after Gideon. Ambrose trailed along behind them out of breath after the amount of power he had used. Nyx wished she had time to ask him how he had known to defeat such a creature. There was so much about the older druid that remained a mystery, and she had so many questions she needed answers to. All of that would have to wait until later.

Gideon didn't stop until he reached his mother's chambers in a part of the palace Nyx had never been to before.

Isabella's eyes widened in shock as Gideon, Nyx and Darius burst into the room. Tendrils of green smoke swirled around her fingers as she stood over a large basin of water.

Gideon gasped. "Mother, are you the one who has fractured the veil?"

The green smoke died away, and she glowered at Ambrose as he staggered through the door. "You killed my Lalpest!" She raised her hand to strike him.

Gideon raised his hand, and his palm glowed with light. "Why did you do it, Mother? You are risking the future of my realm."

Isabella snorted. "What realm? This realm will never be yours or mine, not while Fergus sits on that throne. I had to do something to gain real power," she hissed. "The next dark age is upon us, and we will all perish. Only the powerful survive in this world, boy. You need to learn to accept that." She turned her gaze back to Ambrose. "And you are nothing but an old fool, a remnant of an age long since dead."

Ambrose raised his staff and blasted Isabella across the room with a bolt of energy. "I still have power, witch."

"Guards!" Gideon yelled.

Two guards came in and dragged an unconscious Isabella away.

"I will call Father. He needs to return home at once to deal with this situation. Only he can decide what to do with her," Darius said.

They scoured Isabella's chamber and found the spell she had used to open the rift. Together Darius, Nyx, Gideon and Ambrose used their magic to close the rift once and for all. Nyx and Darius headed out to Migara where she was stunned to find all traces of it had disappeared.

"Is that it?" Nyx asked the druid. "Is it finally over?"

Darius nodded. "I think so. At least until my father gets back and deals with Isabella."

"What will he do with her? Will he kill her?" She couldn't say she would miss the fae queen very much, not after everything Isabella had done.

Darius shrugged. "I don't know. Perhaps he will. He won't like anyone making a play for power against him." He hesitated. "I found something back in my father's vault. My mother wrote about a new energy – someone who can threaten everything on Erthea."

"Who?" Nyx frowned. "The Andovian queen? Who is she anyway?"

"She was the leader here in Andovia up until my grandfather took power and enslaved the Andovians a century ago. She's been dead a long time now. I don't see how anyone could bring her back." Darius knelt and ran a hand over the ground. "Hopefully there is no permanent damage left here. Even so, Ambrose will want to do a cleansing." He rose to his full height again. "I'm glad you're okay. How did you find your way out of the rift?"

"I was able to move through it. I — I went back to the tavern to find my sisters, but they were gone." She wrapped her arms around herself. "I've been so focused on running away and going back to them."

Darius arched an eyebrow. "Why did you come back?"

She hesitated. "Because there are answers here about my past and who I was before I ended up with Harland." She bit her lip. "I've remembered what happened that night — I didn't kill him. The darkling was there looking for me. I've come to realise that this whole thing is bigger than my freedom — at least for now, this is where I belong."

That didn't mean she would give up trying to find the sisters, though.

"I'm glad you've decided to stay." Darius flashed her a smile. "We work well together, don't we?"

"When you're not irritating me, yes." She laughed. "Am I still stuck being your servant?"

"In an official capacity, yes, but I want you to know I consider you a friend now."

Friend. Nyx hadn't had a real friend before, aside from her sisters. In a way, she felt like she already knew Darius better than she ever knew them.

Nyx only hoped their friendship was enough to face whatever came next.

Darkness was coming, and they had to be ready for it.

If you enjoyed this book please leave a review on Amazon or book site of your choice.

***

For updates on more books and news releases sign up for my newsletter on tiffanyshand.com/newsletter

ALSO BY TIFFANY SHAND

ANDOVIA CHRONICLES

Dark Deeds Prequel

The Calling

ROGUES OF MAGIC SERIES

Bound By Blood

Archdruid

Bound By Fire

Old Magic

Dark Deception

Sins Of The Past

Reign Of Darkness

Rogues Of Magic Complete Box Set Books 1-7

ROGUES OF MAGIC NOVELLAS

Wyvern's Curse

Forsaken

On Dangerous Tides

EVERLIGHT ACADEMY TRILOGY

Everlight Academy, Book 1: Faeling

Everlight Academy, Book 2: Fae Born

Hunted Guardian – An Everlight Academy Story

EXCALIBAR INVESTIGATIONS SERIES

Denai Touch

Denai Bound

Denai Storm

Excalibar Investigations Complete Box Set

SHADOW WALKER SERIES

Shadow Walker

Shadow Spy

Shadow Sworn

Shadow Walker Complete Box Set

THE AMARANTHINE CHRONICLES BOOK 1

Betrayed By Blood

Dark Revenge

The Final Battle

SHIFTER CLANS SERIES

The Alpha's Daughter

Alpha Ascending

The Alpha's Curse

The Shifter Clans Complete Box Set

TALES OF THE ITHEREAL

Fey Spy

Outcast Fey

Rogue Fey

Hunted Fey

Tales of the Ithereal Complete Box Set

THE FEY GUARDIAN SERIES

Memories Lost

Memories Awakened

Memories Found

The Fey Guardian Complete Series

248

ABOUT THE AUTHOR

Tiffany Shand is a writing mentor, professionally trained copy editor and copy writer who has been writing stories for as long as she can remember. Born in East Anglia, Tiffany still lives in the area, constantly guarding her workspace from the two cats which she shares her home with.

She began using her pets as a writing inspiration when she was a child, before moving on to write her first novel after successful completion of a creative writing course. Nowadays, Tiffany writes urban fantasy and paranormal romance, as well as nonfiction books for other writers, all available through eBook stores and on her own website.

Tiffany's favourite quote is *'writing is an exploration. You start from nothing and learn as you go'* and it is armed with this that she hopes to be able to help, inspire and mentor many more aspiring authors.

When she has time to unwind, Tiffany enjoys photography, reading, and watching endless box sets. She also loves to get out and visit the vast number of castles and historic houses that England has to offer.

You can contact Tiffany Shand, or just see what she is writing about at:

Author website: tiffanyshand.com

Business site: Write Now Creative

Twitter: @tiffanyshand

Facebook page: Tiffany Shand Author Page

249

Printed in Poland
by Amazon Fulfillment
Poland Sp. z o.o., Wrocław
19 February 2022

068470ef-b1b1-4750-a4c4-a6ebe16c3312R01